THE ONE WE LOVE
A Letty Whittaker 12 Step Mystery

By Donna White Glaser

Credits:

Cover images and design by:
Rickhardt Capidamonte/Booknook and Joleene Naylor
Front cover design by Rickhardt Capidamonte/Booknook.com
Full cover by Joleene Naylor
Editing by April Solberg, Red Pen Proofreading & Editing

Also By Donna White Glaser

THE ENEMY WE KNOW
A Letty Whittaker 12 Step Mystery

To Levi and Leah
my pride and joy

STEP TWO

Came to believe that a Power greater than
ourselves could restore us to sanity

STEP THREE

Made a decision to turn our will and our lives over
to the care of God *as we understood Him.*

CHAPTER ONE

I felt bad about not liking Regina more, especially after she died. Of course, I don't think Regina liked me much either, despite that she'd saved my life. Maybe liking isn't the point.

It would have come in handy at her funeral, though.

Surrounded by most of my co-workers, I sat on a folding chair covered in faded burgundy, trying to come up with topics for conversation. I needn't have bothered. My colleagues left me in a cone of respectful silence, shooting sympathetic looks whenever our eyes met. Mostly I concentrated on facing forward. If I blurred my eyes like when looking at those 3D pictures where a unicorn materializes out of a psychedelic swirl, I could almost believe it wasn't a casket placed center stage with burgundy velvet theater curtains bracketing it.

Except for two wilting ferns provided by the funeral home, there weren't any flowers either, which I'd always found to be a nice distraction at funerals. A person could examine each bouquet, stick her nose in the blossoms for a good sniff, discuss how pretty they all were and which flowers were the favorite of the deceased. Maybe even (silently) compare the estimated cost of the other arrangements to one's own.

Ignore the dead body in the middle of the room, Letty.

Instead, somebody had arranged for "in lieu of" donations, which, while imminently charitable, did not lend themselves to small talk.

I wanted to get up, move around. Oh hell, what I really wanted was to sneak outside for a smoke. I reminded myself I was trying to quit. Besides, at any moment, the minister was going to come forward to ask for the personal anecdotes of the deceased that made everyone smile and nod in fond remembrance. My armpits grew damp, my stomach doing lazy flips in anticipation.

Months ago in the wake of some horrible events in my life, Regina had really come through for me, had forced me out of the bleak dead-zone of depression and back into real life. By rights, I should have loved her for it. Because of it, my colleagues assumed a relationship between us that didn't exist, and naturally expected some folksy, heart-warming Regina stories. Not that they had any of their own.

I guessed I could chat about the choke holds and knife attacks that she'd forced me to escape from or the multiple times she thrashed my butt, teaching me self-defense skills. Although upon consideration, it was probably better not to mention the worrisome little smile that twinkled across her face during the attacks; that didn't seem like funeral fodder. I guessed that also ruled out showing off the yellow-green bruise that still lingered on my ass from the last training session a little more than a week ago.

Or, keeping it light, I could tell about the time Regina took over two racks of the employee lounge fridge so she could slide in her own personal lockbox to secure her imported salad dressing and designer water from those of us who consistently forgot to bring a sack lunch. Regina wasn't what you would call a "sharer."

Unless you counted the thousands of hours of time, energy and expertise she'd donated to the women and children at our community domestic abuse shelter. Or the similar intensity she displayed in saving me from myself after the previously mentioned horrible events.

Now I felt really bad. Again.

Bob, acting supervisor and reigning toad of the clinic we all worked at, plopped down beside me. He was actively losing his own battle with sweaty pit issues, and it showed. Or, more accurately, smelled. I tried blurring my nose, but unlike my eyes, it didn't take.

"Hey, Letty. You'd think they'd have the air on in here," he said, mopping his head with a hankie. Unfortunately, the action misaligned the strands of hair he'd pasted across his balding dome and he had to spend a few minutes patting them back into submission, which further served to fan his eau de la pit-smell. "You're gonna say something, right? For the eulogy?"

"I thought *you* would. I mean, you and she were—"

"Nah, I better not. I don't want to seem like I'm playing favorites. If I compliment one employee, then everyone else gets PO'd. I don't need the hassle."

As a psychotherapist, I knew how to keep my emotions in check, but my training occasionally fails in the face of abject stupidity. This occurred whenever I talked with Bob.

"Bob, I really don't think anyone is going to mind if

3

you say some nice things about Regina at her funeral. Besides, you and she have been friends for a very long—"

He interrupted. Again. "You start it out. I'm sure you've got some good things to say." He gave me a "boss" look underscoring the non-voluntary qualities of his suggestion, then heaved himself to his feet and walked toward the funeral director.

As I glared at his retreating backside, I noticed several more people entering. All women. All with that no-makeup, Amazonian-professional look that secretly intimidated me. As far as I'm concerned, women willing to bare unadorned faces to the world have big juju.

I recognized three of them from the shelter where Regina had volunteered. The shelter that she'd dragged me to after . . . well . . . *after*. I shook myself.

A rustling sound distracted me and I swiveled back to face front as the funeral director—a chubby little cherub—minced up the aisle to the speaking podium. At least I wouldn't have to witness some meek clergyman trying to pronounce Regina's name correctly. Regina always insisted it rhyme with her girl parts, rather than the traditional usage. And if she were alive now, she'd have slapped me for saying "girl parts."

The cherub stood in front, clearing his throat and cloaking his face in decorous restraint. I waited for his assistants to perform the discreet, behind the curtains closing of the casket, but none appeared. The cherub greeted us smoothly, then read a brief eulogy comprised of dry, isolated facts, taken straight from the newspaper obituary. At least he got her name right and he didn't blush when pronouncing it.

Still no sign of assistant cherubs coming to shut the casket.

Moments later, he opened the floor to Regina's loved ones and extended his hand to the first speaker.

Me. *Damn you, Bob.*

Mouth dry and legs shaking, I made my way to the podium. I hoped that people would assume I was overwrought with grief, or even just afraid of public speaking, instead of the truth: I had no idea what to say about Regina; all made worse by the fact that Regina lay directly behind me, casket open to the world. The skin on the back of my neck crawled. I felt like she was going to grade me on my performance. Or leap on the back of my neck like the undead.

The cherub had left a pitcher of water and a small stack of Dixie cups on a stand next to the podium. I stalled, pouring a drink. The water danced in the tiny cup like I had palsy.

"Regina," I began, "was an amazing woman. I hardly know where to begin." *All true, so far. Doin' good.* "She was a skilled and dedicated therapist, a stalwart defender of women and women's rights, and . . . a good friend." *As long as we disregard the "not liking each other" part.* "Regina taught me so much. So, so much. . .um—" *What? What did she teach me?* "She taught me about how to be a strong woman in a very scary world, how to walk with pride and courage. How to trust my instincts."

I was starting to surprise myself. I looked out over the assemblage and saw the nearly all-female crowd nodding. Bob, sitting near the front, was rubbing his nose surreptitiously. I closed my eyes to avoid viewing the actual booger-picking moment.

"How to fight back and refuse to be a victim."

How to kick a man so hard he'd sneeze out nuts.

My eyes flew open in sudden panic, scanning the upturned faces to see if I'd actually said that last bit out loud. I rubbed the nicotine patch on my shoulder hoping to activate a rush of chemicals. Bob, booger free, looked bored, and Clotilde, the shelter's dominatrix. . . er, director, showed neither shock nor, as would be more likely, amusement.

I recognized the woman next to Clotilde. Astrid had once co-led the group counseling sessions that Regina had dragged me to. She leaned toward Clotilde, whispering in her ear. Clotilde, never taking her eyes off me, nodded once. Since it didn't seem to pertain to sneezing nuts, I tried to move on.

More water. Then, "I'll miss Regina." *Surprisingly enough, also true.*

I sat down, tuning out the next few speakers, and waited for my heart to quit its wild thumping as the realization of just how true my last statement had been.

I was going to miss Regina-rhymes-with-vagina very much.

CHAPTER TWO

After the service, I attempted to escape without talking to anyone. Before I made it to the door, however, a slightly older, decidedly sleeker version of Regina caught up with me and grasped my hand. She wore her hair in a fashionable bob, letting it curl around her chin, giving a look of sweetness to an otherwise too narrow face. She had Regina's light blue eyes, but makeup softened and gentled the effect. I wasn't surprised when she introduced herself as Regina's sister, Emma.

"I just had to thank you," she said. "You seemed to know Reggie so well. I wanted to tell you how much your words meant to me. Everybody else seemed so. . ." Her voice trailed off, avoiding actual criticism. "I hope people aren't upset because we didn't have a pastor. Reggie had it all planned out. She always had intense beliefs; I imagine she didn't want to trust it to anyone else. She didn't want anything to do with a religious service, of course, but frankly I don't know what message we were supposed to get from the casket remaining open the whole time."

"Maybe just a reminder?" I fumbled. Reminder of what, I didn't know, but I, for one, wasn't ever going to forget.

Without letting go of my hand, Emma began walking toward the front. Until now, I'd managed to avoid the whole "doesn't she look peaceful?" moment that required staring down at the dead person and commenting on her appearance. For a nanosecond, my legs locked up, attempting to transform into reality the cliché of digging my heels in. Just as quickly, I realized that resistance was futile. Emma was a sweeter version, perhaps, but there was more than just a physical resemblance between the sisters. I might leave drag marks in the thick carpet, but I *was* joining her casket-side.

Regina didn't appear peaceful, which would have been a weird look on her anyway. Whoever had done her up must not have gotten a demo-picture because they'd slathered her face with dramatic makeup and twisted a bright jewel-toned scarf around her neck. The heavy layer of foundation was too dark, making it look like the normally pale Regina had abused a tanning bed right before she'd died. A slash of rouge across her cheekbones only added to the unreality of her death.

She looked so very different that my eyes skittered away as if caught staring at a stranger. They landed on her charm bracelet. I smiled. I'd gotten plenty of close-ups of that trinket when Regina had her hands wrapped around my throat. It would jingle as she demonstrated how to twist an attacker's thumbs to leverage them off my neck. She'd talk matter-of-factly about maiming and blinding and paralyzing with the charms tinkling merrily in counterpoint to her movements.

"I wonder where they got the scarf," Emma remarked. "I don't believe I've ever seen Reggie wear one before. She wasn't all that into style." Emma smiled down at her own chic outfit.

"No, she wasn't," I agreed. I would never in a million years have pictured Regina choosing this scarf, beautiful as it was. It didn't even particularly match her more familiar navy pants suit.

"I guess they needed to cover the wound," Emma continued. "I didn't even know she knitted."

"I'm sorry? A wound? I thought Regina fell. They told us she'd fallen down a set of stairs at the women's shelter."

"She did, but from what I understand that's not what killed her. It might have if she hadn't been able to get help, but what really killed her was the needle."

"A needle?" I felt like a parrot, but none of this made any sense. "A *knitting* needle?"

"Yeah, that's strange, huh? I never knew she knitted," Emma said again.

I looked down at Regina's still form. "Neither did I."

"It just seems like such a strange thing to happen. Of course, when they told me they were doing an autopsy I thought it meant. . .

"Anyway, they assured me that it's a requirement in all accidental deaths."

"Wow, I didn't realize . . . Do they think—"

"Letty?" Bob approached, startling me. He stood slightly off to the side, indicating with a "c'mere" head tilt that he wanted to speak to me. I excused myself from Emma.

Bob said, "I need to meet with you later. Can you come by the clinic when you're done here?

"Um, sure. Are you heading to the cemetery?" I asked.

"Nah, something's come up and I need to take care of it. If you're going to pay respects, that's fine. Just stop by the office afterward." Bob said.

He nodded to Emma. "My condolences." Then hurried off.

I turned to Emma. "I'd better go, too. It was nice meeting you."

She nodded distractedly, then looked deep into my eyes. I waited, assuming she had more to say. Instead, she smiled faintly and turned back to her sister.

It felt strange meeting Bob in our former boss's office. Bob had never liked Marshall, but I . . . I certainly couldn't say the same. I hadn't heard from Marshall since he'd left for Wyoming, and my heart twisted at the sight of Bob sitting in Marshall's old leather chair.

"So, okay, Letty. Here's the thing. Regina left you some instructions. Her lawyer called me this morning before the service. Called me at *home*." He stressed the intrusion, implying that it was my fault. "She had Regina's will, and she faxed it over here."

"Her will? What do I have to do with Regina's will?"

"Not her will exactly." Bob sounded irritated that I'd assumed his use of the word "will" meant. . . well. . .a *will*. Apparently, I should have known better.

He snatched a sheaf of papers from a tilting column on the desk. "Her 'Professional Executor Instructions.' Her lawyer, gal by the name of Perkins, said Regina was supposed to have given me a copy, but I never saw it. You need to give her a call." He tossed the papers across the desk to me.

I left them lying between us, seemingly harmless,

but I'd been fooled before. The A/C kicked on and the papers fluttered gently. I shivered.

"What the hell is a professional executor anyway?" I asked.

Bob shrugged. "Like, you know, the person who's got to cross all the I's and dot all the T's. Contact her clients, review her files, maybe do a little grief counseling. Like that." He pointed to the papers again. "Her client list is in there, too."

"Well, of course, *somebody's* got to do that." With the unexpectedness of Regina's death, I hadn't really thought about it, but it seemed obvious now. Regina's clients, many of them anyway, would need help processing her sudden demise. "I guess I figured we would all pitch in."

"Oh, sure, absolutely." Bob acted as if he'd already thought the process through. Maybe he had. "But with this," he gestured to the papers, "and a lawyer involved, we'll need to honor Regina's wishes." Not to mention that dumping it all on me took Bob off the hook.

"Uh-huh," I said. "Haven't her clients already been notified?"

The clinic had been closed for two days, ever since we'd heard about Regina's accident. All clients, aside from a very few emergency calls that each of us dealt with accordingly, had been rescheduled for next week.

"Not officially notified," Bob said. "We canceled Regina's appointments, but without an explanation. I was waiting to hear from Admin how they wanted us to handle the situation."

Bob loved the perks of the director position; he liked his big office, he liked the respect he assumed he had, and he liked choosing his own hours, which always seemed to combine coming in late with leaving early and allegedly toiling diligently at home under onerous conditions.

But the responsibilities and, worse, the accountability? Not so much. He didn't make any decision without prior approval lest someone—anyone—try to assign blame for any mishap. He didn't venture new ideas and he didn't claim old ones until they'd been proven successful.

Come to think of it, he had more administrative skills than I'd been crediting him with.

A wistful yearning made me ask, "Has anyone called Marshall?"

Bob shrugged. "Why would they? I mean, he's not going to come from Wyoming for a funeral of a former colleague. They didn't even get along. It's the clients we have to focus on."

"What about *my* clients?" I asked. Yes, I admit to a slight whiny quality in the question.

"You'll have to go through them and prioritize. Transfer as many as you safely can to the other therapists for a couple of weeks, and see the ones yourself who might be too fragile to shift over. Go through your client roster this afternoon and get me a list ASAP. But the big thing is going to be reviewing Regina's current client files and contacting each of them. Give referrals to the ones you think need to continue seeing someone and work out some kind of grief sessions for those who need it. You may need to go into her back files and review those clients, too, but obviously the priority is gonna be her current people. Read that," he said, pointing again to the papers, "and call Ms. Perkins so she knows we're on top of things."

I finally picked up the papers. "Professional

Executor Instructions," it said across the top. "For the Disposition of the Practice of Regina L. Wentzler, Psy. D. In the Event of Death, Disappearance, or Disability."

Ugh.

CHAPTER THREE

It took nearly an hour to sort through my client roster. Only a few clients would really have difficulty transferring to an interim counselor while I dealt with Regina's caseload. Two were in full-blown crisis mode, and a third had abandonment issues so severe that she would hang up the phone before the other caller could say good-bye. But the majority was in a relatively good place, either nearing the end of treatment or so firmly entrenched in denial that a couple of weeks apart wouldn't set us back. I hoped it wouldn't take more than a couple of weeks to settle my obligations. Any longer than that and I risked exposing how dispensable I apparently was.

Sighing, I leaned my head back against the worn cloth of the chair. For all my whining, I really did recognize my obligation to Regina. Even without the legal arrangement, I should have jumped at the chance to pay back the debt I owed. Should have.

The truth was I didn't like thinking about Regina because doing so called to mind painful memories, not the least of which involved a certain, hunky, former boss hiding out in the West. I toyed with the idea of calling him, just picking up the phone and punching out the number I'd never dialed before, but had memorized, just in case. Despite their differences, I'm sure he'd want to know about Regina's accident.

But not from me.

I sat up, snatching the papers Bob had foisted on me. *Professional Executor?* I'd never even heard the term before, although the concept made sense.

Unlike most legal documents, this one was comprised of simple, easy-to-understand language. I scanned quickly trying to get a feel for the job. Despite my light perusal, Regina's dedication to her wounded charges rose off the pages as though the ink were scented with her own special brand of fanaticism. I skipped ahead to a section titled "Specific Instructions to my Professional Executor" and slowed to read more carefully. While Bob had touched on the essentials of my new duties, Regina spelled out a veritable to-do list for following up with her clients.

I finally smiled—leave it to Regina to take care of her people from beyond the grave—and started taking notes.

Toward the end of the instructions was a section of general, housekeeping-type information. The form stated where I could find extra sets of keys to her offices, including the file cabinets, closed files storage, malpractice insurance policy, and managed care contracts. Very tidy.

Wait a minute. *Offices?*

I went back to the beginning and immediately self-diagnosed myself with an exotic form of visual processing disorder, because apparently I'd blacked out what I'd read. The will very clearly stated that my responsibilities included her clinic duties *and* those at the domestic abuse shelter. The place where, after I was attacked, she'd dragged me for group therapy and self-defense classes, the place where I'd vowed to never return. The place, after all, where Regina had saved lives and, literally, given her own.

Shit.

Sue met me at the donut shop across the street from the HP & Me club. We could have met at the club, but, Higher Power notwithstanding, the coffee was crap and we'd have had to share our donuts with the two or three grizzled drunks who always hung around the lobby, bitching and cheating at pinochle.

Sue became my sponsor shortly after I'd stumbled into AA, hung-over and desperate, nearly ten months earlier. I would have liked a sponsor who fed me cookies on rainy days and listened to all my sad stories. Someone I could go to when life got too scary, which felt like all the time. Someone whose gentle nature let me grow like a seedling in the sun.

Instead, I got Sue.

In all fairness, I picked her. A retired middle-school teacher, she was born cranky and stayed that way, seeing no reason to change since it was obvious, to her at least, that the world was at fault, not she. I shudder to think what she must have been like drunk. Nevertheless, she guided my sobriety with a combination of tough love, gritty wisdom, and the implicit threat of a beat-down should I fall off the wagon. She was, in a word, formidable.

Unfortunately, back during the days following the attack and Marshall's leaving, Sue had met Regina. And liked her. They got along. They'd conspired to protect my sanity and health in ways that I, in my depressed haze, hadn't been privy to and would probably never understand. In short, they'd formed an unholy alliance.

Although Sue had attended the visitation the night before, she hadn't been able to come to the services this morning. I told her about meeting Emma, Regina's sister, and how different from each other they seemed to be. We pondered the variability of DNA in siblings for a moment. Then, I showed her Regina's will, or whatever it was, and waited while she read it.

"I'll be damned," Sue said. "So, what do you think?"

"I think you'll be damned, too. You swear too much."

My comment elicited a snort and a much bigger cuss word, but didn't succeed in distracting Sue from her question. Sponsors, like therapists and moms, have a bit of bulldog in them. Or in Sue's case, a lot. She gave me the one-eyebrow-raised stare.

"What do I think? I think it sucks. I hate it," I answered. "And I hate that I hate it. I don't want the extra responsibility, for one thing. And yes, I know that's horrible of me—especially after everything Regina did for me.

"I mean," I continued, "she knew how screwed up I've been after Robert's death and all the rest. I'm a mess, and I'm just getting my shit back together. Why would she choose me for this job?"

"Why did she?"

"I don't know." I stared out the window to the AA club. Regina had known I was an alcoholic; she was the only one at work who did. She also knew, better than anyone did, how ravaged my life had been just a few months earlier. *Why* had *she chosen me?*

"She must have trusted you," Sue said, breaking into my reverie.

"But she trusted the women at the shelter more. I saw her with them. That shelter was her life. Why didn't she appoint one of them?"

"Maybe you should ask her lawyer," Sue said. "And you could also ask her what happened two weeks ago that made Regina change her will."

"What are you talking about?"

In answer, Sue pointed to the date on the document: Tuesday, September 2 of this year. Whatever had factored into Regina's decision to appoint me professional executor had occurred very recently. Two weeks ago, as Sue pointed out.

What the hell?

CHAPTER FOUR

After a night spent staring dry-eyed into the dark, I dragged myself out of bed. Siggy, my recently acquired cat, snuggled down in the warm curve of my pillow with a soft grunt. He watched with apparent incredulity as I stumbled around getting dressed in the dawning light. We are not morning creatures, Sig and I.

I slapped a new nicotine patch on my back and set forth to seize the day, stopping for coffee twice on the twenty-minute commute. Between caffeine jitters and the pee-pee dance, I could barely manage typing the alarm code and opening the lock on the clinic door. Thankfully, the bathroom was just off the lobby and I made it in time to avert serious embarrassment.

The clinic was empty. I knew better than to expect Bob before noon, and the rest of the therapists wouldn't be in for another couple of hours. Lisa, our office manager, might be in before that, but I still had the place to myself for a while.

Eerie.

Without clients and co-workers, the place felt like a stage set: empty and devoid of purpose. The phrase "if walls could talk" came to mind, and I couldn't shake a sense of the accumulated anguish that would be seeping out of the walls if that were true. I stopped off in the lounge to set up a pot of highly unnecessary coffee, before hurrying to Regina's office.

Bob had given me the master key, but despite my unease, I hesitated outside the door. A weighted sensation smothered my coffee jitters, making it hard to breathe. My heart thumped against the pressure. *Heart attack? Regina's ghost?*

Obligation.

Forcing a deep breath, I walked in.

Our offices were the same size and furnished with the same crap commercial furniture. Regina, however, had had nearly two decades to place her stamp. She'd filled her room with eclectic folk art, a few travel souvenirs judging by the I-Heart-Ireland coffee mug, and a profusion of small remembrances from clients—the kind that couldn't be refused without hurt feelings, but which fell on the angels' side of ethics.

Even Regina's flooring was symbolic. My clients traversed the standard brown-flecked industrial strength carpeting that ran throughout the clinic. Regina had brought in a handspun area rug—the faded pumpkin background backlit a curling tree in browns and greens: the Tree of Life.

She'd re-covered the loveseat too. Across the back, someone had tossed a celery-colored afghan. It lay there, soft and warm, ready for the next person who, regardless of the current season, might be caught in her own winter of the soul. I picked it up, brought it to my face.

Regina's scent—as clean and crisp as fresh sheets snapping on the line—filled my head. *Had she made this herself?* The weave looked handmade, and I couldn't find a label or tag anywhere. I folded the fabric carefully, setting it back on the loveseat. I'd need to find out who was entitled to Regina's personal effects; I assumed her sister Emma, but I hadn't gotten her phone number and didn't know her last name. The lawyer would know.

Setting my purse on her desk, I pulled out a notebook and my copy of Regina's will. Feeling like an intruder, I sat at her desk, flipped to a new page in the notebook and made a list of people I'd need to call. Regina's lawyer, definitely, and then Emma. Clotilde, the shelter director. I'd need to make sure she was aware of Regina's will and make an appointment despite the fact that I'd never, ever wanted to set foot in the shelter again. Considering a fourth name, I debated with myself. Was I being silly? Overreacting? With a sigh, I wrote "Detective Blodgett."

Didn't want to talk to him again either.

It was too early to call any of them. I pulled out Regina's client list and grabbed the nearest stack of files. I'd have to read each one carefully, reviewing the clinical progress notes before calling each one. It was time-consuming work, work that would require my full attention, my total commitment to people I'd never even met.

This I could do.

I busied myself checking Regina's client list against the files piled on her desk, making notes, creating new lists dividing clients into tentative groups: those to be referred, those to invite to a grief support group, those who might need immediate attention and so on. The task was absorbing, which is why it took me several attempts at cross-checking a particular file with Regina's client list to realize that it didn't belong to the clinic. Didn't belong *in* the clinic, for that matter.

At first glance, it seemed like a typical manila file folder, although rather more beat up than usual as though recycled from a previous use. The stickers were different, too. Every office has its own system, using stickers or some other marking on the exterior of the file to indicate various information. Our clinic used colored circles to indicate activity status; a green circle meant an active client, red meant a closed case. We also had a system to indicate whether the client paid by private means or through an insurance carrier, and, if the latter, which?

The file I held had none of these indicators and, in fact, the client's name had been neatly handwritten in black ink on the label tab instead of printed on a computer-generated label. No case number either.

I didn't recognize the name—Tammy Long— although that didn't mean much. If it weren't for this situation I wouldn't have known any of Regina's clients' identities. There were a half-dozen progress reports inside, all in Regina's slanted, spiky handwriting. I paged past them, coming to the client info sheet clipped to the back of the folder. I was looking for information on the client but the first thing that caught my eye was the letterhead: a deep purple logo—three linked feminine figures protectively encircling a fourth—centered on the header with the agency name, Devlin House for Women, underneath.

What was Regina doing with a shelter file here?

It didn't make sense. Standard practice holds that files are never removed from their parent agency, unless perhaps if they are to be archived at a separate, designated site. Regina knew this.

A quick examination of the stack dredged up five more. Six files, in total, belonging to Devlin House that had no business being here in the clinic. Worse, only three of them were Regina's own clients. One belonged to another therapist whose scrawled signature was both unfamiliar and illegible. Regina had taken them from the shelter, but for what purpose? It seemed so out of character. Regina followed rules. She may have bitched about them or, more likely, walked a picket line against them, but she wouldn't have simply broken them without a very good—an overridingly *important*—reason.

I sat back in the chair, thinking. There were too many unusual circumstances in Regina's death, in the recent changes to her will, in this latest discovery for me to feel comfortable. Yet, what did I really know? The sister Regina had little contact with didn't know she knitted? A couple of files had been misplaced? Perhaps Regina had absentmindedly placed them in her briefcase, brought them to this office. Maybe something was going on with her medically? Something that could account for her distractibility—if that's what it was—and cause her to lose her footing or be disoriented resulting in a fall.

Or I could easily be overreacting. I acknowledged that. On the other hand, I told myself as I gathered up the files and headed to the copy machine, another mysterious "something" had made Regina change her executor of many years to me as recently as a couple of weeks ago. I scanned the records as I fed them to the copier. The dates ranged from March 2007 to this August—all had been closed out. So whatever the reason for her keeping them, it wasn't because they were current clients.

I glanced at the clock. My co-workers would be straggling in any minute ready to start the workday. I didn't want them to find me illicitly copying files from another agency. My actions were just as wrong as Regina's taking them, and I'd never be able to explain the nebulous doubts that I was reacting to. I didn't understand them myself.

My other problem was where to hide them. I didn't dare hide them in plain sight in the file room, something I'd tried once before with disastrous results. Hearing the front door open, I grabbed up the papers willy-nilly and fled back to my office. As I hastily reassembled the paperwork, I realized I should simply take the original files back to the shelter and leave the copies in Regina's office. No one would know they were duplicates since I was the only one with access to both agencies. Hiding in plain sight. Again.

What could go wrong?

CHAPTER FIVE

Before I went to the shelter, I made two of the phone calls from my list. The first was to Regina's lawyer, Ashley Perkins. I had a hard time reconciling the cute, perky name with my idea of a lawyer, but the no-nonsense voice fit. She spent seven minutes on the phone with me and probably billed Regina's estate for an hour. But, then, therapists were among the first to invent the fifty-minute hour, so I shouldn't judge.

At any rate, she didn't need any more time to confirm that yes, I was stuck being the executor and it meant all the duties that I thought it meant, and no, she had no idea why Regina felt the need to change the executorship two weeks ago. However, she did let me know that the previous executor, Lachlyn Brody, had held the spot for well over eight years. Listening to her strong, assured voice, I couldn't bring myself to ask her if she thought Regina's death might be something other than an accident. It seemed silly.

The second call went straight to voice mail, a relief since I had no better idea of what to say to Detective Blodgett than to anyone else. Unless I came up with something more credible than Regina's assumed non-knitting habits, I'd sound like some conspiracy nut.

The suspicions that tickled my brain would sound crazy just as soon as I voiced them. Pondering that line of reasoning, I looked up "paranoid schizophrenia" in my DSM-IV just in case I'd fallen over the line already. It wasn't reassuring.

The drive to the shelter went all too fast despite my efforts to catch every red light. Instead, the fates sailed me through a long procession of green lights and got me there in record time.

Devlin House, an immense, thrown-together duplex, sat at the end of a block of sleek office buildings and looked as misplaced as a dandelion in a rose bed. Despite being two stories, it appeared squat, slightly shabby, and in serious need of a fresh paint job. Shingles, too, when I looked a little closer.

I rested my head back on the car seat and sighed. Time for a little pep talk. I was here in a professional capacity. I was here as the legal representative of a . . . Well, not a good friend, that was stretching it. But still, a legal representative. A professional. Definitely not a victim.

It wasn't working, but I pushed myself out of the car anyway.

The door chimed as I entered the front door of the administrative side of the duplex. Midday, the shelter was quiet, the resident women at jobs or looking for them. Against my will, I glanced to the left, into the group counseling room. A former living room, its walls were painted a light spring green overlaid haphazardly with child-height scuff marks and small, white scars where folding chairs had been pushed back carelessly, gouging half-moons into the drywall. A wooden bookshelf filled with self-help, feel-good books, feminist tomes, and an entire collection of Dr. Phil's words of wisdom had been placed against the back wall. Generic brand tissue boxes were placed on the floor in between every third chair or so, and a yellow legal pad rested on one of the chairs, waiting for the next line of notes to be filled in.

I took a deep breath, trying to relocate oxygen to the areas of my body that needed it. A door shut behind me, and I twisted around. Not Clotilde, the director, although this woman was just as tall and exuded the same sense of efficiency. It took me a moment to recognize her.

"Hi, I'm Astrid. Welcome to Devlin House. You're safe here." She smiled warmly and I felt myself smiling back.

"Thank you," I said. "I'm Letty Whittaker. I'm here to see Clotilde. . ." I fumbled, not remembering her last name. "I worked with Regina. At the clinic."

The smile left her eyes. "Oh, yes. Horrible, isn't it? I still get the shakes when I think about it. I thought your eulogy was very nice."

We stood for a moment, awkwardly, before she gathered herself to respond.

"Do you have an appointment? Clotilde has a lot on her plate, what with this emergency and all. I don't think she has a spare minute today. Why don't you give me your information and I'll have her—"

"Um, no," I interrupted. "I suppose I should have called, but. . ." I let that trail off, because of course I should have called. However, it probably wouldn't help to explain that I wanted to meet them face-to-face in order to evaluate each as a potential murderer. That might be a communication barrier, as we say.

Astrid maintained her welcoming expression, although I sensed an exasperated huff building under the smile. I could understand her irritation; among other things, she probably had two jobs—welcome visitors and guard the boss's time—and I was straining her efforts on both. Despite my reluctance to give out too much information, I was going to have to provide a more detailed explanation or run the risk of being shooed back to my car.

"Regina appointed me executor of her professional duties," I explained. "That includes the shelter as well as the clinic. I'm really sorry to interrupt Clotilde, but I need to coordinate my efforts here and make arrangements to settle Regina's case load. Her lawyer can verify this if there are any concerns."

Astrid's eyebrows shot up and her whole body stiffened. At the very least, I'd managed to pierce the shell of efficiency. "I see," she said. "Well. Wait here. Clotilde is in the back."

She spun on her heel, leaving me standing next to the entry door while she went to alert her boss. I'd lost the advantage of breaking the news myself, but it couldn't be helped. As I stood in the dark entryway, I heard a door at the back of the house open and click shut. Moments later, it opened again and the sound of brisk footsteps brought the shelter's director into view. Astrid trotted just behind.

I'd met Clotilde once, briefly, during the time I'd come here with Regina, and I saw a flicker of recognition in her light blue eyes. Or maybe it was from my short eulogy at the funeral. Neither episode had shown me at my best, but I pasted a professional smile on my face and stuck my hand out anyway.

Her grasp was strong, almost painful, but she released my hand the second before I would've been sure she was aiming for intimidation. I was surprised to find her dressed very smartly. The soft grey suit wasn't Bruno Grizzo, but she hadn't picked up the ensemble at Wally-world either.

"Why don't we talk in my office?" she said, with a glance at Astrid. A look passed between them, too quick to interpret. I followed Clotilde, hurrying to keep up with her long strides, just as Astrid had. A row of offices ran the length of the hall opposite the group counseling room so it was only a distance of about forty feet, which was good because I hadn't been keeping up with my aerobics and I was already sweating from nerves.

Her office was as I expected. A small room, crowded with papers and books, various newspaper photos showing Devlin House over the years hanging in cheap frames on the walls. The furniture was hand-me-down expensive—items that had been donated from wealthy benefactors and put to good use. The only object in the room looking relatively new was the computer.

Clotilde motioned to a straight-backed, wooden chair placed in front of the desk. I sat, feeling the chair wobble on uneven legs. *A power play. Or just another ancient donation?*

"Astrid tells me—" She broke off as the door opened. A third Amazon entered, joining Clotilde behind the desk. She remained standing, reminding me of a bodyguard or a dueler's second. In contrast to Clotilde's smart business attire, she wore a baggy pantsuit in a pea green tone that did nothing for her complexion. No makeup, of course. None of them wore any that I could tell, making me feel like a harlot with my eyeliner and lip gloss.

Clotilde went on without introducing us. "Astrid

tells me that you are here representing Regina." Her voice tilted at the end, making a question out of the fact as though she couldn't quite believe that Astrid had communicated correctly.

"Her professional estate, yes," I answered, pulling a copy of Regina's instructions out and laying them on the desk between us. "She named me executor of her professional duties and listed very clearly what that would entail. In addition to settling her client cases at the clinic where we worked together, I'm to do the same here. I'm sure you're well aware of Regina's organizational skills." I smiled to show we were on the same team. They didn't.

Clotilde nodded noncommittally throughout my little speech. Her bodyguard, however, had no such compunction, frowning at the sheaf of papers as though her eyes could ignite them. Following Clotilde's lead, I kept my face expressionless, a professional mask. She picked up the instructions and began reading. She didn't hurry, and I concentrated on sitting still, projecting an air of confidence on loan from somewhere. Maybe I was channeling Regina. When she finished, Clotilde cleared her throat, glancing up once, enigmatically, at her sidekick.

"Everything seems to be in order," she said. "However, we'll need to decide how to proceed. There are certain protocols that would need to be followed. The shelter and our clients have very specific needs, and I'm sure that Regina, of all people, would want us to protect them."

"I understand," I said, although I didn't. "I don't want to disrupt your program any more than necessary, especially after all that's occurred. Of course, I'll need access to Regina's client list and files, and I'll need to meet with her clients. We're arranging a grief support group at the clinic; I'm sure we could expand it to include any client here who might find it helpful."

"It's just that sort of thing that causes difficulties," Clotilde said. "We don't want our residents to be out in public areas any more than necessary. Their situations are often very volatile, and several are in active hiding from abusive partners. We couldn't expect them to travel across town to another agency to receive services."

I looked over my shoulder as if my gaze could penetrate the walls of the empty shelter. Obviously, the women didn't spend *all* their time in hiding. I knew from my own participation here that most women continued working or otherwise spent the day in the community, only returning at night to the safety of the shelter. One woman in my group, despite all advice, used to go back to her home to keep up with the housework and the laundry.

"That's fine. I could set up a group here as well. No problem."

"I'll need to confer with our board about access to the clients and their files." She met the bodyguard's gaze.

"I don't understand," I said.

I left the statement hanging in the air. Clotilde and I had an ever-so-polite stare down while I awaited her answer. She didn't want to, I knew. Maybe she was used to immediate compliance, but we both knew she had no standing here. The document was legal.

Time for another bomb.

CHAPTER SIX

From my large purse, I pulled the files Regina had appropriated—a much nicer word than "stole"—and laid them on the desk. Two pair of glinty eyes tracked my movements like heat-seeking missiles. "I found these at the clinic. Why would Regina have removed these from the shelter?"

A long silence descended. The air almost crackled with tension as the two strained for an appearance of normality. Clotilde cleared her throat.

"Obviously we can't hazard a guess since we don't know what you have there." She drew the stack toward her. The bodyguard leaned in to read over her shoulder.

"Excuse me? I don't believe we've been introduced." I stood, extending my hand across the desk. "My name's Letty Whittaker. You are. . .?"

She hesitated, which I found interesting. "Lachlyn Brody."

"I see. Then you must already be aware of Regina's intentions regarding her professional will. . . " *Since you were her executor until two weeks ago,* I didn't say. Wanted to, but didn't. Having opposition to something I didn't even want to do was causing a well-spring of petulance to bubble up inside. I would have to watch that. "And I'm sure you're *well* aware of the legal standing of the document."

Nobody's perfect.

"Thank you for returning the shelter's property." Clotilde reentered the fray. "I'm not sure why Regina had these in her possession. Perhaps she was thinking of submitting a paper for review. At any rate, we hadn't discussed it. For now, however, you can leave your contact information with Astrid. I'll get back to you as soon as I discuss the situation with our board members."

Since I was still standing, there wasn't much I could do, but I wasn't ready to slink off, either. "When can I expect your call?"

Irritation flashed across her face. It was probably unusual for anyone to demand an answer from the director, and even more rare for her to expose her emotions. It gave me a childish, zingy thrill. She glanced again at Lachlyn for more silent communion. Maybe they were practicing to be telepaths.

"I should get back to you by the end of this week," Clotilde said.

At the same time, Lachlyn offered, "Maybe by Monday."

I smiled pleasantly, choosing to respond to Clotilde. "Friday, then."

No surprise: Friday came and went with no call from Devlin House. It gave me time to reflect on the meeting and, after the thrill of battle passed, I wasn't entirely pleased with my performance. Not pleased at all, in fact. Despite the momentary rush of surviving a grown-up version of mean-girl wars, I couldn't see any advantage in alienating two persons who could make my executor job difficult, thus extending the time and energy I'd have to invest in order to complete it.

They say that an alcoholic's maturity level gets stalled at the time of life that she started drinking. Which means, despite a graduate degree and a respected profession in the mental health field, I've been a teenager passing as an adult for several years. I'm working on it.

Since I was already immersed in immaturity, my inclination was to blame my response on the Amazons. That felt comfy. Clotilde and Lachlyn had certainly put out strong bitchvibes, but my instinctive bitch-back wasn't going to help the situation, no matter how gratifying.

Plus, with Regina's death and the strange circumstances around it, I was just too emotional to fully trust my gut. Was there some strange purpose behind the power-play going on at Devlin House, or was it simply a battle of wills with two domineering women? Hard to tell.

The delay gave me time to make arrangements at the clinic for the grief group. I also thought to include any of our coworkers who might benefit from attending, but no one took me up on it. Not surprising and nothing to do with how anyone felt about Regina, I imagined. We therapists are just more comfortable being the helpers than the helped.

The clinic reopened on Thursday morning, so many of my coworkers claimed to be too busy for the group that evening. My friend Hannah agreed to cocounsel, though, and that was nice. Hannah is a health-conscious, earth-mother type who was thoughtful enough to bring snacks and tea, which hadn't occurred to me. If it had, I would probably have brought something laden with chocolate. Instead,

Hannah chose to bring in her "special" muffins made, she informed us, with natural molasses and acorns she'd picked up from the ground herself. They required a lot of chewing and were gluten-free.

Clotilde didn't call until Tuesday. At 6:00 a.m. A time she could be certain she wouldn't find me in the office. Her message said that the board had given temporary approval (whatever that was) for me to review Regina's current client list only. I interpreted this to mean I was sort of okayed to do not much. I wouldn't have access to Regina's closed files unless the full board met, reviewed the will, and gave official approval. They were seeking advice from their lawyer, too. Lastly, they required a shelter employee be present to "supervise" my involvement. Apparently, they were insisting on a reviewer for my reviewing. The whole thing reminded me of the Bee-Watcher Watcher in a Dr. Seuss book my mother used to read me. But it didn't make me feel lucky.

Lachlyn was my assigned bee-watcher watcher.

CHAPTER SEVEN

I made sure to get to the shelter later that very evening. No sense in dragging it out, but irritated at the delay over the weekend and the ridiculous restrictions, my inner bitch tugged on the leash a little. She decided we needed to make a point. Sometimes I have very little control over her. It was worse when we drank.

Astrid once again opened the door. This time the group room door was shut, the soft sibilant sound of women's voices dipping and rising just beyond. Astrid put a finger to her lips, shushing me, then motioned me to follow. I couldn't tell if she was protecting the residents' confidentiality or merely trying to keep my presence a secret. We retreated to Clotilde's office. Astrid, still silent, circled around the desk and took a seat. Her expression was a careful blank, no vestige of the welcome that she'd previously extended.

"Clotilde told me to give you the list of Regina's clients. Her current ones, that is. A few of them are still in residence, but the others were seen as outpatients. Their contact information will be in their individual files, but be sure you read the notes sections to make sure that it's safe to contact them at home. We don't want you to put anyone at any more risk than is necessary."

"Of course not. I don't want to put anyone at risk."

"Well, that won't change the fact that you probably will. I don't know what Regina was thinking . . ." The last was muttered quietly as she twisted to reach the file cabinet behind her. Not so quiet as to not be heard, however.

Pulling the top drawer open, she reached in, grabbing a sheaf of papers. "I can't just give you a key. You'll have to arrange a time with Lachlyn since she's in charge of you."

It took an effort to not respond to the "in charge of you" statement, but I managed. Taking a deep breath, I asked how I could get a message to Lachlyn. I imagined another few days of the runaround. Instead, Astrid pointed to the wall. "Her office is right next door." Her expression indicated great doubt that I could manage the five or so feet without visual aids. "She's probably still here. She rarely leaves before 7:00."

"Such dedication." I turned before she could verify whether I was being sarcastic. My vow to resist pettiness was being broken at every step, but I tried to regroup before knocking.

A crisp "One moment" greeted me through the cheap, hollow-core door. A scowl greeted me after it opened. I couldn't see much past Lachlyn's tall, spare frame, but what I could reminded me of a monk's cell. The furniture had been stripped down to a cheap metal desk and a decade old swivel office chair. No paintings that I could see. No knickknacks. Papers arranged with OCD precision on the desk's surface. Lachlyn shifted to block my view.

"Good evening," I chirped. I was not surprised to

discover that Lachlyn was prone to sneering. Here's where my pettiness came in handy because instead of acting as a deterrent, Lachlyn's sourness cheered me immensely. Since I couldn't seem to vanquish my inner bitch, I'd have to make her work for me.

Easy enough.

I followed Lachlyn to Regina's old office, where she unlocked the door as reluctantly as if she were letting me in to ransack her family's burial vault. Like Clotilde's, it was another mishmash of furniture odds and ends. Oddly enough, Regina hadn't added her personal touch here. She did have a couple of generic landscape-type pictures, but nothing that reflected the sense of style and warmth that she had displayed at our clinic.

Lachlyn stood next to the file cabinet and stretched her hand palm up toward me.

For a brief, crazy moment I thought she was asking me to dance. "What?" I asked, mentally backing away.

"The client list?" She didn't bother with sarcasm, but kept her voice flat and dry as though my stupidity exhausted her. Nice touch.

I handed it over, glancing around the office again as I did. It was so very unlike Regina, so plain and stripped down. Inhospitable. Lachlyn unlocked the cabinet and immediately pulled out a small stack of files rubber-banded together. She hadn't even needed to sort through the long row of manila files lining the drawer.

"You've already gone through these, haven't you?" They had gone through the office too, I realized. That's why it felt so wrong. Regina's articles had been removed, her files combed through. Whatever I'd be reviewing was likely to have been sanitized. But of what? At any rate, I still had the copies of Regina's pilfered files, and I would find anything worth finding in those. I hoped.

"Of course we did. We weren't aware of any changes in Regina's plans, and we needed to protect our women."

"When will I be able to review the closed files?"

"Who knows if you even will? That hasn't been decided yet. The full board still needs to meet on that issue. They can't be expected to completely rearrange their lives and their schedules to suit you."

Having spoken her piece, she stalked out the door. I heard her footsteps recede toward the kitchen and sighed in relief.

Short-lived.

Before I could even circle the desk to take a seat, she was back in the tiny room, hauling a metal folding chair. She stuck it in the corner, then sailed out the door again. Moments later, back in she came with a notepad and pen. She sat in the chair looking like she might be ready to take dictation.

Apparently, my file-reviewer reviewer was ready to begin. Sitting at the desk, I pulled the stack of files to me and began checking the names against the list Astrid had provided. Not that I would be able to tell if there had been any tampering. Unless . . .

I pulled open the top drawer, yanking it too hard since I'd expected it to be locked. Stray pencils shot from back to front, rattling like bones in a coffin. No wonder they hadn't bothered with locks. Unless I could read the past in the loose paperclips and food crumbs in the empty space, there was nothing for them to worry about. I slammed the drawer.

"Did Regina have an appointment book?" I asked.

"I wouldn't know."

"Did she use a computer?" I thought back, seeming to remember Regina carrying a red leather laptop case. Of course, our clinic had computers, old and clunky, in each therapist's office, which hooked up to a central server. We were able to check our schedules, although clients set those up with the secretaries in the front office. But here, the only computer I'd seen was Clotilde's dinosaur-era monster. I hadn't noticed one when I'd peeked over Lachlyn's shoulder, but maybe it was out of view.

"No, we can't afford one for everyone. And those that are donated are usually so riddled with viruses that they're next to useless."

"Then how did Regina keep track of her appointments? Did she have a planner?"

Lachlyn's hesitation was so brief it might have been overlooked by someone less familiar with resistance. "I said I don't know. You'll have to ask Astrid. By the way, you only have another twenty minutes before I have to go. Next time, you might let me know what your plans are. I can't be expected to drop everything whenever you decide to show up."

"How do the rest of you keep track of appointments? Does Astrid have them on her computer system?"

My cell phone rang, jarring me from my thoughts. I checked the Caller ID—Blodgett. The detective's timing was as rotten as a fart in an elevator. I let it go to voice mail and repeated my question to Lachlyn.

"No, she doesn't. We each take care of our own scheduling. Are you finished?" She snapped her notebook shut and stood.

"I still have twenty minutes." I pulled the top file

off the stack and opened it. Keeping my eyes riveted to the document, I could nevertheless feel Lachlyn's resentment emanating from across the desk. However, she regrouped.

"*Seventeen* minutes," she said as she sat back down.

I let my eyes rise to hers and gave a fleeting Mona Lisa smile. Then I got back to work.

CHAPTER EIGHT

Sixteen minutes later—yes, I counted—Lachlyn snatched the files out of my hands, locked them in the cabinet and stalked back to her office. Didn't even say good-bye.

I could still hear voices coming from the group therapy room, so instead of leaving, I followed the hall past Lachlyn's lair and Clotilde's office. I paused briefly outside the director's but couldn't hear anyone beyond the closed door. I didn't want to see her anyway. Just beyond Clotilde's office stood another door. I tested it and discovered a set of stairs leading up into Stygian darkness. *Was it this stairway. . . ?*

I shuddered, not wanting to think about Regina's fall, and shut the door a bit too loudly. I half-expected Lachlyn to poke her head out and catch me being nosy, so I hurried on into the communal kitchen. A light burned over the stove, which should have made the room feel cozier. I could feel the chill of the tiled floor through my thinly soled dress shoes. The heat was probably on a timer-switch that lowered the temperature automatically in the evening.

I'd just decided that there was no one around and was envisioning going home to a long, hot bath, when I heard a thump from a room just beyond the furnace room.

"Hello?" I called.

The door cracked open, spilling light into the space. Astrid stood blinking out into the hallway, a warm smile on her plain face. "Yes?"

"Hi, Astrid. It's me. Letty Whittaker?" I moved into the tiny halo of light offered by the stove.

She stopped smiling. "Oh. What can I do for you?"

"I'm sorry to bother you. I just wondered if we could set up some time for me to meet with you. I really don't understand the shelter or its workings, and, well, I don't want to make things worse for the women here. I thought maybe you could give me an overview, kind of help steer me in the right direction."

"Oh!" Surprised at my overture, she moved toward me slightly, her body relaxing into itself, becoming less of a barricade. I'd touched her Achilles heel, one which most of us in the mental health field shared: the need to be needed. I hadn't planned it, but I'd always had a soft spot for support staff in an agency. Secretaries could be formidable allies. They knew where the bodies were buried. So to speak.

Down the hall, a door opened. The sound of several women talking at once rippled toward us as the group let out.

Astrid stepped back quickly, almost guiltily. "Call me. We'll set something up." She shut the door in my face, leaving me stranded in what I thought was the *middle* of the conversation.

"Well, now I just feel cheap," I muttered.

"What?" The light clicked on as two women entered the kitchen, apparently ready to scrounge up an evening snack. They looked at me strangely.

"I, um, said I needed some sleep. Time to go

home!" I sailed past as they traded skeptical looks with each other, their giggles following me out the door.

I didn't call. Instead, I showed up at the shelter at 7:00 a.m. Unfortunately, I was the only one who did. I tried tapping at the office-side of the duplex, but no one responded. After briefly entertaining the idea of knocking on the other side, I decided against it. I was afraid I'd scare the women and really piss off Clotilde. Astrid showed up about an hour and a half later, thus saving me from a nearly exploded bladder and terminal boredom. After waiting for her to park, I hopped out of my car, trotting after her.

"I thought you were going to call," she said, scowling. Apparently, whatever goodwill I'd accrued last night had expired. Maybe she wasn't a morning person.

"Really? I thought you said to meet you here this morning. I'm sorry." I smiled disarmingly.

It didn't take. She stood frowning in the middle of the sidewalk, although since she didn't actually order me away, I pretended not to notice.

"I really don't have time this morning to—"

"Do you mind if I use the bathroom? I really have to go." I whispered the last sentence in one of those confidential, pseudo-girlfriend tones that are supposed to be hard for fellow women to resist. I could tell she was tempted, but when I pretended to eye the shrubbery, she caved.

After using the bathroom, I found Astrid in the kitchen making fresh coffee. The smell of eggs and syrup hung in the air like the ghost of breakfasts-past, making my mouth water. Despite that, the room looked much the same as it had last night; the women had cleaned up after themselves so well that, without the aroma, I wouldn't have been aware they even existed. It also made me wonder why no one had answered my knocking.

"Do the women eat on this side? I thought it was just administrative."

"It is. The stove is broken on their side and we just have to make do."

"This is certainly an amazing place," I said, my voice so buttery I almost imagined it adding to the breakfast smell. "I can see that it's very well run. What exactly is your role here?"

A brief war played across Astrid's face. Half of her knew she should boot me out, but the other? The other half ached to talk about her life's work.

"My role? Well, I guess I'm the one who feeds the women cookies and tucks them in at night."

She laughed and I could tell that she'd used that line many times before. I smiled back at her. "That's nice. They must need someone like you after all the abuse they've been through."

"They do. Many of them can't even remember feeling safe or cared for. That's the first thing we tell them. That's what I told you, remember? When you first came in?" A shadow crossed her eyes as she remembered my purpose in coming to the shelter.

"How does the shelter manage the security issues here?" I asked hurriedly.

"That's my area," she said, almost preening again. Apparently I'd stumbled on exactly the right question to keep from being booted out the door. "It's our biggest expense, really. But there's no getting around it. Come here."

CHAPTER NINE

Astrid led me to a door tucked in between the kitchen and her office. I could hear the furnace humming to life just beyond. Unlike the cheap doors that were used elsewhere, this door was of solid wood. Pulling a jangling batch of keys off a belt clip, Astrid unlocked it. Inside, a furnace did indeed take up most of the space, but a good share of the wall housed an electrical panel that looked like a NASA-level circuit board. Astrid waved a hand at it.

"This is what a lot of our donations go for. It's a good system, but it needs updating. With all that's happened, I'm hoping the board will see . . . Well, never mind." She shut the door again, firmly, and made a show of locking it back up. Then she continued on to her own office, using the keys again.

I followed. The whole purpose of Astrid's domain, about the size of a walk-in closet, seemed to be to house the computer that sat on the desk. Astrid had to squeeze sideways between the wall and desk to take her chair behind it. A clear swath, butt-high, on the dingy paint tracked her route.

"Apparently this is where the rest of the donations go," I said, indicating the computer.

"It's all part of the security system. The video

cameras around the property feed into this computer and record all movement on the perimeter. I can access the system for remote viewing, if need be, and, of course, so can the police. When it's set, an alarm will sound if the perimeter is breached. What we really need, though, is a silent alarm system so if an intruder gains access and it develops into a hostage situation, we can alert the police."

"What if they cut the power?" There was no extra chair so, since we were getting so chatty, I perched on the corner of the desk. Regina had described some aspects of the shelter's security precautions when she'd dragged me here months ago, but not to this degree. She'd also made me participate in a safety drill, which I'd hated. I didn't remind Astrid, though; I needed her to forget I was a different kind of intruder, and letting her show off her expertise was making good headway.

"Most of our utilities are buried, but we also have a backup battery as well. Plus any cut wires instantly set the alarm off and notifies the police and fire department."

"Sounds pretty elaborate. Is that why you don't worry about keeping the shelter a secret?"

"More like the other way around, really. It's nearly impossible to keep a shelter's location confidential for very long, especially in a small city like Chippewa Falls. Too many women and their children come through the doors, the police and fire departments are all in the loop, and eventually any repair work means we have to have construction workers or plumbers or whatever here. This way, we're known to the community. In fact, some of our neighbors help keep watch on our ladies. I've had several of them call the cops on strange cars or men who seem to be lurking. A lot of the problems get handled before the assholes even get on the premises.

"Besides," she went on, "why should the women have to sneak around like they're the problem? Most of their abusers are cowards and bullies who aren't going to risk having witnesses for their actions. This way, we don't have to keep our offices in a separate facility, and we can openly educate the community on domestic violence issues."

"Most of the abusers," I repeated. "But not all. What about the ones who aren't going to be stopped by a bunch of women? A neighborhood watch might not be enough." Having been the victim of a stalker a few months ago, I knew the risk these women were taking. Knew it *very* well.

Astrid sighed. "There are pros and cons to both approaches. If it were up to me, I'd have gone with keeping the place secret. They just went with what seemed the most practical at the time."

I noted the 'I-they' comment.

"But I understand your concerns," she continued. "Let me assure you, I take my job very seriously. At any rate, I keep them safe here at the shelter. The problems start when they go out into the real world, don't they?"

Astrid's eyes were soft and gentle, telling me she knew about my past.

Enough bonding.

"Did the cameras record Regina's fall?"

Astrid stiffened, the tenderness slipping off her face like it had been greased. "No. The cameras aren't. . .well, never mind. What a *morbid* thought."

She stood abruptly, shoving past my knees and out the door in a heartbeat. She held it open, waves of disapproval radiating off her body.

"I'm sorry. That was tactless." Meekly, I followed

her into the dim hallway. "Regina told me to watch out for irritability or sudden outbursts of anger after . . . You know." Tactless *and* heartless. I had no compunction about using Regina's name or Astrid's awareness of my history to my advantage. Not under these circumstances. And Astrid would be well-versed in the symptoms of posttraumatic stress disorder, the changes that occur after one's very life has been threatened. She also knew about my former boyfriend's death. I'd talked about it one night, months ago, when Regina had dragged me to a group here.

It must have worked. Astrid calmed a bit, the blaze dropping from her eyes.

Pressing ahead, I pulled the client list she'd given me the day before from my purse. "You said that this is Regina's current client list. Does that mean that these women are still in residence?" I already knew the answer from my file review yesterday, but I needed to re-engage her.

She took the list, scanning it. "Yes, well, at least most of them are. These two—" she pointed at two names—"were discharged a few weeks ago. They were meeting with Regina once a week for outpatient counseling. I don't see Karissa here, though. Maybe because she left. She took off with her kids the Sunday before last. I'm worried about her. She'd only been here a few days, and I don't think she was at all ready to leave."

"A week ago Sunday? The day after Regina's accident?" I asked.

Before she could answer, a voice from the kitchen said, "Astrid? Who are you talking to?"

We both jumped.

A tall, Junoesque figure stood shadowed in the

kitchen doorway, a cup of coffee steaming in her hand.

"Good morning, Lachlyn," I said, walking forward. My heart thumped as hard as if I was facing an IRS auditor. In fact, that would be preferable.

The figure stepped back as I approached, moving from the dark hall into the morning light of the kitchen. Clotilde—not Lachlyn.

"Oh, I'm sorry, Clotilde. I thought you were—"

"Are you here to meet with Lachlyn?" she interrupted in a distinct, your-explanations-mean-*nothing*-to-me tone.

Almost hurt my feelings.

"Not today, I'm afraid. I'm going to give her a call and set something up. Speaking of appointments, do you know where Regina's calendar is? Nobody seems to know what kind of system she used to keep track."

We eye-dueled for several moments before Clotilde smiled and said, "No, I certainly don't know where Regina's calendar is. Astrid? Do you?"

Astrid shook her head, looking as if she wanted the floor to swallow her up.

"I've already asked Astrid. She couldn't tell me anything, either." I tossed a bone to the woman, not wanting her to get in trouble for talking with me. I really wanted that calendar, though. For one thing, all I had to go on regarding Regina's client list was Clotilde's word, and I certainly didn't trust her. No one had mentioned this Karissa, and her name wasn't on the client list that I still clutched in my sweaty hand. There was no way she would be included on the closed file list if she hadn't left the shelter until the day after Regina died. In fact, it was entirely possible that Karissa, having been at the shelter that night, would have information about the incident.

I needed to find her.

I looked up to find Clotilde staring at me. I shuddered, hoping she couldn't follow my thoughts.

It depended, however, on just how much she had overheard.

CHAPTER TEN

A s soon as I got back to the clinic I confirmed that
Karissa and her children weren't on the roster of
clients that the shelter had provided me. The
question, of course, was why not? I checked the
stash of files that Regina had appropriated and
established Karissa whoever wasn't included there
either.

I really needed Regina's calendar, which I hoped
would contain the facts about Regina's clients. It would
help if I knew whether she carried a hard copy, such as
a day planner, or kept track by computer. A closer
search of her office didn't turn anything up, but I
hadn't really expected it to. I'd gone through her
papers very carefully and had been working in her
office almost daily since accepting the executor's
responsibilities.

But I hadn't been to her house. A sudden fear that
Clotilde or Lachlyn had already gone through Regina's
home made my stomach cramp. There were so many
knots to unravel that I was certainly overlooking some
obvious ones. I searched through the paperwork until I
found Emma's phone number, then held my breath
through several rings, trying to improvise a coherent
message in case her voice mail picked up.

My luck was in. Emma answered and agreed to meet me at Regina's after she got off work Friday afternoon. I didn't have any clients scheduled after three that day so that worked well for me. She asked if I'd mind picking up a box of Regina's personal things from the shelter if she called them to give permission. No. No, I didn't mind at all.

Thursday morning unfolded into one of those crisp autumn days that made me wish I could get out to the woods. Since I wasn't seeing clients today, I decided to go casual and wear my denim jacket and the Timberlands I'd gotten on sale last spring at Gander Mountain. At least I could look hiker-esque.

I'd tried calling Lachlyn after my AA meeting the night before but only managed to get her voice mail. I told it that I'd be stopping by this morning to pick up Regina's personal items and hoped I could get some time with the files. I sounded so submissive I almost puked.

Even if Lachlyn wasn't available, I planned to confront Clotilde about Karissa's missing files. I'd gone back and forth trying to decide if she'd overheard Astrid. Eventually I decided it didn't matter either way. If she hadn't heard us, it was only a matter of time until Astrid filled her in. If she had, she and Lachlyn would probably amp up the resistance to my presence. Either way, I was going to need Karissa's file and contact information. Better yet, I was legally entitled to it.

Before heading over to the shelter, I met with Bob to give him an update and ask if he knew anything about Regina's shelter calendar.

He denied knowing anything—which explained a lot—and gave me an impatient, finger-rolling gesture telling me to get on with it. I debated showing him a different sort of finger gesture, but refrained.

Hannah and I had scheduled the second grief session for the coming Tuesday, even though only a few of Regina's clients had committed to attending. Of those, several would probably be no-shows. It was a start, anyway. Others had decided they'd feel more comfortable in a one-to-one setting, and I'd been scheduling meetings throughout the week. Unfortunately, even more had decided to discontinue therapy altogether. Almost all agreed to return if needed, but I didn't have an established relationship with any of them. Therefore, there was no way of knowing which were close enough to the end of therapy to pick up the pieces and move forward on their own and which were tucking their issues back under the rock of denial until the next crisis overtook their life. In other words, who was bullshitting and who wasn't.

Hearing how many clients had dropped out of therapy clearly annoyed Bob, and we shared a moment of helplessness that therapists experience when a client's fears draw him away from confronting the pain in his life. For the first time, I almost liked Bob.

Of course he had to ruin it.

What I'd interpreted as concern for the clients' welfare was actually bitching about the drop in revenue. What a nub. As soon as I realized my error, the desire to thump him with a blunt object rose like a phoenix from the ashes of my naiveté.

I left for the shelter.

Lachlyn met me at the door and informed me, reluctantly that she had time to supervise while I plowed through the files. Well, actually she said she had time to review them with me, but we both knew what she meant. Perhaps they'd decided that the best way to get rid of me was to let me do my job.

Sillies.

I mentioned Emma's request for her sister's personal effects, but Lachlyn seemed to have no problem with that. She pulled out the same stack of files that I'd looked at two days ago. I shuffled through them quickly, looking to see if they'd added Karissa's. Nope. I worked for several minutes gathering information from the other files while I pondered what to do.

"I believe several of these women are still in residence here?" I asked.

Lachlyn took the list again and placed check marks next to four names. "These women are."

"Have they been reassigned a therapist?"

"Of course. Clotilde and I already adjusted our schedules for now, although we're hoping to have an intern this semester. I doubt if we'll assign any of Regina's clients to her, though. They've been through enough instability as it is."

Lachlyn seemed unusually forthcoming this morning. I didn't trust it.

"So where is Karissa's file?" I asked.

Her face barely quivered, but her breath quickened and she paused several beats too long to be natural.

"It isn't there? I guess you'll have to ask Clotilde."

At least she hadn't insulted me by asking who I meant, but she didn't look surprised either, which made me certain that Clotilde had filled her in.

"Is she in?"

Lachlyn glanced up at the wall clock: 10:02. "I'm sure she is, but I don't think—"

Before Lachlyn could voice her thought, I was speed-walking to Clotilde's office. I pushed the door open, hoping to startle her. She sat at her desk working with an accounting file opened on the computer. She tilted the screen away from my view with a scowl.

"Haven't you ever heard of knocking?"

"Oh, gosh," I said, smiling. "I just figured you for an open-door kind of person." If I were ever to stop, I would miss lying almost as much as drinking.

She smiled back—if gritted teeth counted—and folded her hands in fake patience. I bypassed the wobbly chair and leaned my butt-cheek on the edge of her desk, just enough to be obnoxious but not enough to be called on it. My inner bitch was amused.

"One of Regina's clients was in residence when Regina died. Her name is Karissa. She left the day after. What happened to her file?"

"I have it," Clotilde answered without noticeable pause. One corner of her lip twitched, however, a fleeting sign of contempt, and her hands squeezed sharply together as though she'd had a brief yet satisfying fantasy about strangling me. I scooted my butt two inches farther onto her desk just to egg her on a bit.

"Any reason it wasn't included with Regina's other clients?"

"She left abruptly, without a forwarding address. We have no way of contacting her, so it didn't make sense for her to be included."

I let her words hang in the air between us—a therapeutic technique normally used to allow the speaker a moment of insight. Or, in this case, to emphasize how ridiculous she sounded.

After a long, prickly silence, she flicked her

eyebrows once in annoyance and pulled a manila folder from the bottom desk drawer. "If you want to waste your time, go right ahead. In my experience, these women respond better when their rights to seek or decline therapy are respected. Chasing after them can be dangerous. I don't advise it."

"*Dangerous?*" Maybe my intrusive butt had pushed her over the edge.

"For them, of course."

"Of course."

CHAPTER ELEVEN

Lachlyn was waiting in the office where I'd left her, lips two white slashes as though, in her impatience, she'd pressed hard enough to leach the blood from her face.

"Found it." I waggled Karissa's file at her. This did not appear to elevate her mood as much as it did mine.

"Wonderful," she drawled. "How much longer are you going to be?"

"Not too long. About another hour, maybe."

"Well, make it quick. I have work to do."

To my credit, I did not snap off a salute in response, but sat quietly and began to take notes. Lachlyn watched closely like she'd expected me to try to steal the paperwork. A ridiculous notion. Regina had already spared me the effort.

Karissa Dillard's file was thin. She and her children had been at the clinic for three weeks, and she'd seen Regina for individual therapy once each week. There was also a case note in Regina's spiky scrawl for a group session that had taken place the second week. Four other group notes had been written by Lachlyn, another two by Clotilde and one by a Joyce-somebody. A quick read-through of the individual sessions didn't turn up anything unusual. Regina and Karissa had focused on developing a safety plan and had begun to set goals. Nothing much more than that, which wasn't surprising, given that they'd only met a few times. Besides, in this type of setting, much of the deeper therapeutic work would go on in the group sessions. Peers guiding peers, much like in AA I set the group notes aside for a more careful review and picked up the intake forms.

Aside from a crossed-out phone number, the face sheet, where most of the contact information should be found, was conspicuously blank. A string of three "O's" had been handwritten next to the phone number, which I deciphered as "out of order." I copied them down anyway. Nothing else, not even an emergency contact number, had been filled in on the form.

Except. . .

I squinted at the paper. There *had* been another number. Now that I wasn't scanning the form for information, I realized what I was holding was a copy. Somebody, possibly even Karissa, had erased a phone number from the original and then had the form copied. Whoever it was hadn't managed to erase the digits completely, however. Wisps of lines rose like ghosts from the paper. I squinted harder. I could just barely decipher the area code: 7-1-5, but the rest was too faint. I thought I could see 2-4-7, but the first number might have been a three and the seven was especially iffy, morphing into a one or a nine depending which way I looked at it. The last number was completely indecipherable.

I grabbed the other papers from the file, looking at them harder. All originals, as was the rest of the intake packet. As far as I could tell, only the front page, with the all-important contact information, had been altered.

I looked up and found Lachlyn's eyes boring into mine. Fine. She knew that I knew. I knew that she knew that I knew and all that gibberish. So no need to pretend.

"Who copied this page?"

"What are you talking about now?" Her eyes dropped briefly, flickering to her notepad, then back to my face.

"This page." I held it up.

She didn't even glance at it, although it seemed to cost her some effort to avoid looking at it. Her whole body was tense, but then Lachlyn always held herself like a coiled snake. It was hard to pick out the nuances of her body language since her emotions didn't seem to fluctuate beyond anger or disdain.

"Somebody copied it," I repeated. "*Why?*"

Rising, she strode to the desk and snatched the form out of my hand. She gave it a cursory glance, then tossed it back on the pile of papers strewn across the desk. "I would imagine Karissa did. Clients are understandably upset when they first come in. Don't you get it? They're in fear for their lives. They aren't thinking clearly. She probably started to write down her abuser's number and then realized it would be dangerous to use that one. So I imagine she erased it."

"So why make a copy?"

"How should I know? I didn't do the intake." She stopped abruptly. Took a deep breath. "Look. You really don't get it. We do good work here. We save lives. Regina was a part of all that practically from the beginning. She might have worked at your clinic, but *this*"—her finger stabbed down at the desk—"this is where her heart was. So go ahead. Do your job. Close out her files, whatever. But do it quick because we have *real* work to do here, and you and your snotty, little attitude are keeping us from doing it." Spinning on one heel, she strode out of the office, slamming the door behind her.

I sat in the silence of her abrupt departure, surprised to find myself feeling guilty. The pile of papers and reused, recycled manila folders stared up at me in reproach. She was right; this was where Regina's heart had been. I knew that. Even Regina's anger mirrored the other two administrators, although hers seemed slightly tempered. Possibly working at the clinic had given Regina a different perspective. At least it would have given her some respite from the work going on here. The really important work. Saving lives, yes.

We saved lives at the clinic. We did. But the work here had a grittier feel, a realness that was hard for me to face. The people I worked with at the clinic had problems and they needed help, no doubt about that. The women here, however, were in literal fear for their lives, and their *children's* lives, in some cases. I'd recently lived through similar circumstances, which I assumed was why Regina had reached out to me. Why, when we'd never even really liked each other, she'd saved me.

The cheap furniture, bare walls, the cheeseparing approach to services, the miserly pinched pennies: all reminders that the shelter served people with no other place to go. No other resource. No voice. Only these bitterly dedicated women scrabbling to keep the place afloat on ever-reducing budgets, infrequent donations, and willpower.

Were all of my suspicions wrong?

A soft tapping at the door pulled me from the pity pot I was stirring. Astrid poked her head in. "I have a box for you." She thumped a dilapidated box on the desk. "Regina's things," she explained. "She didn't keep much here. Unfortunately, things have a nasty habit of getting stolen. I suppose it's the children, mostly, but I don't know. The moms are having such a rough time that it's hard to say what they'll do. I mean, they're like in survival mode, you know?"

I nodded. Shoving papers back into their files, I handed the stack to Astrid. "Can you make sure that Lachlyn gets these? She might be worried that I'd. . .well. . .you know."

"Steal them?" She laughed. "Yes, we've had a rash of that lately, too, haven't we? The board is extremely upset with the situation. Will you be at the meeting Saturday morning?"

"I plan on it." Well, I planned on it now, anyway. "That was at what time?"

"At 6:30, which is just crazy, but it's the only time they could get a quorum."

"Sounds pretty official. They *must* be upset."

"Well, security is the most important part of our services. If word got out that we'd been missing files. . ." She let the thought trail off, apparently unwilling to give voice to the consequences. "I can't imagine what Regina was thinking of, can you?"

"Maybe it was all just a big mistake," I said.

CHAPTER TWELVE

I sat in my car trying to think of the best way to make use of the time I had before meeting Emma the next afternoon. My mind was in a swirl trying to decide whether my suspicions had any basis or if I was simply acting paranoid, a not unlikely state of mind after nearly being killed by my co-worker. *Why do therapists always avoid analyzing ourselves?* I decided I needed a second opinion and resolved to get hold of Detective Blodgett sometime today. Aside from the "I'll call you back" message he'd left two days ago, I hadn't heard from him. Maybe he'd meant I should call him? Or perhaps he was working a big case and just got too busy. I'd wait another day and then try again.

In the meantime, I decided to delve deeper into the files that were causing such uproar at the shelter. Regina had broken policy by removing them, and she must have had a pretty significant reason. I pulled my car into the sparse traffic of midday Chippewa Falls and headed back to the clinic to retrieve the files. I'd work at the library so Bob wouldn't question why I was working on shelter business rather than the clinic's.

It had been years since I'd been at the public library. After finding a parking space on Bay Street, I took a moment to poke through the odds and ends in the box Astrid had given me. A coffee cup with a picture of a golden retriever on it; a framed, black-and-white picture of two young girls—Regina and Emma, perhaps; a worn copy of the DSM-IV, the manual we use to diagnose mental disorders; a handmade, dried clay mug that had obviously held pens and pencils.

No calendar.

I closed the flaps of the box, grabbed the files and headed in. It was just as quiet and restful as I remembered. That was good. I needed restful quietude. I found a study carrel in the corner of the nonfiction section and spread my things out.

Regina had snuck six files out. Three were her clients, the other two had been seen by Clotilde and Lachlyn. Regina's most recent file belonged to a woman named Monica Skolnik. I flipped the cover open and found myself confronted with a Polaroid photo detailing in exquisite detail the injuries one human could inflict on another. Monica's eyes were so black and swollen that the only way I knew they were open was because of the glitter of blue trapped in the center of the blackened voids. Her nose, presumably intended as a Slavic ski slope, had morphed into a jagged slalom course, proof of having been broken more than once.

Forcing myself to read on, I discovered at only twenty-three years old, she'd already been to the shelter twice; this latest time she stayed for nearly four months. I paged through her file, feeling sadness wash over me as I read the meager details of her young life.

She and her live-in boyfriend had two children, who'd been removed by child services more than a year ago due to the violence in the home. The kids were allowed regular visits with their mom at the shelter, but the court had ordered supervised visits for their dad.

According to the case notes, Monica had been doing well in group and had managed to get a job as a receptionist at a local dental office. She'd also placed a deposit on a studio apartment. Things were looking up. Unexpectedly, however, she'd moved back with her abuser. Despite the professional language of the notes, the disappointment of both Regina and the other workers was palpable.

Despite the fact that D-N-C was written in big block letters, I jotted down her phone numbers and address before closing the file. It was gut-wrenchingly sad, but I couldn't yet see why Regina had felt the need to sneak the file out of the shelter. There didn't seem to be any unethical behavior on the part of the shelter workers, which is what I had expected to find. No complaints had been filed, at least, not internally. I'd have to check with the state licensing board, but I doubted I'd get a clear answer. Maybe it would be smarter to have Regina's lawyer check that out.

I debated whether I should call Monica myself. Technically, I was supposed to review each client and determine the need for continued therapy, but with that big DO NOT CONTACT request, I could be putting Monica in danger just by contacting her. One look at her fractured face was evidence enough of that. Flipping back through the file, I found the address of the job she'd applied for. Perhaps I could track her down there and avoid the home situation altogether.

Pulling the second file toward me, I took a deep breath before opening it to another white-bordered photo of misery.

It took two hours to work all the way through the

files. It would have gone faster if I hadn't kept getting distracted by my own reactions to the horrible stories the files held. With each story I could feel myself understanding more and more Regina's passion and how she or any of the shelter staff could become so dedicated to helping these shattered lives. And how they could become so bitter as well.

The similarities from case to case were striking. The women were kept isolated from family or friends and usually had young children, which added to the hostage mentality. Where could they go? Where could they run? Only to other women, it seemed. Women dedicated to their safety, determined to help, ready to give all of their time, maybe even their very lives, in order to save their sisters. To women ready to sacrifice their own sanity as well?

I was certain a cigarette would help me make sense of this.

That might be my addiction talking.

I sighed, shoving the files into my tote bag. I'd compiled a list of names and numbers for the women in the files, but I was still uncertain about contacting them. Only one, Monica Skolnik, could be considered a recent client having left the shelter this last August. Regina had died—or been killed—just over two months later, but if there was a connection, I couldn't see it. The others were all more than a year old, one going clear back to March 2007.

Still, for whatever reason, Regina had been concerned enough about these women to have stolen the files and secreted them in her clinic office. I wasn't ready to give up yet.

Since I was in the library, I decided a little research was in order. I moved to the computers. A quick search popped up thousands of hits for Devlin House. Not surprising since the shelter depended on donations and grant money. It also explained why they couldn't maintain complete secrecy for the operation and Astrid's subsequent emphasis on security.

A shelter newsletter popped up about seven hits down, so I clicked it open. It was a typical newsletter, half information, half appeal for money. There was also a national study that examined the compliance with aftercare services in women who left the shelters before treatment had been completed versus those who left after meeting treatment goals. Not surprisingly, those who went AWOL hoping their partner had "changed" refused follow-up counseling and, more often than not, returned to the shelter bruised and battered. *How awful.* I shook my head sadly.

The newsletter also had a listing of the board members, along with cameo pictures of each. One woman looked familiar, but I couldn't quite place her. Her name, Beth Collier, didn't help either. Shoulder-length auburn hair, emerald green eyes, a nice smile that reached her eyes. The association tickled the edges of my memory but refused to come to the fore. I printed the newsletter, hoping it would come to me later.

For the next hour, I clicked my way down the search hits without finding anything that seemed unusual. Another thought struck me: the shelter predated the age of Google by at least a decade and a half. It was time for some old-fashioned research.

A nice librarian led me to the newspaper archives and, once she was certain I could manage the microfiche machine, left me on my own. From the newsletter I'd just downloaded I knew the year the shelter opened, although not the month. I'd reached September before I found the article I'd felt certain would be there. By that time I had a raging headache from the strobe light effect of the flipping screen. It was worth it, though, if only for the photo.

The article's headline ran "A Safe Haven For Women." The paper had granted two columns for the story, a surprisingly generous allotment. Next to it, a grainy black and white photo captured the moment. Streamers and banners decorated the front of the structure, lush flowers bordered the walkway, the paint looked fresh. Quite a difference from the run-down facility that housed the women now. I doubted it had been painted since.

Clotilde and Astrid each stood with wide smiles on either side of an obviously handmade poster board welcoming the women of Chippewa Falls to Devlin House. Behind the poster, beaming like sunshine on a summer lake, stood Lachlyn in full nun regalia. I gaped at the screen trying to reconcile my mind to Lachlyn as a nun, much less a *smiling* Lachlyn in a nun's habit. But there she was. There they all were. Three women— young, idealistic, strong—each basking in the joy of achieving their life's dream. Or no, I thought. Not achieving it. *Beginning* it. They looked like adventuresses, fearless, ready to stride off to battle, as indeed they were.

Strangely, perhaps because of the black, cloak-like habit, it was Lachlyn that drew one's eyes. Lachlyn, who despite the bright smile, gave the ensemble an aura of austerity, asceticism, harsh determination. She loomed tall and stately as she stood with Clotilde and Astrid on either side of her like stewards to a warrior queen. An optical illusion, really, because the three were so nearly the same height and build that they could have been sisters.

    I blinked and the image cleared.

    I needed a meeting

CHAPTER THIRTEEN

Thursday isn't my usual night for a meeting, but I was too stressed to stay at home. After feeding Siggy, I took off for the HP & Me club downtown. I'd only been sober ten months, but the dilapidated old building already felt like home. Various greetings ranging from warm welcomes to raunchy catcalls greeted me as I pushed through the door and looked around for my friends. Sue, my sponsor, and a few other women from my Wednesday night group stood next to the coffee counter. As I approached I remembered the photo in the shelter newsletter that had seemed so familiar. In addition to being a mainstay at the club, Sue was a retired teacher and knew an amazing amount of people and their families. It didn't hurt that she'd lived in Chippewa Falls all her life and was related to half the county. When I showed her the newsprint, she recognized the auburn-haired woman right away.

"That's Beth C."

The initialed last name told me that Beth was a fellow AA member. "Why don't I know her?"

"She goes to the Sunday morning group. She's been sober for maybe five years? Six? She only comes once a week, but she's still very regular. She's good people."

That was a solid endorsement from Sue. She didn't like most people. Sometimes I wasn't even sure if she liked me.

"Why are you asking about her?" she asked.

"She's on the board at the shelter where Regina used to work. They're having a board meeting on Saturday, and I'd really like to talk to her before then. If you think she would be, um, sympathetic."

"Like I said, she's good people. But it would depend on exactly what you're asking her to do. I'll give her a call and pave the way for you. You're on your own after that."

"Good enough," I said.

"It better be. Now, unless you want to talk about your Third Step, you better hustle your bony butt into the meeting."

I hustled.

Grabbing a chair between Stacie, a young friend who'd gotten sober the same day as me, and Trinnie, a newbie, I plunked myself down at the banquet table. Trinnie looked liked she'd lost weight; something she could ill afford. She had a murky cigarette smell that, despite the staleness, was captivating to me. Addictions are a bitch.

Unaware of my vicarious inhalations, Trinnie leaned forward. "Letty, I need to ask you something."

"What's up?"

"Would you be my sponsor?"

"*Me?* I can't. I haven't gotten through the steps yet myself." An understatement.

"Just temporary then. Until I find someone I can work with," she said.

"How come you don't have one yet?"

"I haven't been able to decide who I like best. But I really need to get started. I had kind of a rough weekend."

"Did you drink?" I asked. Sounded like a sponsor already.

"No, but it was close. I need to get phone numbers, too."

"I guess I could be a temporary sponsor, but you really need to find someone with more time. *Soon.* And you need to talk about your weekend when it's your turn tonight."

Stacie and I passed her our phone numbers, then hushed. The meeting was starting.

I didn't know if I'd done the right thing, but I guessed as a sponsor I was better than nothing. Not by much, but still. Especially not with the way I'd been avoiding working on my own program.

I liked Trinnie. She reminded me a lot of my younger sister, Kris.

I mentally shook myself and turned to focus on the speaker. Daydreaming through a meeting wouldn't exactly be setting a good example.

Later that night, I laid on my couch waiting for the local news. Siggy was curled in a warm, vibrating mass on my chest. I blew softly on his ear, making it twitch. He stretched, then re-positioned, tucking his face under my chin. Although he looked like a rich dessert, cream-colored with cocoa-tipped points on three paws and the tip of his tail, it was the chocolate smudge under his nose and chin that made me name him in honor of psychology's father, Sigmund Freud. His purrs rose and fell with his breathing, a sound I call "sleep buzzing."

The phone rang, startling me and upsetting us both. Sig hopped down, tossing a reproachful look over his shoulder and stalking into the kitchen for a nighttime snack.

"Hello?" My voice sounded wary even to my own ears. The only persons I knew who would call this late were family. Hence, the wariness.

Detective Blodgett's gravelly smoker's rasp boomed through the tiny phone speaker as though he'd never accepted the phone's ability to project his voice. I snatched the phone away from my ear, frantically jabbing the volume button. Even with the phone six inches from my ear, I could still hear him.

"Don't you ever call back?" he asked. "I was just getting ready to put out a BOLO on you."

"Nobody needs to 'be on the lookout' for me, but thanks for worrying. Besides, I called you."

"I wasn't worried, and I texted you back."

"You *texted* me?"

"My grandkid taught me. I'm hip."

I thought about Blodgett's stretchy, hound dog face and baggy, mismatched suits, and squelched a giggle.

"What kinda trouble are you getting yourself into now?"

Not worried. Right. Despite suspecting me in my boyfriend's murder, Blodgett was one of my mainstays following my attack. *After* he'd decided I hadn't killed anyone. But he'd stayed involved in my life and I had the feeling that wasn't a typical reaction for him. I'd grown close with his wife, Diana, a sweet forbearing woman who was awaiting Blodgett's retirement with eager plans. She'd put her years in raising children— their own four as well as an assortment of foster kids— and she was ready for some serious cross-country visiting. An elaborate motor home stood parked in the side yard ready to go, a travel itinerary all laid out. Diana claimed the only thing she had left to pack was her recipe box. She planned to cook each person's favorite treat as soon as Blodgett slammed the gear shift to D. Secretly, I pretended to be one of her adopted daughters.

"It's going to sound stupid," I said to Blodgett.

His sigh rattled in my ear. "I'm a detective. I'm used to stupid. Lay it on me."

So I did. He already knew about Regina's death. In fact, he'd been to the wake. I assumed he knew the manner of her death, but I went over it anyway, mentioning the strange fall, the knitting needle. Then I filled him in on Regina's recent appointment of me as her professional executor. He grunted at that, but didn't interrupt, which I took as cop-speak for "I'm listening; please go on." Either that or he was sitting on the john.

"And then," I continued, "I found this stack of client files that Regina took from the shelter. She wasn't supposed to do that."

"Maybe she was just going to work at home."

"They weren't all her clients. In fact, they weren't even recent cases. Plus, taking the files from the site is a breach of confidentiality. In many agencies, that would be a firing offense. You just don't do it. Regina would have been well aware of that. She didn't have permission either, because Clotilde, the director, was pretty steamed when I gave them back."

There was a pause, then, "You gave them back?"

"Of course I did," I said, virtuousness dripping from my lips.

Another pause. "I'll want to see the copies. What

else?"

I didn't bother asking how he knew I'd made copies. He was a detective, after all.

"There was a woman at the shelter the night Regina died. She took off the next morning, which isn't really surprising, I suppose, if she's afraid of getting involved. But I was supposed to have access to all of Regina's clients and they kept her off the client roster. I found out about her inadvertently."

"So, you've got an accidental death and a bunch of misfiled files?"

"Well, no."

He waited.

"I've got a creepy feeling too."

"Uh-huh. An accidental death, misfiled files, and you're creepy."

"A creepy *feeling*. Look, if you don't want—"

"Get me copies of the copies. I'll look into it." He hung up.

Why did I love rude people so much?

CHAPTER FOURTEEN

I'd hoped Blodgett would share info from the autopsy or give me a hint as to what the cops were thinking. Wrong. Information only traveled one way with Blodgett. I snuggled down under my comforter getting ready to do my own sleep buzzing when a new thought crept into the fuzzy edges of my mind.

Blodgett sent me a text?

I tried to ignore it. Siggy had settled into the hollow at the back of my knees, providing kitty-heating-pad warmth. I didn't want to bug him again. Feline attitude can be scary.

But a text message from Blodgett would have definitely caught my attention. If it had gotten through, I should be hearing the beepy alert telling me I'd missed a call.

I pulled the covers up to my chin, burrowing deeper into the cozy softness. Obviously Blodgett's grandson hadn't done a good job of instructing him. Not surprising. Blodgett, despite his self-delusions, was not on the cutting edge of communication technology. He kept up with just enough to understand how things might impact his job, but I'd never seen any evidence that he used any of the myriad of technologies available in his daily life.

Besides, I would have heard the damn alert.

I gave up, trudged into the kitchen where my phone was charging, and stared blurrily at the home screen. Even in my groggy state I could see that there were no little icons for missed texts or messages. I clicked over to the MISSED CALLS screen and there it was.

DET BLODGETT

He'd called at 10:04 this morning. I clicked over to the messages screen and found—nothing. Which didn't make sense. Blodgett's text had obviously come through. I checked the volume in case I'd forgotten to adjust it after my last therapy session. Except I hadn't had therapy with anyone today, and I knew the phone worked because I'd gotten several calls on it.

Maybe Blodgett had called but hadn't properly sent the message? Was that even possible?

And yet . . .

Where had my phone been when Blodgett had called?

Or better question: where had *I* been? If it rang while I was with Clotilde, I wouldn't have heard it. I would, however, have since heard the beep indicating I had voice mail or missed a call. I hadn't heard that.

My usual habit was to leave my cell on the desk next to me while I worked. If it's out on my desk I was more likely to remember to turn it to vibrate before meetings. There is nothing as embarrassing as a cell phone ringing in the middle of a therapy session. But if I had followed my usual habit—and I thought I had—it would have been sitting on the desk . . . including the time I met with Clotilde. On the desk in the therapy office where Lachlyn waited for me all by her lonesome, growing more and more irritated.

Where, in fact, Lachlyn could have seen that my buddy, Det. Blodgett, was returning my phone calls. She must have wondered why I had a police detective in my phone directory. Had she deleted the message?

So much for sleep.

Friday was a struggle. I managed, barely, to stay focused on the back-to-back clients I had scheduled that morning. On the positive side, being so busy kept my mind from anxiously swirling out of control. Not only had the doubts raised last night kept me awake, but Siggy had picked up on my tension and refused to sleep with me. I'd have to learn better stress management techniques or I'd lose my snuggle buddy.

Eventually the time for my appointment with Emma rolled around. On the way over to Regina's house, I stopped at Blodgett's house and left copies of the files. Neither he nor Diana were home, but he left the screened-in porch unlocked and he'd told me to leave them on top of the freezer chest.

I'd never been to Regina's and didn't know what to expect. I had always pictured her living in a sleek, ultra-modern condo with stainless steel fixtures and having somebody else to do the maintenance.

Instead, I discovered that she lived in a restored Craftsman style bungalow in a quiet, well-tended neighborhood. Emma waited on the covered porch, a soft, pumpkin-colored sweater draped over one arm in concession to the early autumn air.

As I climbed the steps, she smiled. "Thank you for coming over. I don't know how I would have felt doing this by myself."

I wasn't altogether sure what she meant by "this"

but assumed it had to do with entering Regina's home by herself. I answered with a simple "no problem," and we fell silent.

Emma unlocked the front door and entered first. The house was filled with a silence so foreboding, it had texture. Yet somewhere close by, a clock ticked. The furnace hummed to life. We stood in the entryway as though expecting someone—*Regina?*—to call out a welcome. The door clicked shut behind us.

"Are you looking for anything in particular?" Emma asked.

"Her scheduling calendar. An appointment book or something on her computer. I couldn't find anything at the clinic or the shelter, either. It's probably stupid, but it just seems strange that I haven't found it. I want to see if she has any work files, too." I didn't mention that it would have been unethical if she had brought the files home, but it had occurred to me that I might find more misappropriated files here. Who knows? Perhaps the normally principled Regina had made a habit of carrying files around. People are strange.

I also didn't mention my concern that we might not be the first to sort through Regina's belongings. My fears weren't evidence.

"You'll probably want to start in her office," Emma said. "It's at the top of the stairs on the right. If you come across any personal papers—insurance, bills, and so forth—I'd appreciate if you'd set them aside. I need to go through all of that. In the meantime, I'm going to start in the kitchen cleaning out the fridge. I hope it's not too smelly."

I left Emma to deal with the spoiled food and made my way up the stairs. Regina's home office had the same eclectic feel as her clinic office, which made me wonder again at the stark bareness of her space at the shelter. Here, Regina had created a serene palette out of cool blue tones and white accents. It felt like the inside of a breeze.

Built-in shelves stuffed to overflowing with books lined two walls. Regina's desk, a golden teak monstrosity, took up a good third of the room. The top of the desk was orderly, but not compulsively so. If someone had searched it before me, there were no obvious signs. A laptop sat in the center.

Hallelujah.

I opened and let it power up. Unfortunately, that was as far as I got. Why would Regina password protect her own computer, especially since she lived alone? On the other hand, if she also used it at the shelter, it might make sense to use a password.

I sat back in the chair and took a moment to settle my mind. I had to get in it somehow. Closing my eyes, I took several deep breaths and consciously relaxed my taut muscles. Emma rustled around downstairs, but despite that, a peace descended over me. The sunlight cast a red glow against my closed eyelids. Since I wasn't sure how I felt about the whole God-thing, I didn't feel right about praying, but I tried to keep my mind open, receptive; to *what*, I didn't know. Maybe to Sue's God. Maybe to whatever Higher Power was working in my sobriety. Maybe to Regina.

Her perfume scent drifted over me. I hadn't smelled it when I first entered.

Freaked. Me. Out.

I scrambled to my feet, sending the chair tumbling and made it to the doorway in three ostrich-sized strides. Heart banging wildly, I clutched the door frame to keep from falling head first over the landing and down the stairs.

"Letty?"

I made a squeaky "eep" sound and almost wet myself until I realized it was just Emma.

"Sorry. I dropped, uh, a chair. Everything's fine."

"A chair?" Her face appeared at the bottom of the stairs, looking concerned.

"I backed into it. Sorry. Didn't mean to scare you." I chuckled, then after hearing how fake it sounded, tried to turn it into a cough.

"Well, let me know if you need anything." She didn't look convinced, but was too well-mannered to push the point.

Taking advantage of her indecisiveness, I gave a little wave and moved back into the office. "Great. Okay, um, I better get busy."

I shut the office door behind me and immediately regretted it.

CHAPTER FIFTEEN

Regina alive was scary enough. I couldn't handle a ghost. I walked cautiously back to the chair and decided I really didn't need to sit in it after all. Anything I needed to do could be done standing. And leaning toward the door. Just in case.

I could ask Emma if she knew the password, but the two sisters didn't appear to have been that close. I wondered if Regina, despite the warnings not to, kept a notebook with passwords written down. I did. Who could remember them all?

The middle drawer held the usual pens, paper clips, blank sticky notepads. The next two drawers yielded nothing of interest to me, but I discovered a stack of bills which I set aside for Emma. The lower drawer had a hanging file system that made my heartbeat quicken, but I didn't discover any client records. Instead of names, the tabs read AUTO INSURANCE, BANK, CREDIT, and so on. More for Emma, and I left them alone.

I didn't find anything in the desk. Before I left the room, I scanned Regina's book shelves. She had crystals and rocks scattered attractively on various shelves. As for the books, a good portion were political in nature, but she had a nice selection of literary novels, biographies, and a smattering of clinical psychology texts that were probably left over from college. With as much as the college textbooks cost, most of us couldn't admit how worthless they are after graduation.

Thwarted by a stupid, locked computer, I wandered back out into the hall, crossing to the tiny, white tiled bathroom opposite. Regina's scent was back, but since a nearly empty perfume bottle squatted next to the toothbrush holder, I didn't need to fear a ghostly specter. I picked the bottle up.

Prada Infusion D'Iris?

She didn't own a pair of tweezers, scorned makeup, yet she was willing to spend more than sixty bucks on a bottle of perfume. The thought that Regina was a secret girly-girl made me smile. However, I wasn't likely to find any clues in here, so after availing myself of the facilities, I checked out Regina's bedroom.

Again, I was surprised at Regina's choice of decor. Instead of the eclectic use of space that she'd displayed in her offices, her bedroom was surprisingly plain. Neat, clean, but plain.

I went downstairs and found Emma in the kitchen, elbow deep in the produce drawer, a garbage bag of spoiling food at her side. She wrinkled her nose at me.

"I'm glad I didn't wait any longer," she said. "Things are just starting to go bad."

"Smells like something already has."

"That's the milk. Did you find what you were looking for?"

"Kind of. Regina has a laptop, but it's locked. You don't, by chance, know the password, do you?"

Emma shook her head. "I wouldn't even know how

to guess."

"I'm hoping she kept a list of her passwords or usernames. You know?"

"I wouldn't know that, either." She sat back on her heels, looking infinitely sadder, and fell silent.

"Do you mind if I keep looking?"

She waved a latex-gloved hand at me. "Go right ahead. There will be strangers going through everything soon enough. I'll probably donate most of it. In fact"—she pulled her head out of the fridge to look at me—"if you find anything you'd like as a remembrance, let me know. I'm sure Regina would want you to have something. There are a few furniture pieces I'm keeping that are family—well, I don't know if I'd call them heirlooms—hand-me-downs maybe. But other than that, it'll all just go to St. Vincent's."

She smiled up at me while I struggled with what to say. A remembrance? Of Regina? I smiled weakly and said thanks.

"Do you have Regina's car keys?" I asked. "I want to be thorough."

"Good idea. I have so much crammed into it, my car is a rolling office." She retrieved a set of keys from her purse.

Regina drove a minty-green Prius that I found parked outside the detached single-car garage behind the house. One peek into the garage windows told me why. It was crammed to the rafters with junk, making me wonder how long Regina had lived here.

Unlocking the car, I slid into the front seat. Despite the fall temperature, the interior of the car was toasty from sitting in the sun. There was a small stack of papers on the passenger seat: a gas charge receipt, junk mail, a month-old copy of the Buck Shopper—a weekly advertising circular. No calendar. Feeling a twinge of unease, I popped the glove compartment and found nothing more dangerous than old maps and Regina's insurance card. Nothing under the sun visor either. Shifting sideways, I peered into the backseat. A red leather laptop case sat on the floor wedged behind the passenger seat. Still looking for a clue to the password, I plundered the pockets. Except for the wall charger, I found nothing.

Disappointed, I made my way back to the kitchen.

"I hope she didn't keep her financial information in the computer," she said. "Do you suppose there's someone we could take it to?"

I liked the "we" part. "I could probably find someone who can hack into it," I offered. I didn't expand, but AA was a delightful repository of (hopefully) retired criminality. Our people have skills. Somebody would know.

Emma, far more trusting than her sister had ever dreamed of being, agreed without hesitation.

CHAPTER SIXTEEN

I continued my search in the living room, checking end tables and between couch cushions. Found lots of crumbs, proving that even ice queens like Regina ate in front of the TV. I also found a tote filled with various balls of yarn and assorted needles next to the armchair. I lifted a tangle of yarn on top. A six-inch wide strip unrolled a couple of feet. A scarf?

Huh. I was wrong about dismissing knitting as Regina's hobby. I turned a slow circle, scanning the living room. Something seemed off, but I couldn't place it.

Hoping it would come to me if I didn't push it, I stretched full out on the floor, trying to peer into the darkness beneath the couch in case the calendar, if it even existed, had slipped underneath. My nose tickled from the rough fibers of the carpet.

Why not *choose something to remember Regina?*

I stopped fishing under the couch and lay still, my arm jammed full length under the three-inch clearance of the couch. Regina had practically saved my life. My sanity, at the very least. I'd been steadily discovering more about her over the last few days, having to jettison the cardboard picture of some fanatical feminist that I'd cast her in when she was living.

I sighed, sucking up dust and inciting a sneeze that almost ripped my still-wedged arm off. Regina was never going to leave me alone. I'd inherited her.

I trudged back up the stairs to her office and stood staring gloomily at the bookshelves. I picked up the ugliest rock I could find--a gravely, gray lump, the size and shape of a halved orange.

Turning it over, I discovered a scooped-out shell filled with twinkly crystals. Sunlight from the window sparkled off a multitude of brilliant lavender shards like a visual echo of laughter. Regina's laughter, set in stone.

Just as I turned to leave, I noticed a small, red spiral notebook jammed between two volumes of poetry.

Aha.

Heart thumping, I opened it and discovered an alphabetized list of passwords and user names. I did a little victory dance primarily consisting of butt wiggles and hooting sounds.

I went to the top of the stairs, hollered "Found it!" down to Emma, then trotted over to the laptop. It took a few minutes scouring the notebook to find the right one, but eventually I lucked onto it: Gloria5teinem.

Of course, it was.

Moments later I was clicking happily through Regina's calendar. She hadn't used names, just initials, keeping confidentiality. She seemed to work three nights a week. Tuesdays, Thursdays, and Fridays— which made sense. I'd never seen her at the clinic on those evenings, and Tuesday was my late night.

Dates had been filled in through the week of September 19th, a scattering of others scheduled ahead in the subsequent weeks. Regina had died—or been killed—on Saturday, the 13th.

The week prior to her death didn't appear to be unusual, but I'd have to study it more closely. I'd also need to compare the initials against the list the shelter had provided to see if any others besides Karissa's had been conveniently left off.

I copied off the results for the last year and included her contacts for good measure. Next, I went to her Documents folder, but there was nothing I could tell for certain was connected to the shelter. I'd need hours to examine it all.

I decided to show Emma my discoveries. A sly whiff of scent registered in my nostrils before I made it to the top step. Once again, it filled my senses, the scent more effective than a ghost in reminding me of my commitment. If I'd had a tail like the Cowardly Lion, I'd have been clutching it.

Instead, I turned into the bathroom, picked up the Prada perfume, and squirted a bit on myself. Now I had an excuse to keep smelling Regina. I tucked the bottle into the back pocket of my jeans and bounded down the stairs chanting, "I *do* believe in spooks! I *do* believe in spooks."

Not wanting to look like an idiot, I paused in the living room until I'd calmed down, then joined Regina's sister in the kitchen, where I gave her the notebook and showed her the "remembrances" I'd picked out.

Emma liked my choices. She smiled and held the rock up to the light, making rainbows dance across the interior. "That's Reggie, all right. Beautiful on the inside, but a little spiky, too."

"You must miss her," I said.

"I do. That feels strange to say, because we never really got along. We weren't the type of sisters that share confidences or call each other and talk all night, but still . . ." Her voice trailed off.

"She was your sister." I thought of my own sister and our recent estrangement. My sobriety was a slap in the face to her, but what could I do? The emotional distance wouldn't make it easier if something were to happen to Kris. In fact, it would make it worse.

Emma sighed, and grabbed the garbage bag of rotting food. She hauled it over to the door, where she balanced it carefully. Nobody likes their garbage spilling out all over the floor.

I took the hint.

Hours later, I lay stretched out on my bed with Siggy ensconced on my stomach, his head nestled on my chest. Better than a man, let me tell you. And lighter, too. The only problem was he listened about as well as most men, which is to say, Siggy was sound asleep.

"You're no help," I told him.

His whiskers twitched.

I had so many questions swirling around my head that I was giving myself a headache. Or maybe it was from Regina's perfume. It would be just like her to haunt me with something that gave me migraines.

"Did I mention the tote?" I asked Siggy. "She had a tote full of yarn, but I couldn't find any other skeins. Don't real knitters hoard yarn? Or is that quilters and fabric?"

That had been the thought that had bothered me when I'd first found the tote. Regina had been killed with a knitting needle, but neither Emma nor had I known she'd knitted. Admittedly, neither of us were exceptionally close to Regina. Lying there, I mentally went back over the rooms trying to remember any sort of knitting paraphernalia: a stash of leftover yarn, patterns, scissors, *anything*. I couldn't recall any.

Had someone planted the tote?

Maybe it didn't mean anything, but why were the laptop case and power cord out in the car? And had Regina hidden the notebook on purpose? I couldn't imagine any other reason why she would hide it in the bookcase. From the desk, it would certainly be inconvenient to have to get up and cross to the bookcase, but then again, somebody burglarizing the place wouldn't stop to hunt for such a thing either. My gut told me that Regina had placed it somewhere inconspicuous on purpose. It made sense that, if she had indeed been hiding the password, it meant she had something else stored on the laptop. Maybe Emma would be willing to let me examine it for an extended period of time. I'd have to ask. It also meant that Regina knew something dangerous enough to get her killed, and what she knew was linked to the shelter files. Which were in my possession. Which meant. . .

I sat up, tossing Siggy once again. He was getting sick of this, I could tell.

"This is serious, Siggy. We could be in danger," I called after him.

He gave me the tail.

CHAPTER SEVENTEEN

Sitting at my desk in the living room I pulled out my notes from the shelter files and began comparing them to the information in the calendar.

In addition to Karissa Dillard and the group sessions, Regina had been seeing seven women at the time she died. I found their initials penciled into time slots in the weeks prior, each of them seeing Regina at least once a week, but more often twice, for therapy. Karissa's initials were on evenings that matched the dates listed in her files, so it didn't appear that anyone had tampered with those details, but there was still the matter of the altered contact info.

Tracing back to the beginning of the year was a steady stream of initials—women who Regina had seen that the shelter didn't consider open files. Hopefully, I'd be able to convince the board tomorrow morning that they should be.

Not expecting anything, I paged through Regina's address section. Flipping through to the last names of my co-workers didn't turn up any familiar names, but I found the shelter women's easily enough. Huh. I kind of liked having access to Lachlyn's address and home phone number. Ashley Perkins, Regina's lawyer, was also listed.

And more initials in this section. *Surprise, surprise.* I smiled to myself. Even Regina bent the rules a teensy bit.

She'd continued to use initials, but the addition of phone numbers made the information potentially identifiable, and therefore, arguably, a breach of confidentiality. It made sense, from a practical point of view. If rescheduling a client became necessary, Regina wouldn't have to have a shelter volunteer contact her appointments. She could do it herself.

Under the D-F section, I found "KD-715-555-3477." A tiny "c" after the number made me hope that it would be safe to call Karissa since it appeared to be a cell phone. A thought occurred to me, and I dug through my notes until I unearthed the number I'd jotted down from the altered face sheet. When it matched, I pumped a fist in the air, sparking a second look of disgust from Siggy. Cats don't respect enthusiasm.

A second number had been added directly under Karissa's with the acronym MGM after it. As a therapist, I knew that, in this case, it didn't stand for a movie studio but for "maternal grandmother." Nice.

I now had two phone numbers, but I still hesitated before calling, remembering Lachlyn's warning about endangering the women. As much as I hated to admit it, she had a point. If there were some way I could check out the situation before calling or meeting Karissa, I should try that first.

Googling Karissa's number didn't net me anything, but the grandmother—Bernadette Stanhope, I learned—was listed in the Chippewa Falls White Pages along with an address.

It was too early in the season for Daylight Savings

Time change, but the light-filled days of summer were long past. I only had about an hour of daylight left and I hadn't eaten supper yet. A drive-thru meal was a necessary evil. I tried to feel guilty about all the transfats my body was ingesting, but Big Mac sauce is as addicting to me as liquor and, if my ever-tightening jeans were an indication, just as dangerous.

Karissa's grandmother lived in a trailer park a few miles south of Chippewa Falls. I debated attempting a private eye-type stake out, but the close proximity of the neighboring trailers made me change my mind. They didn't need an official neighborhood watch committee in this community. They all watched. All the time.

A decade-old green Wrangler occupied the patch of dirt that doubled as a driveway for Lot 7. Despite the rust pitting the wheel wells and the thick coating of dust, it looked a lot snazzier than the trailer. Decrepit wooden steps leaned against the side of the home looking as if they'd gotten tired of the job and wanted a rest. I wasn't sure they would hold my weight, and I found myself regretting the sugar-carb diet that had so recently replaced my drinking habit.

Thinking light, airy thoughts as a gravity-defying defense mechanism, I knocked at the door and almost fell backward when it was snatched open by a young boy. It would have been hard to guess his age by looking at him—his body size and ancient eyes told different stories—but the file had stated the eldest boy was nearly six years old. Michael was his name, I knew, although I'd forgotten the baby's.

"Is your mom here?" I asked. Michael turned and yelled a long, drawn-out "Mom" over his shoulder. My heart thumped despite my legitimacy. A sharp gust of wind rattled through the oak trees, causing me to glance up at the branches in case Clotilde and Lachlyn, hovering like harpies, were waiting to snatch me away from my goal.

Footsteps brought my attention back just as a twenty-something woman reached the screen door. She was almost my height, 5'6", but had the aid of two-inch wedge sandals to reach that. A strange choice for the end of September. She also wore a caution-yellow tank top and loose-fitting jeans. The dripping blood, barbed wire tattoo circling her upper arm didn't scream "mom," but maybe I was old-fashioned. She held a bright red Elmo in her hand that looked too new to have been toted around by a kid yet. She thrust it at her son.

"Here, Mikey. Take Elmo to Grammy." The voice, sweet and girlish, did not match her exterior, but her eyes, like her son's, had seen the rough side of life.

Mikey scowled, refusing the toy. "No. That's not Mo-mo. And 'sides, I'm too old for Elmo anymore."

"Yes, it is Mo-mo. It's a better one. Take it to Grammy and go check on Myka. *Now.*"

He grabbed it by a leg and took off into the darkening interior, carrying it along without any enthusiasm. She may have won the battle, but he wasn't giving up the war. Mo-mo hadn't won his heart.

"Can I help you?"

"Karissa Dillard? My name is Letty Whittaker. I'm, um, a friend of Regina's." I tried not to turn the last sentence into a question. I confess I was a little distracted by the cigarette smell she carried. I rubbed my patch. It itched. "I'm a therapist, too, and we worked together at the clinic in town. She appointed me as the executor of her patient files. That means she wanted me to check in with her clients and make sure they're all okay."

As I spoke, Karissa's face shifted from guarded to scared, briefly, and settled on pissed. The knuckles on the hand clutching the screen door whitened, veins popping in her arms with the pressure she exerted. I half-expected the metal to buckle.

I took a step back, almost solving Karissa's problem by falling off the decrepit stairs and breaking my neck. I teetered a little but kept my balance. Trying to defuse the situation, I lifted my hands, palm out in the ancient I-carry-no-weapons pose. "It's okay, Karissa. Nobody knows I'm here. You're safe." Although I wasn't so sure I was. Now that I thought about it, perhaps telling her that no one knew I was here wasn't such a good idea. Despite her diminutiveness, this woman looked capable of stuffing my dead body under the trailer and letting some lime and a couple of pine tree air fresheners hide the deed. Mikey would probably let the new Mo-mo keep me company.

She stayed tense, her muscles bunched, but she didn't slam the door in my face. Yet. Behind her, I saw another person moving swiftly through the dark interior of the trailer. I braced myself.

A tiny wisp of a woman slid under Karissa's arm, standing in front of her like a shield. Not a particularly effective shield, since the top of her grey head only came to Karissa's chin, but I had no doubt whom I needed to fear most. She wore a blue flannel shirt, probably intended for a twelve-year-old boy, and a pair of psychedelic, tie-dyed pajama bottoms. Funky Grammy. A gnarled finger thrust up to the tip of my nose, making my eyes cross as I tried to follow it.

"Who the hell are you? What do you want with my Rissa?"

"Um. . ."

"Gosh darn it! I'm tired of people thinking they can just walk all over her!"

Behind her, Karissa laughed, enjoying the show.

"No, no. I'm not," I said.

"You gosh darn better not be!" She whipped around, tilting her head back to glare at her granddaughter. "Get in the house, missy. Don't just stand here in the doorway letting her push you around. Get inside."

The puff of wind from the slam of the door blew several strands of my hair around my face. Stunned, I meekly returned to my car and sat, trying to figure out what had just happened. Attack-by-grandma had been remarkably successful. Between the two, I hadn't stood a chance.

As I looked back at the trailer, I saw a grey head pop up in a window, every wrinkle in her grizzled face shaped into a mighty frown. I saw her mouth move silently, behind the glass pane. I didn't need to be a lip reader to know what she was saying. The very un-grandma-like middle finger salute clarified, in case I had any doubts.

I left. But just before I drove away another head appeared in a window farther down the side of the trailer. Mikey. At least he waved with all of his fingers.

CHAPTER EIGHTEEN

I hated getting up early on a Saturday, especially when I hadn't been sleeping well lately, but I couldn't miss the board meeting. I almost didn't bother with business clothes, but forced myself into a pair of decent slacks and an autumn-colored sweater when I remembered I was trying to impress people with my professionalism.

While I'd been out prowling, Sue had left a voice mail telling me she'd tracked down the board member, Beth Collier, and filled her in on my situation. She said Beth had been receptive, but couldn't promise anything until after she'd met me and heard the shelter's concerns.

Great. An ethical alcoholic. Why did I have to keep tripping over all these ethical people these days? I wished I'd had a chance to talk to her myself. Living an honest, sober life sure made navigating problems a lot trickier. Took more energy, too.

On the flip side, I wasn't waking up with sweaty jitters and puking my way across town to the meeting. Pros and cons to everything, I guessed.

The board met in the group therapy room. Based on the varied appearance of the members I could have worn whatever I pleased. There were six of them—an even split of three men, three women. Two of the men, crisply suited, looked as though they were hustling back to the office as soon as they could wrap things up here. The third, however, wore baggy shorts, an eye-jarring Hawaiian shirt, and leather thong sandals. His thinning hair was pulled back in a grey braid as thin as my pinky.

The women had taken the middle road, casual, although there were wide differences in the amount of money each seemed willing to spend on achieving that effect.

I recognized Beth from the newsletter photo. Stylish, auburn-haired, and decked out in a trendy, boucle jacket, she winked at me as I came in. I smiled back.

Clotilde and Lachlyn were already seated. Just for giggles, I tried picturing Lachlyn as a nun, mentally cloaking her in the habit she'd been wearing in the newspaper photo. The effort made my head spin.

Astrid trotted in, balancing a tray of fresh baked cookies, a fistful of yellow pencils, and a stack of papers clamped under her armpit. The papers started an ominous slide, forcing Astrid into a strange contortion as she tried to clamp harder while not losing any cookies. I hurried over and rescued the papers just as they slithered free. Beth saved the cookie tray, and between the three of us, we managed to get the supplies over to a side table where a large coffee urn bubbled darkly.

"Let's get started," Clotilde announced over the top of Astrid's expressions of gratitude. I took my seat as Clotilde ran through quick introductions. Since I'd perused the shelter newsletter, I was familiar with the names and only had to match them to the faces. Sean Benson, the lawyer, caught my attention first of all, because I assumed he'd have the most say in my situation. He was, of course, one of the besuited gents. He was also really hot in an I'm-a-power-hungry-stud kind of way. The other suit, Steve Riccio, was the shelter treasurer and a professional accountant. He handed me his card. The aging hippy was Dr. Brian Feldman. "Retired," he clarified as he shook my hand. Soft, limp grip, but a friendly smile. I'd already pegged Beth. She was the wealthiest looking alcoholic I'd ever seen. Despite that, she appeared down-to-earth, and just as friendly as Dr. Brian. The second woman, Amy Myers, looked crisp and professional and slightly irritated at the delay. Her bright smile surprised me, though and I decided I was projecting. Last of all was Joyce Trent, a former shelter resident turned employee, who sat on the board as a resident representative. Months ago, when Regina had first brought me, I'd heard whispers about Joyce's past. She towered over me by a good four inches and embraced the no-makeup look of the shelter women. She also looked like she could bench press a small cow.

"I need to bring up one item before we go over Regina's case load," Joyce said. "I need the board's approval for a Buddy tracker on one of our kids. There is—"

"What's a Buddy tracker?" I asked. Okay, it had nothing to do with me, but hey, I was curious.

Joyce went mute, letting Clotilde answer. "It's a GPS tracking device. We use them in extreme situations when we fear a parent might abscond with a child. It needs board approval."

"There is a restraining order in place between the father and mother," Clotilde continued, "but the court has allowed supervised visitation. Dad has already tried picking the boy up at daycare, so we can see how well he respects court orders. The boy is only three and a half years old and can't be expected to refuse a surprise visit from Daddy, even if he's seen the man beating his mother once a week for the last two years. He has a teddy bear that we can plant the Buddy in."

Lachlyn sighed. "I wish we could home school every one of them. It's ridiculous that their lives are in such danger and we blithely send them out to school or daycare while we sit back and pretend their fathers can't get to them."

Beth spoke up. "Well, we can't isolate them forever, Lachlyn."

"Why not?" Lachlyn smiled ruefully.

"If it's okay with the board, I'll get you the Buddy tracker this afternoon, Joyce," Astrid said.

After the board approved the motion, Clotilde broached my role as Regina's professional executor. Astrid passed around copies of Regina's arrangements, although I noted that Sean Benson, the lawyer, already had one. Feldman and Beth both asked him a few questions clarifying what a professional executor's role was. His answers meshed with what I'd learned, so I didn't interrupt.

"So, what do you need from us?" Beth finally turned to Clotilde. Her forthrightness verged on abruptness, but she softened it with a smile. Riccio nodded at her question, glancing at his watch. Time was money and apparently he needed to go count it.

"We need to know just how far this document reaches," Clotilde answered. "Are we talking about Regina's case load at the time of the accident? Or is this more far-reaching? I'm particularly concerned that Regina's unusual choice . . . " she turned to me with an aside. "No offense."

"None taken," I lied.

"Regina's choice is an outsider. Someone completely unfamiliar with shelter policies and practices, which, of course, could be dangerous to our clients."

"Regina must have felt a high level of confidence in Ms. Whittaker," Beth countered. "Are there problems with her qualifications?"

"No," Clotilde answered almost reluctantly. I could tell that she had researched that end carefully.

Feldman entered the fray. "Maybe not, but Clo has a valid point. Our clients are in a precarious position. We can't allow anything to jeopardize that or even increase their sense of vulnerability. They have enough against them. I'm against anything that risks that. Why can't one of you follow up with Regina's clients?"

Time for me to jump in. "Because that goes against Regina's expressed wishes. My understanding is that this document is legal and binding. Assigning a professional executor is a practice that the American Psychological Association strongly favors, and its practice is specifically addressed in the Code of Ethics." Damn, I sounded good. And pulling the APA's Code of Ethics was an especially nice touch, I thought. It had the added sweetness of being the truth, too.

After a brief pause, Benson asked, "What is the current arrangement?"

"We've allowed Ms. Whittaker access to the files of Regina's open client roster. Lachlyn has been supervising her during the file review. As far as actual therapy, Lachlyn and I have divided the case load in the interim and are providing group therapy."

Joyce asked her second question of the meeting. "Isn't that a strain? You're both so busy already." Although she'd obviously meant well and had displayed a reasonable concern for the director and Lachlyn, they both frowned at her, not wanting to admit to the burden.

Joyce dropped her eyes to the floor.

"That's a valid point," Beth jumped in. Her eyes had narrowed slightly and, legs crossed, the topmost foot jiggled in midair with irritation. "I really don't understand what the problem is. We've granted that Whittaker's credentials are legitimate, we've acknowledged Regina's professional discretion in choosing her executor, and we've also acknowledged the legal and ethical realities of the situation. My feeling is that we need to allow Letty to get on with her obligations. I'm sure she has plenty of other things going on in her life that she could be attending to."

A long, stiff pause ensued as the others grappled with Beth's blunt summary. I liked her. As long as she was on my side, that is.

"It looks like much of this has already been worked out," Amy Myers spoke up for the first time. "May I suggest that as Ms. Whittaker finishes reviewing the files, she'll let our people know if she has any immediate concerns for any particular resident's well-being. It doesn't make sense to transfer the women back to yet another therapist, though, does it?"

She was right and I told them so. "However, I'm not comfortable with limiting the review to the few clients Regina was working with when she died. Given the frequency of women returning to the shelter in the first three years, it would make sense for my review to extend that far back."

I knew that newsletter would come in handy. They would find it very difficult to argue with the results of a national study that their own newsletter had cited.

Another pause. Then, Clotilde rallied. "Three years is entirely unnecessary. For one thing, we don't have the staff to supervise for as long it would take you to get through that many clients."

"I'm not clear on why you think I need to be supervised anyway," I interrupted. "I don't want to take Lachlyn away from her duties any more than she does. In fact, it makes it difficult for both of us to have to coordinate our schedules. It also makes for a very scattered approach on a task that I could already have finished by now. For instance, my duties at our clinic are very nearly wrapped up."

"Maybe so, but the shelter has vastly different concerns than does a clinic," Benson said. "We will certainly comply with Regina's wishes, but it will be done in keeping with the shelter's policies and with our residents' best interests uppermost."

That sounded very lawyerly to me. Very cover-my-butt and you're not-getting-what-you-want, as well.

"So, how far back are we willing to let her go?" Beth chimed back in. "And what safety measures will Letty need to follow?"

"Three months," Benson said. "Lachlyn supervises a file review of Regina's clients going back three months. No contact with any of those residents unless you have a specific, defined reason for approaching her, and you'll be required to have written approval from Clotilde beforehand."

Clotilde kept up the facade of reasonableness that she'd erected. Her lips thinned slightly when Benson announced the time period, but no other emotion snuck through. Apparently, even a measly three months galled her. Lachlyn, on the other hand, shook her head, refusing to look at me. I bet if I mentioned that I'd already tracked down Karissa and her kids, I'd get her attention. And not the positive kind, either.

"The board will expect a report on your progress at the next board meeting," Benson concluded. "When is that?" He looked at Astrid, who had been taking notes.

"October 3rd," she answered briskly. "At 9:00 a.m."

"There you go," Benson said. "Any questions?"

"I second it," from Riccio.

The meeting wrapped up quickly, Beth tossing me a discreet wink as she left. Nobody else said a word to me, although I heard the buzz of conversation as soon as they cleared the doorway.

The room emptied, leaving Astrid and me. She had gathered all her papers and was moving efficiently around the room tidying up. I debated helping, but realized I'd just have time to make the Saturday morning meeting at the club if I hurried.

CHAPTER NINETEEN

I was glad I made the effort to get to a meeting. Sue was there, so I was able to tell her about the board meeting.

"You got more out of them than I expected," Sue said.

"Not really. It's all paperwork. They gave in just enough to say they complied, but that's all. My impression was that the lawyer wasn't confident that they could just ignore Regina's will. But they were adamant that I not have any contact with the nonresident clients. And since they've divided the current residents between Clotilde and Lachlyn, it doesn't look like I'll have any face-to-face time with any of them, either. They have to be feeling pretty stretched. From what I can tell, Clotilde's main duties before this were community outreach and fundraising while Lachlyn managed the day-to-day stuff. You can't keep a facility like that running without a constant inflow of money, and that takes personal attention. Lots of it."

"What exactly are you looking for, Letty? Is this just a power struggle or do you have a definite goal in mind?"

Good question. Before I could answer, a familiar voice hooted a greeting to me from across the room. "Hey, Letty! Hey!"

Tall and gangly with a sheaf of blond hair, Paul still looked like a corn stalk, but since getting sober he'd filled out a bi. The added confidence of belonging somewhere had also calmed his twitchiness somewhat. I had gotten skilled at sidestepping his attempts to ask me out, but it was a constant balancing act between salvaging his feelings and not getting hooked into a date.

Unfortunately for me, Paul had displayed unswerving loyalty and even a burst of self-sacrificing courage during that horrible period of my life. Whether I liked it or not, I owed him. Besides, he was such a vulnerable, social misfit that I couldn't bear to do anything that might hurt him regardless of how uncomfortable I felt with his fawning.

Paul took a lot of energy.

After the meeting, not wanting an encounter of the Paul-kind, I scooted out of the club as quickly as I could. This might be a good time to return to the shelter. The board members had scattered immediately after their meeting and I'd watched Clotilde drive away as well. That left Lachlyn, but if she was there perhaps she'd let me get started on the files.

No surprise, none of the administrative staff had hung around. Joyce, however, was still there, scrubbing out the stove in the communal kitchen, but she wouldn't relinquish any of the files without Lachlyn being present. Couldn't blame her really.

I wanted access to the resident side of the building, hoping I could maybe talk to a few of the women without Lachlyn breathing down my neck. "Would you mind if I explored the shelter a bit?"

She paused so long I thought she was ignoring me. "You can't go on the residents' side. If you really want to help, you can go upstairs and get some blankets," Joyce finally answered. "A new girl came in this morning. First room on the left at the top of the stairs." She pointed down the hall in the general direction of the therapy offices.

There weren't too many rooms on the administrative side that I hadn't been in. The one area that I had no reason to enter, and frankly, hd no desire to, was the upper story. I knew I *should* examine the stairs and what lay beyond. I just didn't want to. I got the feeling Joyce's request was inspired by her own desire to avoid the site of Regina's death. She stared at me, stone-faced, awaiting my decision.

The door leading to the stairwell was next to Clotilde's office. In all the times I'd been here, I'd never seen anyone go upstairs.

Holding my breath, I made it past the spot where Regina's body had been found. I promised myself that if I caught even one whiff of Regina's fancy perfume, I'd haul ass out of the shelter and *never* come back, pushy ghost bitch or not.

They were steep, too, those stairs. My foot barely fit on the tread, so I had to go up angled sideways. They shot straight up like a ladder into the darkness above. Apparently back when the house had been built, people had had teensy, tiny feet and strong-like-bull thigh muscles. Three-quarters of the way up, they took a hard right.

Stars danced in front of my eyes by the time I reached the top. I told myself it was from holding my breath, but the button of my slacks digging into my belly argued a different cause.

Spooked and in active button-denial, I turned into the first room I came to. Somebody had decided that this was the room where furniture came to die. A jumble of mismatched wooden chairs had been shoved against the far corner, their legs entwined incestuously. An ancient, too-cheap-to-be-antique bureau squatted, gap-toothed, against the wall, several drawers missing and a pile of chipped ceramic planter pots stacked haphazardly across its surface.

Dust thickened the air, dulling individual color into a homogenous skin over the objects. Even the wall paint and window curtains had aged to a tired taupe.

Made it hard to breath, too. Cupping my hand over my face, I glanced around for blankets, even though the state of the room made it an unlikely place to store linens. A space had been cleared in front of the closet door, however..

I cracked the door open and peered into the darkness. It was a deep closet, not quite a walk-in but deep nonetheless. Files cabinets lined the back, five across. Dust coated most of their surfaces, except on three cabinets where recent finger marks had left clear swathes. I pulled open a drawer on the closest and, unsurprisingly, found it stuffed with manila files, jammed so tightly I couldn't fit a finger between them. The second drawer down showed a disturbance. A section of files jutted up, an obvious irregularity.

These must be the shelter's archives, although they couldn't possibly hold all the files since the shelter first opened. Maybe those had been recycled. Agencies only had to hold on to their files for a certain number of years—seven, I thought. I performed a hurried check to see if the disturbed areas matched the files Regina had appropriated.

They did.

CHAPTER TWENTY

Had Regina been attempting further research the night she was killed? Unbidden, visions of the women's faces—their poor, broken faces— rose in my mind. I didn't have time to explore deeper. Heart thumping, I clicked the closet door shut as quietly as I could, suddenly feeling like Bluebeard's most recent wife.

How long *had* I been up here? I tiptoed toward the door, hoping that the creaking floors hadn't given away my presence. Unfortunately, I didn't prove to be a proficient tiptoer. In my haste, my feet tangled and I fell full out on the musty, threadbare carpet almost breaking my nose on an extended leg of one of the wooden chairs.

Bet they heard *that.*

Air huffed out of my lungs and I lay there gasping a vile dusty air mixture. From this vantage point, I could see the pile of chairs wasn't just any old pile. Somebody had made a fort with just enough wiggle room for a child to squeeze through to the cavernous space in the middle. I would have smiled at the memories of my own childhood forts—Kris and I using upended couch cushions and the old quilt to fashion a snug hidey hole— except that a swath of red fur caught my eye.

Recognizing the missing Mo-mo really did make me smile. Returning it to Mikey would earn me bonus points as well as giving me an excuse to return to Karissa's trailer. I pulled it out, feeling the lumpy stuffing of a well-loved toy. The smile died when a glint of silver alerted me to the tiny bauble caught in a terry cloth loop. A charm. A fat, sassy little cow with black enamel spots. I'd seen it many times dangling from Regina's wrist. The whimsical nature of the charm bracelet had always surprised me, but even more so, this cow. It seemed so. . . well. . .Wisconsin-y.

Finding it there, under the chairs, meant Mikey had probably been there at the same time Regina had. Maybe they'd even had some kind of interaction. Maybe she'd handed the toy to him, snagging the charm. Maybe she'd discovered his hiding place when she'd come up to research the archives. Hell, maybe they'd been playing hide-n-seek; staff often organized play activities for the shelter's children. Maybe, maybe, maybe.

Maybe he'd been here, tucked away in his fort, when Regina had plunged to her death.

I practically levitated off the floor, OD-ing on adrenaline: hot and dizzy, ears ringing, a tinny flat taste in my mouth. Clutching Mo-Mo, I stuffed the bauble in my slacks pocket and fled. In the room across the hall, I found lots of blankets—stacks and stacks of them on a banquet table running the length of the back wall. Pillows, too.

A door creaked from the lower floor. Snatching up a set of sheets and a blanket, I stuffed the toy between their folds, wiped sweaty palms on the uppermost, and scurried to the top of the stairs.

Lachlyn emerged out of the murky darkness of the stairwell like a bubble rising to the surface of a stagnant pond, her eyes fixed on mine. My poor overworked adrenal glands had no more juice to give. I stood there, dumbly.

"What are you doing up here?" She didn't actually hiss, but in my mind, she did.

With a throat so dry I feared it would spontaneously combust, I husked out a reply. "Joyce. . . There's a new girl. She, um, said she needed a blanket. So I got it. For her. Joyce, I mean." I held the linens up.

"Uh-huh. Well, now that you have them, you don't need to loiter. This area is off-limits, except to staff." She stood back, silently indicating I should precede her down the stairs.

Let her walk behind me on the stairs that Regina had been pushed from? Not. Gonna. Happen.

"I'll be right there." I plopped down on the top riser. "I have something in my shoe. You go ahead." I pulled off my flat and shook it wildly. Nothing fell out, but neither of us believed I was telling the truth anyway, so no surprise there. Her lips did that bleached white thing, but she started down the stairs.

"Meet me in the group room in ten minutes," she tossed over her shoulder. "Since you're so *help*ful."

I had just enough time to hide the stuffed animal, toss the bedding on the kitchen table, and dart into the bathroom to quietly urp in the toilet. I multitask.

I wasn't in any shape to co-lead a group session, but after bitching about the need to interact more, I couldn't very well say no.

Strangely, the metal folding chairs had all been pulled back from the circle and stacked tidily against a wall. Four sets of wary female eyes stared at me when I walked in. Lachlyn was at the opposite end of the room and didn't bother to look up. For the first time, I noticed she was wearing sweats, hair scraped back from her head, feet bare.

Everybody else was in some form of loose clothing,

mostly sweats with Green Bay Packer logos, although one woman wore pajama bottoms and a stretched-out tank top. If it weren't for Lachlyn's casual apparel, I wouldn't have been surprised. It was Saturday, after all, and the women could be expected to dress for comfort. Not Lachlyn though. Emotionally, she just wasn't the relaxed-casual type.

Obviously we weren't going to be running a therapy session. Aerobics, maybe? Lachlyn was still fiddling with something across the room so perhaps she was setting up a CD player. Secretly, I was rooting for a meditation session. Relaxation and stress were some of the few activities I'd liked about my own recuperation. I could sure use some deep breathing right about now.

I said hi to the women, smiling and introducing myself. Each gave her name, which I promptly jumbled up. There was a Sharon, a Candice, and a Barb, but they were all wearing green-and-gold and milling around. I was pretty sure Jan was the one in pjs.

At any rate, I was overdressed.

And oh, so wrong about the activity.

CHAPTER TWENTY ONE

Lachlyn was teaching a self-defense class. Definitely *not* my favorite activity. Despite Regina's rigorous drilling, I always flinched when she screamed to disorient me, cowered when she rushed at me, and got the giggles when she pinned me to the mat.

I was light-years away from ninjahood. And I sure didn't like the look in Lachlyn's eyes either. Her "pleasant" expression didn't lie comfortably on her face muscles, unused to the emotion as they were. Her eyes, however, retained the usual pissed. Nothing new there.

The other women clustered several feet away from me. As hyper-vigilant to anger as they were, they sensed enough to stay out of Lachlyn's sight line. Self-preservation ran strong. Couldn't blame them.

Lachlyn turned to me with a smile. Not what I would call a friendly smile, but it did seem genuine. That made sense since she was about to thrash my ass.

"All right, ladies, let's get to work. Today we're looking at choke holds—a favorite of a lot of abusers. They like to get up close and personal. Letty? How about volunteering? You can be my victim." Lachlyn laughed as she made the suggestion.

I didn't. I didn't break eye contact with her either, letting her know I was on to her game. One of the few things that Regina tried to teach me that took was *show no fear*.

I was sick and tired of fear anyway.

"Geez, Lachlyn, don't look so eager," I said. "You're not trying to scare me, are you?"

The residents giggled nervously. Lachlyn's smile lost some of its genuineness, but none of the malice.

We faced off.

"OK, first off, it's important to remember that while there are always exceptions, generally speaking, a strong man can render an average-sized woman unconscious in five seconds. Five *seconds*, ladies. Count them off, one-thousand one, one-thousand two... That's not much time at all. Ten seconds after that, you could be dead. Fifteen seconds, start to finish. Keep that in mind."

She motioned to me, my cue to choke her. *Finally.* And I had permission and everything.

Face to face, I wrapped my hands around her throat, but lightly. There were witnesses, after all. She smiled, eyes narrowing.

"You have to protect your airway," she continued, angling her head back. She was taller than I, giving me an instant disadvantage as her height pulled my center of gravity up. "That's first. It's imperative. Don't try jerking away or scratching at him; he's too strong and you don't have enough time. Don't try fancy footwork; you'll only end up tripping yourself and your clumsiness will help him finish you off. Tilt your head back to increase air flow, and *get to the thumbs.*"

Bringing her arms outside my own, she reached in, grabbed my thumbs and levered down *hard.* I slammed to the floor, pain singing through my knees as I landed. "See how vulnerable your big, bad attacker is?" Lachlyn said as she smiled down at me. "Look at all the places you can hurt her. I mean, him." She air-jabbed at my eyes and throat and feinted a kick at my midsection.

Then, she stood.

I rose slowly to my feet as she nattered on about heel strikes to the nose, palm strikes to the carotid artery, and the ever popular kick-him-in-the-nuts-and-run. It was nice to see someone enjoy her work.

My turn. I waited until she was done with her mini-lecture, and then said, "Mind if I try?"

"Of course. By all means."

"OK, so I'm getting choked." Lachlyn wrapped her fingers around my neck. Long and cold, I felt their strength even though they rested lightly on my skin. "So I tilt my neck back . . . Then reach through, get my thumbs between yours and . . . twist." I moved slowly through the steps—not fast, not hard—carefully matching a running commentary to the actions.

When I finished, Lachlyn smiled and said, "That's ri—"

"And I could do this, right?" I grabbed her by the back of the head and her chin, and spun her around. Pretty easily, too; bodies, after all, tend to go wherever the neck goes. But not *too* hard. Manslaughter would not look good on the old resume. "Because he would be all vulnerable and everything. In fact, if I really thought he was trying to kill me or go after my kids, I could just snap his neck like killin' a chicken for dinner."

As soon as I released her, she spun around, face red, mouth pulled into a snarl. Adrenaline spiked through me like a cocktail, my lips snarling into a crazy-ass smile.

Astrid materialized, shoving her body between us, pushing me sideways and grabbing Lachlyn's arm. "That's wonderful! Wow! What a treat we've had tonight. Ladies, let's give these two a round of applause for their hard work. Look at you two. You're both tired out. Lachlyn, can you pour the lemonade out? You look thirsty." Turning her back on me, she herded Lachlyn over to the table holding cookies and drinks.

I stood there, panting, as a cold sweat popped out of my skin. I felt nauseous. I looked around for a chair, but despite a wave of weakness washing over me, I changed my mind. I really didn't want to stay any longer. My glance caught on a glint of silver lying on the floor. *The charm.*

I snatched it up, slipping it back into my pocket, then looked around quickly to see if anybody had seen. Lachlyn's gaze burned at me from across the room.

CHAPTER TWENTY TWO

I could feel the bruises gelling under my skin on the drive home, and when I turned my head to the left too sharply, there was an ominous twinge in my neck. I looked forward to a long Epsom salt bath until I realized that no amount of hot water would ease the anger-rich tension from my muscles. Lachlyn hadn't scared me away; she'd royally pissed me off. At least now we knew where we each stood.

Once home, I grabbed the copy of Regina's calendar and set it with the files on my coffee table. Siggy jumped up to inspect the pile, then followed me into the kitchen to supervise my coffee-making preparations.

"This might be a long night, Sig."

He blinked up at me, then walked over to his food dish as though reminding me to get my priorities straight. I hadn't been spending enough time with him, and he was not averse to heaping on the guilt.

"I know, I know," I told him as I poured his favorite cat food into his bowl. "Maybe you could sit by me and help solve the case like those cats do in books, huh?" Ignoring me, he hunkered over his food like a prison convict, tail lashing, ready to kick butt if anyone tried to take his salmon flavored Kitty Krunchies.

Useless.

Before sitting down, I detoured into my bedroom, where I sorted through my jewelry looking for a chain thin enough to fit the charm's tiny fastener. The only one that worked was one that Robert had given me a month or so before he was killed.

Sadness swept over me. And guilt. I hadn't loved Robert—nor he, me—and our break-up had occurred mere days before his murder, but after I'd finally realized what an ass he was and how little we had in common.

But his death was a direct result of his involvement with me. There were people at the club who still blamed me. Hell—*I* still blamed me.

Returning to the couch, I placed the files on my lap, stomach churning. Skolnik, of course; I set her file back on the table. I didn't remember the next one—Bailey— from the closet boxes. My heart banged at the next though: Church. It went on top of Skolnik's. As did the next file—Tammy Long. Jordan and Tshida didn't ring any bells, and I was pretty sure that Tshida hadn't been one of the labeled boxes.

I started going through the paperwork slowly, taking notes, trying to find a common denominator that perhaps I'd overlooked the first time. If there was one, it eluded me. They'd had different therapists; none of the time periods seemed to overlap; after-care services were varied; they didn't live in the same part of town. I puzzled on it until the information started swirling in my head—something joined these women together. Regina had seen something, knew something. And it had gotten her killed.

Frustrated, I set the stack of files to the side and picked up Regina's calendar. I paged through to the beginning of September, a couple of weeks before Regina's "accident." I found Karissa's initials penciled in various places, seeming to correspond with what I remembered of her sessions. Other initials had been

recorded as well, and a few "Gp Tx" abbreviations
indicated when Regina had led the group therapy
sessions. I paged back a month to August. More of the
same. She'd also made a habit of listing phone calls or
tasks she needed to complete. One date, with a telephone
number, caught my eye.

I knew that number. I'd called it numerous times last
spring when a nasty client had filed a false complaint
against me to the state licensing board. I'd consulted
with Regina over the issue, but that had all been settled
by late spring.

If the licensing board note didn't have to do with
me—and I didn't see how it could—who did it concern?
Was Regina being investigated? I'd have to check with
Bob, but if it wasn't connected to the clinic, he wouldn't
know. Maybe the shelter? Could that be why Clotilde and
Lachlyn were so edgy? I'd never get a straight answer out
of them, and I doubted that Astrid would spill the beans,
either.

It was possible, likely even, that if Regina was being
investigated she would have consulted her lawyer. I
made a note to call Ashley Perkins.

There was another possibility, however. If Regina
wasn't the target of an investigation, maybe she was the
initiator of one. In which case, she would have pissed off
someone.

Between the discovery of the archives and this new
possibility, I had more than just an icky feeling to show
Blodgett. If it wasn't so late I'd call him, but unless he
was working a case he preferred to be in bed by 10:00. I
didn't want to scare his wife Diana, either. She'd put up
with enough over the years; she didn't need me calling at
close to midnight. On the off chance that I'd catch
Blodgett at work, I dialed the police station.

And learned my friend had just been rushed to the hospital.

The hospital, of course, gave me even less information than the desk sergeant had. I ended up calling Sue—a truly courageous act on my part—and made her call her on-again, off-again beau, Pete Durrant, an officer with Chippewa PD. She claimed the reason they fought was for the spicy, make-up sex. A nice way to rationalize being a bitch. At any rate, even though they were in an off-period, she was willing to call him to see if he'd track down information about Blodgett's admission.

It would be awful if Blodgett had a heart attack just a few months before retiring. If his heart didn't kill him, Diana would.

Pete Durrant called back within twenty minutes. It wasn't a heart attack. Blodgett had been attacked— knifed from behind—while off-duty. Diana had found him lying on the sidewalk leading to their back door. Although he was unconscious by the time she'd found him, the blood trail showed that he'd managed to crawl from his Chevy truck. He'd lost a lot of blood. He was still in surgery.

Even though I made it across town ten minutes quicker than the law allowed, Pete was there before me. He met me at the Emergency Department entrance—the only doors unlocked at this time of night—and led me through the hospital maze to a waiting room where Diana sat, the only soft pair of eyes in a sea of flint.

Blodgett's colleagues had shown up en masse, an undercurrent of anger creating a subliminal hum of energy. One of the few things that TV cop shows apparently got right was the rage incurred when one of their own was hit. I sat next to Diana and took her cold hand. We waited.

CHAPTER TWENTY THREE

Over the course of the next few hours, most of the cops trickled off, back to work or home or wherever, leaving a trio of older men, each looking as close to retirement as Blodgett, who sat stoically waiting for news. Blodgett's oldest son and his wife made it to the hospital just before the doctor came to talk with Diana, so I hung back and let them be. As soon as the doctor left they informed the rest of us that Blodgett had come through the surgery well and was in recovery. No visitors allowed, of course, except for immediate family.

One of the three men approached Diana. As they murmured quietly together, she nodded several times, her face tired and grayed out under the flourescent lighting. Knowing how anxious his colleagues would be to question him, I imagined Blodgett had just acquired a "long-lost brother" who would take his turn with the family. There would be no time wasted in tracking down the person responsible for attacking their fellow officer.

I hesitated, trying to decide if I should talk with Blodgett's buddy. Despite my quasi-friendship with Blodgett I had a long family history of learned cop avoidance. My mother, in particular, would have crapped kittens if she'd known my cell phone had a cop's personal phone number residing in close proximity to her own. Called him more often, too.

Besides, all Blodgett had been doing for me was

looking up records. Although I couldn't imagine his attack was connected with Regina's death, my stomach felt queasy. Maybe it was all the coffee I'd been chugging.

Undecided, I gave Diana a kiss on the cheek, told her I'd call, and left.

My body craved sleep, but my brain was buzzing like a frenetic mosquito. I briefly debated going to the Sunday morning AA meeting. I'd have to wait a couple of hours, but I could curl up on the couch in the lobby and maybe nap. The thought of dumping my problems and wallowing in my safe place was almost as intoxicating as the booze I used to drink, but the couch had seen more asses than a county fair judge and I rethought the nap plan, which left two hours of even more stale coffee and brooding.

Instead, I stopped home to explain my absence to Siggy (who was sound asleep and oblivious to the fact that I'd been gone all night), fed him (this, he cared about), and grabbed Mikey Dillard's stuffed toy.

I hoped Mo-Mo would get me past Karissa's elderly bodyguard, maybe even earn me some goodwill.

The Jeep was gone from the parking slot. I again braved the precariously leaning set of stairs and knocked on the trailer's metal screen door until my knuckles screamed in protest. No one answered; I sensed emptiness beyond the flimsy door. The windows were too grimy to see very much so I didn't try. Besides, I didn't want any neighbors calling the cops, although it was so early in the morning I doubted many would be awake.

After following the PARK MANAGER signs, I found myself, despite the early hour, knocking on yet another door. This one had the name Tallie Brandess, Manager stenciled across the front. I heard movement within as someone, presumably Tallie, shuffled up to answer my summons.

The woman who answered was a tiny bird of a woman with a smile that captured the joy of a new morning. It was impossible not to smile back.

"Yes?" she asked.

I introduced myself. "I'm sorry to bother you so early, but I'm looking for the family from Lot 7. The woman's name is Bernadette Stanhope, but it's actually her daughter Karissa that I'm looking for."

"Oh, dear," Tallie said. "You just missed them. I talked to Bernie yesterday morning and everything seemed fine. Next thing I knew they were loading up and long gone just before midnight. One of our neighbors ran over to tell me they were packing up 'cause it looked like they were sneaking out. Thing is, though, Bernie had already paid up her October rent and, of course, I have her deposit. Not much I can do if she's paid up."

"Was there an emergency, do you think?"

"I don't know what the problem was. Bernie is very private, and I never really met her daughter. Bernie was renting that trailer, and she wasn't supposed to have anyone staying with her long term. I was willing to ignore it as long as no one complained. Times are so bad we all have to look the other way on some things. But I don't think it was that. Nobody had complained, and if Bernie just wanted a bigger place, I would think they would have stuck out the last month or asked for part of the rent back."

"Did she leave a forwarding address?"

The manager was shaking her head before I finished my question. "No, she said she'd contact me. If you ask me, they were more focused on leaving than on where they might be going."

Another thought occurred to me. Could they have even fit everything in the old Jeep that I'd seen? A Wrangler isn't the roomiest vehicle. I asked Tallie.

"No, just the Jeep."

"Was anybody helping them? Did you see anyone else?"

"Nope. Not then, anyway."

"I guess it's possible that they'll come back before their rent runs out? Maybe they aren't gone for good."

"Maybe so," Tallie agreed, but her little bird face scrunched up with doubt. I could tell she didn't expect to see Bernie back at Lot 7 in the near future. I stood there pensively, trying to come up with some more questions.

"You said, 'not then,'" I repeated. "Was there somebody here earlier? A man?" If Karissa's ex had shown up, it would make sense that they were on the run. It would be a hassle for me to try to find them, but at least it would mean that it didn't have anything to do with the shelter. And if *I* couldn't find them . . .

Tallie's face closed like a cloud covering the sun.

I held still. It looked like she wasn't sure if she should mention whatever it was that she'd started to say. I didn't push for it. Sometimes it was better to just wait patiently.

"They had a visitor," she finally said. "Not a man, though."

"I see," I murmured. It's a therapist thing. Works, too.

"I only caught a glimpse," she continued. "But I've been half expecting a social worker to show up there, so I wasn't surprised. Anyone could see that Karissa was having some troubles, and when there's kids involved, well, quite often someone official comes by eventually. I used to teach. We could usually tell."

"So, you think it was a social worker?"

"I don't know, really. It could have been. She was tall, you know, but professional looking. Real short hair like those women who don't want to bother with curlers. I just don't know. Really, you know, I shouldn't have said anything. I hate spreading gossip, especially when I don't know if there's anything to it. She could have just been a friend of the family."

She did look distressed, so I reassured her as best I could. I gave her one of my business cards and asked her to call me if she saw Bernie or Karissa, but I could tell that she was regretting her openness. She mumbled good-bye and retreated into her trailer looking far less happy with her day than she had before she'd met me.

I hated having that effect on people.

CHAPTER TWENTY FOUR

Back at home, I settled in on the couch with Siggy and called the hospital. Diana answered in Blodgett's room, sounding tired but happy. She told me the doctors were pleased with his response to surgery. Diana was waiting for her son to get back from the cafeteria, and then she planned on going home to rest for a few hours.

"They have an armchair here next to Del's bed that I've been cat-napping in, but I need a shower and their soap here smells like cleaning fluid. Well, I guess it is at that, but I don't want to smell like sanitizer all day. Besides, I need to feed Whiskers. He must have been scared to death with all the ruckus."

"If you need me to run over to the house, I'd be happy to feed Whiskers, or stay with him, whatever you need."

Siggy turned his emerald-green eyes to me and glared. Stopped purring, too.

Diana declined my offer. She had plenty of family in the area, not to mention their extended police "family." I had to forcibly stifle my need-to-be-needed gene, but Diana promised she'd let me know if anything came up. She also promised to call as soon as Blodgett could have visitors.

That left me with nothing to do but suffer under Siggy's jealous stare and nap.

Lachlyn had agreed to meet me at 8:30 the next morning, but I got there a wee bit earlier. Forty-five minutes early, actually, but I wanted to have some wiggle room to get up to the second floor if I could. Unfortunately, Astrid was fluttering around the kitchen while the residents yakked and finished breakfast. I couldn't manage it without a half-dozen witnesses.

I also wanted the opportunity to study Lachlyn's face when I asked her point-blank why she'd gone to Bernie's trailer. Of course, it was possible that it had been Clotilde, but, if so, I was certain Lachlyn would be well aware of it. After waking up from my nap, I'd spent the previous evening brooding over the mystery woman who had shown up at the trailer so conveniently just hours before the family fled. What I couldn't decide was how they'd tracked Karissa to her grandmother's home, unless they'd withheld information from the file they'd allowed me to see. Wouldn't put it past them.

I also didn't know whether the mysterious visitor had been initiated at my discovery of Bluebeard's closet or if that too was just a coincidence.

I didn't much believe in coincidences.

When Lachlyn finally arrived, twenty minutes late, she looked like she'd been sprinkled with an extra dusting of pissy powder. After saying good morning to the women—and pointedly ignoring me—she turned to me and snapped, "I have an emergency. I won't be able to monitor you this morning. You'll have to reschedule."

Without bothering to wait for a reply, she spun on her heel and made for the door.

"Lachlyn, wait!" For once, my voice tone—with a *fine*, commanding ring to it—matched my intentions. The women at the table hushed, eyebrows raised in astonishment. Astrid froze like a field mouse under a hawk's shadow as Lachlyn slowly turned back. "We need to talk. Here or in your office is fine with me. You choose."

For a moment, the air crackled around us. Lachlyn's eyes narrowed at the challenge, then slid toward the table full of watching women. Taking a deep breath, she forced a syrupy smile across her face. "Of course, Letty. The office will be fine."

She held the door open for me. Unless we were to enter into one of those "after you" games, I'd have to walk with her at my back. Reasoning that she wasn't likely to bludgeon me to death in front of witnesses, I proceeded forward, but my back itched where I could feel her laser eyes scorching a path up my spine. By the time we made it to her barren office, much of the delicious bravado had leached out of my skin, and I was back to my usual passive-aggressive, sarcastic self.

Lachlyn closed the office door with a snap. "What is it that's so important it can't wait?" she asked. "I have things to do."

"I'm sure you do. In fact, I understand you were pretty busy Saturday, too."

Her eyes flickered from disdain to doubt, then to something else that I couldn't quite place. "I don't know what you're talking about." She managed to pack a lot of scorn into one sentence.

"Sure, you do. How did you know where to find her? Couldn't have been from the file . . . unless there was something missing from it. Maybe something you held back? A contact person? An address? That, if you removed it from the file, would be illegal, by the way."

"This is ridic—"

"But that's not the biggest question, is it? No, what I

want to know is what you said to her. What is she so afraid of that the whole family had to pick up and take off again right after you went to see them? Every one of them—back into hiding. Isn't this supposed to be a safe place? Aren't you supposed to be the one they run *to,* not away from?"

Her face had run a whole gamut of emotions during my speech—irritation, shock, guilt maybe—but not confusion. And last, not surprisingly, was rage.

Don't know what I'd hoped to accomplish, but it felt damn good.

"You have no idea," Lachlyn sputtered. "You just have no ..." She bit her lip, visibly willing herself under control.

I wanted to keep her off balance without bringing Mikey into it, so I kept the focus on his mother. "Did Karissa see something that night? Maybe hear something? Was Regina sticking her nose into something?"

It didn't matter. However off balance my first accusations had made Lachlyn, she recovered quickly.

"I don't have time to waste on your theatrics. Now please remove yourself from my office. Immediately."

I left. Wasn't much more I could achieve anyway. But I'd gained more than just the fleeting look of complicity that I'd seen flash across her face.

Lying with military precision in the upper right hand side of the desk, I'd also seen the work order request for a local locksmith. A solitary red and white cardboard box perched like a paperweight on top, so it didn't look like they were changing all of the locks. Just one. The door leading to the stairway maybe? Or the upstairs storage room? Either one would be effective at preventing accidental visitors to the Bluebeard closet.

CHAPTER TWENTY FIVE

I'd parked out back, so I went through to the kitchen. Astrid was up to her elbows in dish water. She jumped and peered over her shoulder when I came in.

"Oh, it's you! I thought you'd gone already." She smiled sheepishly. "Don't tell the others that I'm doing the dishes. The residents are supposed to take care of all their household chores, but every now and then I give them a break. They're going through so much."

"It'll be our secret," I said. "Besides, they're not exactly my best friends."

"There's just so much you don't understand. I know it must be hard for you, coming in like this. It even took a while for them to warm up to Regina, and that was early on. It's just ..." She struggled to find the words as she dried her hands on a towel. "They've both been at this so long. We see so many women, so many children—they're all hurting. As soon as one gets out, two more show up needing our help. Or, worse, they go back to their abuser. It's like it never ends.

"Lachlyn's own daughter . . ." she continued, "Well, I won't get into that, but I'll just say this: it's not just a theory with us. It's not just a political stance or whatever. We've *lived* it. All of us. Most women have, as far as that goes."

"Lachlyn has a daughter? Really?" My mind almost fritzed out trying to mentally reconcile Lachlyn as a mother. "I thought she was a nun."

"She *had* a daughter and she *used* to be a nun. She was discharged or whatever they call it. It was her choice. I guess she decided it wasn't her calling."

"Was she pregnant?"

"That is none of your business, now is it?"

"I'm sorry. You're right. I just can't picture Lachlyn in either role."

"She was a wonderful mother. Kaitlyn was practically raised here at the shelter. Lachlyn used to bring her in. Not to the groups, of course, but Kaitlyn played with the children here. She was such a happy, little girl. Very loving. And she didn't have just one role model—she was surrounded by strong, intelligent women. Courageous women—especially her mother.

"You should have seen Lachlyn when she was younger. She's grown bitter over the years, but who could blame her?"

"What happened?" I murmured.

"A man, of course. Isn't it always? Kaitlyn grew up, met a man—an absolute jerk, I might add—and decided she could save him."

"He was abusive?" I asked.

Astrid ran more hot water, added dish soap, and set the frying pan to soak. "We couldn't prove it. Not at first. But he was never good for Kaitlyn. Drugs. Drinking. He completely destroyed that girl. When Lachlyn tried to get her to see what was happening, Kaitlyn turned her back on her. Clotilde and I tried to intervene, too. We were like aunts to her, after all. But she wouldn't listen to us either. I know Lachlyn felt helpless. We could see what was going to happen. And then . . . it was too late. She was gone."

I waited several moments before saying, "That must

have been Lachlyn's worst nightmare."

Astrid turned back to the pan with an air of finality, scrubbing vigorously. "That was a long time ago. But you can see why I don't blame her for being cranky. She's earned it. And she does such good."

"What about you?" I kept the conversation going. "How come you haven't grown . . . cranky?"

"I have my days, believe me. But I don't know. Their jobs are a lot more stressful. I think I'd go crazy if I had to deal with all the funding issues or the people in the community who *say* they want to help abused women, but then protest the shelter or a group home in their own neighborhood."

"Is that an issue here?" I asked. "This shelter's been here forever. I would think that any protests would have long since died out."

"Don't you believe it. Every time somebody new moves in, it all gets stirred up again. Strange as this may sound, it was a lot easier when this was a low-income neighborhood. When folks with money started buying up property and remodeling, well, it all started up again. They don't want 'transients' in their neighborhood. What if some crazy husband goes on a shooting spree and takes hostages or something? It's just ridiculous. Every six months we have to spend good money on yet another community open house so we can answer questions, show off the security system, and just reassure so-called educated people that the boogy man isn't going to eat their children. A new family moves in and back to ground zero we go."

"I can see where that would be frustrating, especially when the money can be used in so many different ways. But in this case, the boogy man is real, isn't he? I mean, you don't keep this place secret, right? One of the abusers could show up at any time."

"Yes, but that's not as common as you might think."

"But it *could* happen," I insisted. I'd had my own experience—very recently—with an abuser who was happy to use me as a substitute when he couldn't torment his girlfriend.

"True." Her turn to smile softly. She knew my history. "Well, don't tell the neighbors—I've got enough to do without planning another open house."

Just as I was about to risk delving deeper into Lachlyn's history, Clotilde walked in. Her glance flicked back and forth between us trying to get a read on the conversation. God forbid Astrid wasn't being suitably nasty to me.

"Letty, I'm glad I caught you," she said. What was it with people refusing to say good morning to me? "I've had several discussions with board members, and there are some points we need to clarify. We can't allow the disruption to our program to go on indefinitely. It's unreasonable to pull Lachlyn from her duties in this fashion. In light of that, we'll need you to be finished with your task by the end of the week. After that, I suppose we could consider you to be on-call if one of Regina's former clients re-contacts the shelter in an emergency. If that should be necessary." From her tone, it was obvious that it would never "be necessary."

"That's going to be rather difficult since Lachlyn keeps canceling appointments with me."

Okay, that only happened once, but I didn't appreciate the bum's rush I was getting. I needed more than a week, especially if I was going to maneuver my way back to the archives. And I needed to get Lachlyn off my back.

"Since we're only looking at a few days," Clotilde

said, "I can ask her to be more flexible. I feel certain she'll agree when she understands the parameters."

Perhaps she would have more time if she weren't running around trailer parks scaring off witnesses. Thought it. Didn't say it. "I'd be happy to be finished by Friday as long as I can do the job ethically. I'm sure you wouldn't want anything less for your clients, would you?"

She didn't allow herself to be baited. "Astrid, if you've finished with the dishes"—she gave Astrid the evil eye—"perhaps you could get started on the board meeting notes." To me, she said, "Have a good day."

And then I was alone in the kitchen with the lemony-soft smell of dish soap masking the taste of bitterness left in my mouth.

CHAPTER TWENTY SIX

A typical Monday. This one came with a trifecta of unpleasantness. Bob had astonished us all by arriving at the clinic well before his usual I'm-in-charge-and-nobody-better-report-me 10:00 a.m. start time. The early appearance coupled with his jittery behavior started a swirl of rumors, the most likely of which was that somebody from administration was descending on us for a "surprise" inspection. This, in turn, set off a whirlwind of paperwork straightening and frantic filing in the front office.

Surprise visits were rarely a true surprise since there wasn't a supervisor in existence who could make a move without his secretary or office manager knowing where he was going and when he was due back. And of course they'd call Lisa, our office manager, and sound the alert. We might not get a lot of notice, but there was usually enough to make ourselves presentable.

Today, however, the normally reliable network of support staff snitches had seemingly failed, and Lisa hadn't heard anything. However, when Bob had come in early, she'd called the main office and learned that Dr. Felding—the big boss—hadn't come in yet. Another highly unusual occurrence. There were just enough discrepancies to the usual routine that Lisa had become convinced that Felding was making a sneak attack. The dreaded words "audit" were spoken, and the front office was in a tizzy.

I wasn't completely convinced since it would be highly unusual for an administrator to choose a Monday morning to venture forth into the field. Monday mornings were for drinking coffee and mourning the demise of the weekend. Besides, human nature almost guaranteed that visits be scheduled on bright, sunny afternoons when the boss could take his motorcycle out for a spin to the outlying sites and call it work.

I was the only one not freaking out. Since I'd been spending the last couple of weeks immersed in files, I knew that both mine and Regina's were in tip-top shape. Felt quite smug until Bob trudged up front clutching a mug of coffee and asked me to meet with him.

Actually what he said was, "Letty. My office." Then, he clomped back to his office, leaving a trail of dribbled coffee in his wake.

"So, what's going on with that group?" he asked after I sat down.

"We've held two sessions. Two people showed up for the first, and one for the second. Most of Regina's clients who decided to continue in therapy preferred individual sessions. Hannah and I decided we'll offer one more session tomorrow evening and see if anyone shows up, but it's doubtful."

"Well, no one can say we didn't do what we were supposed to. How many of her clients dropped out? Any way we can make some calls and get them back in?"

I wasn't about to start telemarketing former clients, but I had planned to do follow-up calls in a month or so with those who had terminated therapy prematurely. I told Bob this, but he still seemed antsy.

In fact, Bob really didn't look well, and I was doubly surprised that he'd shown up today. For once, he looked like if he'd called in sick, he wouldn't be lying. Since he *had* come in, I figured it was nerves. Maybe admin had caught on to the lackadaisical approach embraced by their newest temporary director or there really was a surprise inspection in the offing.

A new thought occurred to me. Maybe his unease had to do with the licensing board issue that Regina had been involved in. Whatever that was.

"Do you know whether Regina was involved in an investigation with the state?" I worded my question so that it wouldn't matter if Regina had been the subject or the initiator of an investigation, although I highly doubted the former. Still, I'd been finding out lately that I didn't know Regina as well as I'd thought. Bob, however, had been fairly close to her, at least until he'd taken up the director position.

He looked like my question had given him instant heartburn. "What? What are you talking about?"

"I found Regina's calendar and she—"

"You what? Her calendar is on our computer."

"Yes, but she had a separate one for the shelter. Remember, I asked you about it? And she had the number for the licensing board written in it. I'm trying to find out why she was in contact with them."

"If it's for the shelter, then I don't care. That's not my problem."

"I don't know for certain that it involved the shelter. Did she ever talk to you about it? Or maybe to Marshall before he left?"

"Oh, I get it. This is about Marshall, huh? I heard he was back in town. Is he trying to stir up trouble for me again?"

"What?" My turn to feel sick. "Marshall's back? When did he—"

"Listen, Letty, I don't know what shenanigans you
and Marshall got up to back then and I don't want to
know. You're both adults and if you like to take a shot at
the boss, well, you wouldn't be the first gal, ya know? But
you can't come running to me if he takes off on you. Of
course, leaving the state is a little extreme, but that's his
business. If you're trying to track him down you should
be talking to one of your girlfriends. I hear they had
quite the blowout Saturday night."

I left the office in a daze. *Marshall was back?* I
made straight for Hannah's office.

Sweet, serene Hannah knew what I was about to ask
before I'd even opened my mouth. She pulled me into
her office and sat me in one of the comfy armchairs. I
pulled a plush pillow into my lap and began kneading the
velvety fabric.

"Is he back for good?" I asked.

"I didn't go out with them, but I don't think so." She
didn't bother pretending either. She was kind that way.
"I think he had some business with the cabin to wrap up.
He's having trouble selling it. I think he's planning on
heading back to Wyoming soon."

"Who all went out?"

She shrugged and named a few of our co-workers,
including some colleagues from around town. I wasn't
particularly close with any of them, which explained why
I hadn't heard until now.

We sat in silence for a while as I absorbed the
information. Marshall was back, but not staying. And he
obviously didn't want to see me.

On the other hand, he hadn't been entirely secretive
about his trip, either. Chippewa Falls was a small town
and the mental health community was a tight one. If he'd
wanted to sneak in and sneak out, he wouldn't have gone

out with people I knew.

"Letty, listen." Hannah broke into my reverie. "I know that you've been going through a lot, especially with Marshall leaving and then Regina's accident. Plus you've had a lot of responsibility thrust on you. How are you doing with all of that?"

"I wish I knew."

"What do you mean?"

I sighed. "Marshall's leaving? I'm dealing with that by not dealing with it. I don't know how to feel about it, I guess, so I can't really pick a response to it. Should I be angry? I guess I am. He left without saying a word to me. Just fled the state," I heard myself repeating Bob, and almost gagged. "But after all that happened and everything he went through? I can't blame him either. Besides, he and I weren't really . . . I mean, there really wasn't anything . . . It was all a maybe, you know? Maybe we could have had something together. But maybe not. It doesn't matter.

"As far as Regina's death," I continued, "I *am* dealing with that. She was such a cranky bitch and so wonderful, too. The more I'm taking care of her business, the more I'm understanding what her loss means to me." I didn't want to get into my suspicions about the nature of her death, however. Not yet. "Anyway, the added responsibility is keeping me busy and out of trouble."

Ha.

Hannah smiled, understanding. Work disguised as therapy—we were all prone to it. "Well, if you need anything, if you need to talk . . ."

I reached over and squeezed her hand. "Thanks, Hannah. I'll keep that in mind. Promise."

I felt a little better after talking, not that it lasted. On top of adding several of Regina's clients, I'd started seeing all of my own again. On the one hand, it felt good to get back into my usual routine, and as I'd mentioned to Hannah, I often used work as a panacea. But it also meant less time to figure out what was going on at the shelter. There were so many questions: *What had happened to Regina? What had Mikey seen, and where had his family fled? And how was I going to finagle my way into the shelter where everyone else was trying to shove me out?* I decided I would skip my AA meeting tonight and go home and hit the computer, dig deeper into the files.

Back-to-back clients should also have meant less time to brood about Marshall, but I managed to slip that in at fairly regular intervals. Like every time I took a breath. Eventually, with enough distractions, I managed to regain some of my equilibrium.

That lasted until I walked out into the front office and found Marshall leaning against Lisa's desk, chatting with several of my co-workers.

CHAPTER TWENTY SEVEN

M y first thought was *Damn, he looks good.* My second thought was . . . Well, I wasn't very coherent after that, so I went back to concentrating on my first thought. I'd forgotten how dark his eyes were and how he'd let his chin get scruffy if he wasn't working. His jeans, faded from years of hard, outdoor work, snugged his butt nicely. *That* I remembered. On top, he wore a black t-shirt with a silhouette of Jimi Hendrix blazoned across his chest.

He looked startled, too, although he should have expected to see me. After all, I worked here. Lisa saved us both by taking charge of the conversation, something she does regularly anyway. After five long minutes of saying "uh-huh" to things I wasn't listening to, I made an excuse and fled back to my office. Unfortunately, it had been the end of the day for me. I wasn't expecting any clients, my files were all caught up, and I had nothing to do but stand with my ear against the crack in the door trying to listen for his voice.

I couldn't quite make out the words, but I could hear his deep rumble and frequent bursts of female laughter. I started contemplating different escape routes, but they all involved crawling through windows or setting off the alarm system that had recently been put in. Nothing stealthy about that. Besides, the alarm system would remind Marshall of why he left in the first place. It was one of the last boss-type things he'd done.

I flopped down at my desk and rummaged through my desk drawer looking for my stash of emergency Snickers. This situation called for serious chocolate.

Marshall, with that innate sense of timing that he'd always had, waited until my mouth was stuffed with chocolate, peanuts, and that tasty nugat stuff before tapping on my door. It swung open, not even giving me a few extra moments to deal with the candy bar lump that distended my cheeks by at least an inch.

Options were limited.

I could spit the wad into a tissue, but I suspected that maneuver would disclose wide, slurpy tendrils of chocolaty spit, not to mention what the half-masticated gob would resemble after it was deposited.

I could pretend that I didn't look like a troughing pig, chew for the next seven minutes methodically breaking down the mass until I could appropriately ingest it, all the while holding up a polite "just one moment" finger.

Or I could swallow it down en masse and risk choking to death.

I didn't die, but I wished I had. Marshall had entered with a concerned, we-should-talk look on his face, but my candy bar contretemps loosened him up. He slumped in the chair laughing helplessly. We were both close to tears by the time I finished. He from mirth, me from scraping the inside of my throat raw by ingesting a jumbo size clump of peanut-studded candy.

"Are you finished?" I finally asked.

"I'm sorry."

"I might believe that if you weren't laughing so hard. It ruins the sincerity vibe."

"I'll have to work on that." A residual grin brought

his dimples out.

"Yeah," I said weakly. I loved those dimples. "You do that. What, uh . . . Why are you here?"

"I came back to go over some things with the realtor. It's not exactly the best economy for selling a house. I've got to decide if I'm going to wait or take a loss."

"I'm sorry to hear that. Is there something you ..." I stopped. I couldn't ask if there was something he wanted when he so obviously didn't want *me*. "Why are you here?" I stabbed my finger at the floor to differentiate "here in Chippewa Falls" from "here and sitting two feet away looking more delicious than an Easter basket full of chocolate bunnies."

He didn't answer right away. His laughter faded, leaving him looking sad, maybe a little wistful. Which pissed me off. What right did he have to be wistful? He was the one who ran away.

"Look, Marshall—"

"I wanted to see you. I just . . ." He sighed, dropping his eyes and running a hand through his dark brown hair. It ruffled nicely, damn him. "I'm not proud of myself. Okay? I know I didn't handle everything very well."

"You fled the state. Took off cross-country. You absconded."

"Yeah, I did." He smiled ruefully.

"You wouldn't let me come visit you at the hospital. You put me on a *list*. No Visitors." My voice got more strained, ending in a raspy whisper. "Like I was some kind of *criminal*."

"Yeah. I did." No more smile. "I did that. Look, Letty, I'm sorry. I am. But I'm also . . ."

"What?"

"Confused. I know what happened to you wasn't

your fault, but at the same time, there were things you did that didn't help the situation, you know? I mean, come on! You drugged me. You thought I was a killer."

Okay, yeah.

"I didn't know what to think, Marshall," I said. "There was a lot going on."

We both grinned at the understatement. Through all of the terror and craziness in the past, we'd been able to laugh together. It was one of the things I loved . . . and missed.

"I remember," he said. Then his smile faded again and his hand rose to rub at the spot where my stalker had shot him in an effort to remove any rivals for my affection. "I remember," he said again.

I felt helpless. How could I fight a memory? What reassurances could I offer? As crazy as it sounded, I was after a killer again. I couldn't tell him he had nothing to worry about. I couldn't tell him *anything*. I think he knew I was holding something back. His dark brown eyes—no wonder I was addicted to chocolate—searched mine looking for an answer to a question I was forced to evade.

He left soon after and his leaving felt as awful as it had two months ago.

I changed my mind and went to an AA meeting. By the time I got to the HP & Me club, I was almost overwhelmed with frustration. I was being blocked at every turn, denied the things I wanted, obligated to things I didn't.

I hadn't even cleared the doors before Paul bounced up to me. He'd gotten new glasses, transforming his held-together-with-masking-tape wire rims into techie-nerd fashionable. Usually his abject adoration bugged me, but today his sunny smile felt like balm. *He* wasn't trying to get rid of me or trying to thwart my every move. *He* wasn't all conflicted and angst-y about his feelings for me.

Might be why, when he asked me out for coffee, I said yes.

Mistake.

I watched the joy spread through his body, causing multiple system failures as it flowed. His mouth and eyes formed perfectly symmetrical O's, I could hear his breath hitch, and his Adam's apple did a fine Mexican-jumping bean impersonation.

"Paul? Wait. It's not—"

"No take-backs!" he said. It took him a while because he stuttered over the consonants in his excitement. "You said yes. I'll see you after the meeting."

He took off, heading for a group of guys in order to rejoice with the fellas. Publicly, at length, and in great detail.

Sue joined me. "What's going on?"

I experimented in my mind with various ways to phrase the situation. They all ended up sounding like "date."

"It is not a date," I said.

Sue played along. "Right. Not a date. Of course not."

"It's *not.*"

"Right. What's not a date?"

"It's just coffee. With a peer. That's all."

She followed my petrified gaze to where Paul was practically yodeling with joy.

"Coffee?" she said. "With *Paul?*"

For once, perhaps for the first time ever, Sue was stricken silent. I was too dazed to enjoy it.

CHAPTER TWENTY EIGHT

It could have been worse. Paul was what I call an "easy talker." Not always a linear one—his eagerness often led to tangents—but mostly all I had to do was sit back and listen. I'd forgotten how much we had in common. Paul was planning to graduate with a social work degree as soon as he completed his internship program. He'd also known my attacker on a first name basis, but he was sensitive enough to refrain from bringing it up.

Once I got him talking about his schooling, he chattered on and on. He was having trouble landing an internship placement, and I felt bad telling him that our agency wasn't taking any on this semester since Marshall had left. Bob wasn't "into" training and, hopefully, admin had better sense than to set up an impressionable intern under his supervision anyway.

Listening to Paul was kind of bittersweet. I couldn't remember ever being as idealistic as he was, even when I was in college. Maybe it had to do with my childhood, but I'd never had the kind of faith in people that Paul obviously had. Maybe I would have been a better therapist if I had.

I couldn't help feeling that Paul was in for a let-down. Part of me wanted to warn him, but who was I to burst his world-view bubble? In first grade, Bailey Bronson had taken it upon himself to inform me that a certain jolly, fat man didn't exist. I punched him in the nose and cried all the way home. Nobody loves a prophet.

The other refreshing thing about Paul was his interest in other people, specifically me. But it would serve him well in his future career, too. I found myself telling him about the shelter. Not about my real fears, not at first, but about how my coworker had died and named me as her professional executor. He was fascinated. They hadn't covered the issue in school, not even in his ethics class, so he asked lots of questions. Good ones, too. Ones I wished I'd thought of asking.

"This would make an awesome paper," he said. "I bet no one else has thought of writing about providing aftercare for your clients after . . . you know."

"After you die," I filled in the blank he so delicately avoided. He'd have to get over that. "Maybe I should make a will. Especially now."

"Why now?"

"Huh?" I stalled.

Paul streamlined all of his manic, high-powered energy into focusing on my answer. 'Huh' wasn't going to get it. "Why now? Why would you need a will?"

"Look, I don't really want to get into it. I'll sound crazy."

"No, you won't. Not to me. Well, not unless you start talking about little green men taking over Washington or something."

"What? You don't believe in aliens?" I said.

"I don't believe they're green. But I'll believe *you*. What's going on?"

I debated how to answer. "There are some strange things going on in that place. Instead of arranging for me to assess and refer Regina's clients myself, they went and transferred them to the two administrators. I can kind of understand that, even though it goes against Regina's instructions. The women and kids they serve have very specific needs, and Clotilde and Lachlyn have been working with them for years. But I'm supposed to at least have access to Regina's clients and their files. Yet they're limiting it to just the last three months. And I've come across some things that suggest they've altered records, too."

"Really? That's illegal. Is it some kind of insurance scam?"

Hadn't thought of that. "I don't think so," I finally said. "I don't think many of these women have private insurance. Even if they did, I doubt it would cover a residential stay. The shelter pretty much exists on government grants and donations. Besides, the pages I think they were messing with had nothing to do with financials. Very little in the client files did."

"What do you think they're hiding?"

Paul was looking very distressed. In his world, helpers helped. They didn't forge or hide documents, didn't ignore the wishes of the deceased, and presumably didn't decease the wisher. Good thing he didn't know my suspicions there. His world would crumble.

"So enough about that, Paul. How long have you been sober now? Couple of months, huh?"

His expressions warred between wanting to pursue the subject and well-deserved pride in his achievement. I let him ramble happily on while I sipped coffee and brooded.

Tuesday was just as chaotic as Monday. To get caught up, I'd even scheduled a client for my lunch hour—something I normally tried to avoid.

Lisa popped into my office while I was writing up progress notes in between my 10- and 11:00 clients. As usual, she out-styled me, wearing a combination of layered shirts in ice-blue tones and a magenta scarf that I would have never thought to put together. Since the Snow Queen rarely left her lair in the front office, I gave her my full attention.

"What's up?" I asked.

"Got something for you." She handed me a file. My stomach lurched, thinking she had found another of Regina's stolen shelter records. Almost immediately, however, I recognized our clinic's system of stickers. If I'd had any doubt, a faded yellow sticky note in Marshall's cramped writing had been stuck to the front. FOR REVIEW, it said. I checked the client's name: Bettina Reyes. Didn't recognize it.

"This isn't mine." I tried to hand it back to her.

"It is now. It's one of Regina's. One you haven't seen."

I sat back with a thump and almost flipped ass-over-tea kettle in my rickety office chair. *Another one?* "Why haven't I seen this one? Did someone tell you to keep it from me?"

"Paranoid much?" Despite her hurry, she took a moment to scoff at me. Enjoyed it, too; I could tell. "It's just been lost."

"Lost? *You* lost a file?" My turn to scoff. I liked it, too.

"It was set aside for review. After Marshall left, it must have just sat there. I found it yesterday when we were cleaning up for the audit that never happened."

"What kind of review? Internal or for the licensing board?" A quick flip through the documents didn't disclose anything out of the ordinary.

"I don't know. I guess if anyone knows anything it would be Marshall. Maybe, um, you could ask him?" She waggled her eyebrows mischievously.

"I think it would be more appropriate to talk to Bob. I'm sure he would have been made aware of the situation." I refused to meet her eyes.

"If so, he never followed up on it. Big surprise. Look, I think the ball got dropped when Marshall left so abruptly. Regina had her hands full between the clinic, the shelter, and you." Lisa gave me a look that was equal parts pointed and tender. How did she do that?

I had more questions, but a glance at the wall clock told me I was already five minutes late for my next client. She was impatient, bipolar, and working on anger management skills. I supposed I could tell her this was a test.

But tonight, no matter what, I'd dig through everything one more time. Just me, the stolen files, and this new one. Maybe some popcorn, too. Siggy liked popcorn.

CHAPTER TWENTY NINE

I allotted Siggy four kernels of unbuttered and unsalted popcorn, but he was not impressed. He kept leaping daintily up on the coffee table where my popcorn bowl rested, trying to snag a pawful of buttery contraband. Miffed at my stinginess, he refused to sit next to me on the couch. Instead, he slunk to the middle of the room, staring with eyes like the hungry children commercials on late night TV. When that didn't work, he gave me the tail and stalked off down the hall toward the bedroom.

I started with the file Lisa had given me: Bettina Reyes, age 47, married. She'd been seeing Regina weekly since January for marital concerns; the last session, just after Labor Day. The psychosocial history looked unremarkable. Bettina and Frank Reyes had been married twenty-seven years and had two grown children, both within driving distance. Regina noted that Bettina had denied any domestic violence or abuse, something I'd thought might connect this file to the shelter.

According to the early progress notes, it looked as though Bettina's primary concern was on how to "reconnect" with her husband. She reported that he was frequently irritated with her and she didn't know how to please him anymore. Frank, resistant to therapy in general and female counselors in particular, refused all invitations to attend sessions with Bettina, something that makes couples therapy almost impossible. Regina recorded that she'd offered Bettina a list of male therapists in the area, but she hadn't included a copy, so I didn't know to whom she'd referred the couple.

Two weeks after getting the referrals, Bettina reported that Frank had made an appointment with a psychologist. Again no mention of who Frank was seeing, but later notes indicated that Bettina participated in a few sessions with Frank and his new counselor while remaining in individual therapy with Regina.

Shortly after, an unexplained break in therapy occurred—not uncommon, although six weeks was a bit longer than usual. When Bettina returned, Regina noted a significant mood change from anxious and weepy to giggly and lighthearted. Bettina denied any changes in her life, seemed disinclined to talk about Frank or their relationship, and was elusive about her current activities. Regina wrote "secret?" in the margin and circled it. I tended to agree. Bettina sounded twitterpated, and cranky Frank was likely not the source.

They continued in this fashion for another three weeks until finally, in late May, Bettina conceded she was having an affair.

With Frank's counselor.

I read the passage twice, brain reeling. This had to be it. This is what Regina was in contact with the licensing board about. Sexual contact between a therapy professional and his client is strictly prohibited. In my opinion, Bettina would be considered a client since she had met with her husband and his therapist, but maybe I was wrong. Or maybe, like so many other abusers, the therapist had justified his actions by splitting that theoretical hair.

Only three more progress notes remained, each

documenting Regina's efforts to educate Bettina about the nature of the therapeutic relationship and how the other therapist's actions constituted abuse. Bettina disagreed. She was an adult and she wasn't his patient. He "understood" her and was helping her overcome her intimacy issues, which could only help her marriage. Conversely, she and her analytic amour agreed that it would be "anti-therapeutic" to inform Frank of their efforts on his behalf.

No kidding.

Regina, bless her, stayed firm, advising her client to report the relationship. I could sense through Regina's terse notes that she was becoming frustrated with the situation. In the recommendations section of the second to last note she wrote that she planned to seek consultation. I wondered with whom? Marshall?

Not surprisingly, the last session didn't go well. Regina informed Bettina that she felt obligated, legally and ethically, to report the violation to the authorities and that she was seeking professional advice about her options. However, she didn't want to act without at least trying to obtain Bettina's cooperation and hoped they could continue discussing the dilemma. Regina offered to hold off for a month while they talked through the emotional repercussions of taking action.

Bettina "became enraged and terminated the session abruptly." Apparently she didn't want to conversate. She wanted to fornicate.

But "who with?" was my ungrammatical but pertinent question. And "would somebody kill over this?" was the next.

I'd been reported to the licensing board on completely bogus charges and had to suffer under an investigation even though my accuser had a documented vendetta against me. I'd had enough evidence attesting to my innocence that I hadn't even bothered hiring an attorney, although Regina had advised that it couldn't hurt. I couldn't imagine what it would feel like to have the board come down on me in a situation where I really was guilty.

I had to find out who Bettina's husband—and Bettina herself for that matter—were seeing. The first thing I'd do at work tomorrow would be to follow-up with Bettina and see if she would meet with me. It was a long shot, maybe the affair had already run its course and she'd had a chance to rethink her position.

Since I was stymied on the Reyes file, I turned to the others. I'd already gone through them twice, but I was certain there was something tying them together. Third time pays for all, they say, and so it did.

I came across a set of initials on the bottom of each discharge summary. Three letters: RTA. I couldn't imagine how I'd missed them, but they were tiny, block printing, and placed at the end of the narrative portion of the form. I started paging back through the layers of papers, searching for someone with those initials. I knew it wasn't Regina. Her last name was Fleisher. Just to make sure, I dug out the little funeral notice that gets handed out to mourners. Regina Edith Fleisher.

No RTA in that.

I moved to the computer, pulling up the shelter website. The "About Us" page had a directory of staff and volunteers with the separate page listing the board of directors by name. No RTAs.

Sighing, I set that question aside for later, and, since I was at the computer anyway, I decided to Google the women's names.

Starting alphabetically and because the name

seemed vaguely familiar, I typed in "Cherly Bailey." In this information era I figured I'd find something, maybe a social networking site, something from the community, things like that. Instead, I found a lot more.

CHAPTER THIRTY

Cherly Bailey had been killed last spring, explaining why her name sounded familiar. Her husband, a high-profile, defense attorney, had been accused, tried, and acquitted. Most of the more recent stories had to do with the lawsuit he was currently filing against the police department, the local newspaper, the county, the state and whomever else he could think of. Despite his scary propensity for revenge litigation, the news articles still identified him as the main suspect although they tossed in the words "recently acquitted" to cover their butts.

Much of the case had unfolded just after my own brush with death, so I wasn't as familiar with the details as I might have been. Scrolling down the accounts of the murder, I learned that Cherly Bailey had been found strangled on the floor of her kitchen. A tape of her husband's remarkably composed 911 call had been made public and probably had much to do with the rush to convict. The defense later claimed that, as a trial lawyer, Bailey was used to sordid crime and was so caught up in his desire to get help for his beloved wife that he suppressed his own emotions during the initial part of the discovery.

Might even be true.

I printed several of the more comprehensive articles covering the murder and the most recent one on the lawsuit before plugging in the name of the next woman: Amy Church.

Amy Church was dead, too. This time by suicide three years ago. It probably wouldn't have made the papers except she hadn't been discovered for several days—a gruesome fact on its own—and there had been some speculation about the cause of death. Apparently she'd cut her own throat and done a remarkably efficient job of it. Her mother, Sandee Church, was quoted in the article. "Ain't no way Amy killed herself. She hated the sight of blood, especially her own." Church's mother had gone on to organize a fundraising banquet to "get to the bottom" of her daughter's death.

I sank back against the couch, thinking. A mother in denial wasn't unusual, but the bit about "hating blood," if it were true, seemed to be a point in her favor. The other thing that bugged me was the method Amy used. Throat slashing, while not unheard of, is more often used as a threat, resulting in a wickedly ugly scar. It's surprisingly difficult to carry out.

I pulled her file, leafing through to where her therapist, Lachlyn, had recorded her mental health history. According to this, she'd never attempted suicide before. At least, none that she'd admitted. Her depression scales were moderate, but she was compliant with her medication and, according to Lachlyn, denied any suicidal ideation.

I could feel the popcorn twisting into a greasy clump inside me as I typed in the next name. Kelly Jordan. Found stabbed outside a local bar. No mention of a trial, although the police reportedly had a suspect. She'd been Lachlyn's client as well.

Tammy Long, killed in April 2007, was seen by Regina. Her boyfriend at the time was tried and convicted of her murder. She'd been beaten to death with a crowbar. Witnesses in their apartment building claimed to have heard an argument, and one reported the boyfriend, Lyle Chester, as storming out of the apartment in a rage. Chester admitted arguing, but claimed he left Tammy in order to keep from hurting her, and stayed overnight at his mother's. When he returned the next morning to get his work clothes, he found Tammy lying in a bloody mess on the kitchen floor. He called the police. Currently, he resided in the Stanley Correctional Institution hoping for an appeal.

Monica Skolnik: left the shelter just this July, killed in August. Her husband, the primary suspect, hung himself in his jail cell. Whether that closed the case or not, I didn't know.

The only one that Google failed to provide details for was Jean Tschida. Hers was also the oldest file, dating back to March 2001. She'd been Regina's client, and the last note indicated that Jean was returning home and had refused a termination session.

Five out of the six women whose files Regina snuck out of the shelter were dead, victims of violent or suspicious deaths. I assumed Jean Tschida hadn't had a happy ending, or else why would Regina have dug the file out? She must have remembered something.

Clotilde had set Friday as the deadline, but I needed a lot more time than that. The only ones who could supersede her wishes were the board, but even with Beth's influence I couldn't imagine that happening. Unfortunately, I had nothing to offer that would influence their decision to wrap up Regina's cases. In my experience, the only thing that reliably swayed boards of directors was money. Lots of it.

In this economy, everyone was hurting and the

governments, state and federal, were adding hoops within hoops for organizations to jump through before cutting a check. Grant monies were drying up faster than a drip of spit on a sidewalk in August.

Money was a guarantee, but sometimes political influence—a slower, less certain pressure—could work, too. I tried to think if I knew anyone at the state level who had the power to divert a trickle of the cash flow to the shelter. I didn't; along with Garth, all my friends were in low places.

Besides, nowadays there were so many checks and double checks at the front end of the money and outcome reports and efficacy studies at the back end that keeping the money was just as difficult as getting it.

Wait.

Efficacy studies. More and more funding sources were requiring studies that proved the money was doing what it was supposed to be doing. Not a bad thing, really, but they were demanding those results at a time when less money meant less staff to execute the studies.

So wouldn't a volunteer who was willing to systematize an evaluation process come in handy? Someone willing to do the grunt work that kept the money a-comin'? Someone willing to dig through the records to chart how the women fared after leaving the shelter?

Someone like me.

CHAPTER THIRTY ONE

I spent Wednesday morning at the shelter holed up in Regina's old office, finishing up the last of the paperwork. As I had passed the stairwell door, I'd taken note of the new padlock—menacing and ominous despite its bright, efficient shininess—that now graced the door leading to the second story.

Contrary to my recent blustering, I took care to keep a low profile. Lachlyn wasn't there, but Clotilde surprised me by allowing me to proceed unsupervised. Of course, if they'd already vetted the new stack of files, they had nothing to worry about. I had no way of verifying they were complete. None had the RTA notation on the discharge page, though.

Obviously, she wanted to get rid of me as soon as possible. On the two occasions when I crossed paths with her, I kept my face a careful blank, not wanting to give away any sign that I was engineering a coup. Between forcing myself to be patient and the suspicions that roiled around my brain, I worked up a splitting headache.

Despite that, I found myself looking forward to the AA meeting later that night. A women's group, it had been meeting for more than a decade. I counted myself lucky that at less than a year of sobriety, I had access to such a wealth of sober experience. Plus, since we took turns meeting at each other's houses, the coffee was infinitely better than at the club and there were usually delicious, homemade munchies. So good, in fact, that we'd had several men try to infiltrate over the years. Technically we couldn't exclude anyone, but after an evening spent listening to the minute details of menstrual cycles and comparisons of cervical dilation records in birthing, the brave soldier would usually decamp, vastly preferring rancid coffee and vending machine candy over "that woman stuff."

This month we were meeting at Rhonda's. She shared one-half of a tiny duplex that felt crowded with three people gathered, but her peanut butter chunk brownie recipe was to die for. She'd crammed five extra folding chairs—the metal kind that chills your butt when you first sit down—alongside a couple of lawn chairs with dubious webbing. There were so many of us that we ended up sitting five to a couch, but we all had warm brownie and a smile.

My smile had much to do with the ominous ripping sound that I'd heard when Sue claimed one of the lawn chairs. She pretended not to hear it, but I noticed her trying to sit light, bracing herself on the metal arms and using her leg muscles to attempt a David Copperfield-style of levitation. Betting that her thighs would give out before the ragged webbing, I was busily calculating the trajectory of her brownie (in case it needed rescuing) when Rhonda passed out the readings.

I would have preferred the Promises, but I got the Twelve Steps instead. Could've been worse. Charlie got the boring Traditions, but after eight years of sobriety, she demonstrated more maturity.

I started reading but hadn't even gotten through the second step, "Came to believe that a Power greater than ourselves could restore us to sanity," when I felt someone staring. I glanced up and found Sue giving me a Sponsor Stare of Death, which was supposed to alert me to an issue relating to my sobriety that I should be attending to. I knew what she wanted. She wanted me to talk to the group about my current struggles with the Second and Third Steps. The whole "Higher Power" thing scared me to death and I'd been avoiding it. Sue had been trying to get me to look at why.

And I might have. Except just then her chair bottom, with a sound like two mating monkeys, split wide open. Maybe even three monkeys. It was *loud*.

It took four of us to pull Sue to her feet and an extra person to uncouple her from the aluminum chair frame that had embedded itself on her nether regions. We had to pause in sheer wonder at the originality, velocity, and intensity with which she described her feelings about being victimized by patio furniture. I wanted to take notes.

Eventually we wrestled the thing off her butt and got her settled on a sturdy dining room chair with a new brownie since her last had gone flying. After all of that, the meeting was a lost cause. Every time we'd start to settle down, someone would get the giggles, reigniting the rest of us. Except for Sue, of course. She refused to see the humor in the situation.

Later, as we gathered our things to leave, Sue pointed a stubby finger at me and said, "We need to meet. Soon. You're going to talk about the Third." With that pronouncement, she sailed out the door, leaving us an unrestricted view of the missing brownie's final resting place.

Not pretty. The death of a brownie is a sad thing.

Unfortunately in all the hoopla, I'd forgotten to get

Beth's phone number, which forced me to call Sue first thing the next morning. She didn't mention the brownie or "Attack of the Chair Night," as it was later called. I didn't either. I'm not stupid.

I didn't even argue when she pushed for our meeting. Facing God and the Third Step was far less scary than my sponsor. We set it up for the weekend.

I waited until I had a half-hour break between clients before making three calls—one to Beth, where I left a message; the next to the hospital, where the only thing they would tell me was that Blodgett was stable; and, lastly, to Bettina Reyes.

I hated to break the news on the phone, but I didn't know how to ask her to come in for a session without explaining the situation. Not telling would be unduly mysterious and, to a certain extent, manipulative. Besides, she probably wouldn't have come. Still, telling someone over the phone that her therapist died has its own set of problems.

I did the best I could. Initially, she refused to meet with me. She claimed that, although surprised and saddened, she didn't see the need for further counseling. However, when I explained my role in closing out Regina's affairs and how the ethics review was still moving forward, I sensed her beginning to waiver. The "Oh, shit. This again?" comment was my clue. Eventually she agreed to meet with me and we scheduled her in for 4:00 that afternoon.

Beth back called twenty minutes later. She was available for lunch and we decided on Northwoods Pub. Everything was falling in place.

CHAPTER THIRTY TWO

By the time I arrived, Beth had snagged a table and two menus. Seemed a little strange for two alcoholics to be meeting in a pub, but they had a chicken breast sandwich with sauteed mushrooms and Swiss cheese that made whatever risk there might be worth it. We ordered and then Beth sat back waiting for me to open the conversation. Fair enough.

"You probably know Clotilde gave me a deadline to finish up the review of Regina's files," I said. "That's up tomorrow. I'm hoping that I can get that extended. In fact, I have a proposition that I believe will really benefit the shelter as well as let me complete my obligations." If I expected her to pick up on the bait, I was mistaken.

"Can't you finish up by then?"

"I could." I hedged, wishing I knew her better. When we'd first met at the board meeting, Beth, although shorter and curvier than fashion dictated, had seemed to fit right in with the professionals. Today she had her auburn hair pulled back in a pony tail and looked right at home wearing a faded, well-worn Packer sweatshirt. In a way, she reminded me of Siggy—a scrappy survivor who had come into some good luck. They had the same elf-green eyes and don't-give-me-shit attitude. Like most AA members with a few years under their belt, she seemed a straight shooter. I needed to walk a fine line between telling her enough to buy me more time and dumping the whole "I think there's a killer running around the shelter" bomb on her. That, I was certain, would be a surefire way to get all avenues shut down.

"The thing is, while I was going through Regina's clients, I noticed a surprising lack of documented outcomes. The shelter just doesn't have any way of knowing how—or *if*—their interventions and techniques are effective. Anecdotally, of course, we can say that the women make progress, but there's no real proof. It's an easy enough thing to fix, too.

"In fact," I continued, "I'm surprised that the shelter hasn't already implemented a system of tracking their results. More and more, grants are requiring outcome studies. And, of course, they're a great tool for attracting donations. People want to know that the money they're giving is being used effectively."

Our food arrived and we sat back as the waiter set the plates down. Smelled delicious. Beth was watching me, a speculative gleam in her eye. I busied myself with the napkin and pretended to be unconcerned with her scrutiny.

"So, what's the plan?" she asked. "What are you looking to do?"

"I thought I could set up an efficacy study. I could, um, review the files—Regina's included—and do some follow-up with former residents. Find out what happened to the women, how they've fared, how the shelter impacted their lives. Meanwhile, I'd put together a survey. It would be given to a woman when she's first admitted. That gives us a baseline. She'd fill out a second copy right before she leaves, if we know beforehand. Sometimes they just take off. That one could double as an exit interview. Then when she leaves, we'd send a survey with her, with maybe a stamped envelope, so she could pop it in the mail on her own. I don't know, though. The last one would be tougher since we really don't know what will be going on with the woman after she leaves, especially if she returns to her abuser. By the way, we don't know for certain how often *that* happens either."

Beth had finished most of her sandwich while I talked. I took a hasty bite of my own while I waited to hear her response.

"Why?" she asked.

Since I had a mouth full of mushrooms and Swiss cheese, I just raised my eyebrows in a "why, what?" look.

"Here's the thing," she said, crumpling her napkin. "I think it's a great idea, but I'm more interested in what's behind it. Something tells me there's more to this than charitable impulse. No offense. What aren't you telling me?"

I started re-evaluating my stance on psychic abilities. This woman was scary perceptive. Sue had warned me not to try bullshitting her. I swallowed and took a deep breath.

"I can't explain the whole thing," I admitted. "Part of it is wanting to make amends to Regina. She did some things for me that I didn't truly appreciate until after she died. I was so busy being pissed at her that I never told her thank you.

"Another part of it is just stubbornness, I guess. Clotilde and Lachlyn seem to have gone out of their way to let me know that they don't want me there, and it bugs me. I just want to do my job, fulfill my obligation to Regina, and get out. Maybe if I were as fanatical as they are, they wouldn't discount me. But I don't have to drink the shelter's Kool-Aid to do a good job. Even Regina recognized that."

"Maybe that's what bugs them," Beth said. "I know what they're like. In fact, I'm pretty sure Clotilde has higher aspirations. I've been on the board nine months, and you're right about their . . . I wouldn't call it narrow-mindedness, but they're certainly devoted to the shelter. That's a good thing, by the way." She raised a sardonic eyebrow at me.

"I know it is. I'd admire them for it if they weren't so annoying. What do you mean by higher aspirations?"

"Political. I think Clotilde's been positioning herself for a run at the state senate. She would certainly be a powerful ally to women in this community, but think how much more could she do at a higher level? She seems to be grooming Lachlyn to take over as director, but I'm not satisfied that Lachlyn is, well, versatile enough to handle the people-pleasing side of things."

"Wow. I hadn't realized that. I'm not really political," I said.

"Regina shared their fervency. I know you're the therapist and everything, but are you sure you're not working out some kind of Freudian thing here? Trying to make amends to the dead or something?"

I grinned. "Maybe. There are definitely some loose ends that I need to pull together. I guess you could say that I'm just trying to 'do the next right thing.'" I invoked the AA slogan that acknowledges the lack of a plan, but a motivating force of good intentions.

"So what's the part you can't explain?"

Huh. Like a bloodhound scenting truth she'd circled back to the one point I'd tried to obfuscate. I sighed.

"I can't tell you, because I don't know if it's true. Looking over Regina's files, I found some things that don't add up. I think Regina was looking into it, too. Look, if I'm wrong, just the suggestion of it could destroy the shelter's reputation. I'm being honest." Well, now I was. "I need more time at the shelter. I need a freer hand with the files, not just Regina's. As for the rest, I just can't tell you more than that."

Beth's turn to sigh. Shaking her head, she looked off into the distance, weighing my words. We sat in silence for so long that I'd about given up. And maybe I *was* asking too much. She didn't know me. Her allegiance was to the shelter. The aura of AA could only invoke so much loyalty.

"Anybody looking for a high-risk lifestyle should try honesty," she said turning back to me. "It's a bitch, ain't it?"

I nodded.

"Okay, here are the rules. We'll go with your survey plan. It makes sense and it would be good for the shelter either which way. They've moved the board meeting up to tomorrow so I better scramble if I'm going to get more support for this idea. It can't just be me behind this, although I hate that kind of behind-the-scenes politicking. Anyway, you meet with me in two weeks and tell me exactly what's going on, in *detail*. If your suspicions"—her fingers twitched quote marks—"turn into fact, you call me right away. Don't wait. Last, if any of this harms even one of our residents, then you'll answer to me. And I don't play by the rules. Get me?"

I did.

After some stilted good-bye noises, we divvied up the check and left. In the parking lot, just before I angled off toward my car, she said, "Letty? Be careful what you ask for. You might get it."

She never did tell me why she was willing to let me go ahead.

CHAPTER THIRTY THREE

The whole encounter with Beth, particularly her parting shot, had left me unsettled. As 4:00 neared, I tried to pull myself together. The meeting with Bettina Reyes was going to be tricky, and I needed my wits about me.

For a woman in an illicit affair, Bettina was rather dumpy. And crabby, too. Couldn't really blame her for the latter attribute since she hadn't wanted to meet with me in the first place, and she most certainly didn't want to hear what I had to tell her. Still, I had to give it a try. At the very least, I needed to find out who her amorous counselor was. Since Regina hadn't included his name in the file, I wouldn't be able to pursue the ethics review without more information. Not to mention, I didn't want to lose sight of the fact that Regina's knowledge could have been very threatening to one of our colleagues.

Enough to kill her?

After greeting Bettina in the clinic lobby, I led the way to my office. She walked uncomfortably close behind, so much so that I could smell her breath mints over my shoulder. Motioning her to a chair, I tried to discreetly uncrinkle the leather of my shoe heel where she'd trod on it. Twice. She hadn't apologized.

"Thank you for coming in," I started. "I'm sure this is diffi—"

"I just want to get this over with."

"I underst—"

"No. You don't. None of you seem to understand that this isn't any of your business. I'm a grown woman. I'm *not* being abused. I'm not being mistreated. For the first time in my life I'm very happy. I thought that's what you the-*rapists* want for us."

It took me a moment to realize she'd bifurcated the word: therapist. Freud would have had a heyday with her word choice, given "the-rapist" lover. Client or not, the temptation to respond sarcastically was hard to resist.

As I struggled, I was hit by an uncomfortable realization. Either Bettina Reyes was my client—in the same way she was The-Rapist's client—or she wasn't. I couldn't have it both ways. No matter how badly I wanted to know who the therapist was and whether he'd had anything to do with Regina's death, that didn't override my responsibility to Bettina. Not even if murder was involved. *Bettina* had to be my priority. Otherwise I was just using my role to manipulate her into a position she didn't want to be in. The-rapist, indeed.

So for the second time that day I had to resort to the telling the truth. I truly hoped it didn't get to be a habit.

"I don't know the name of the other therapist. Regina never recorded it. I have no way, without your cooperation, of following through with an ethics complaint."

She blinked. "Then why did you have me come in?"

"Because I needed to give you the chance to talk about what it might mean to you when you heard that Regina died. Especially since you two were in disagreement over your, um, lover. I wanted to make sure that you know the door is always open if you need to talk about the situation. I won't lie ..." Well, not under these circumstances. "I totally agree with Regina that he should be reported. I do believe that his actions are unethical and that you are being mistreated. But unless you tell me his name, I can't do anything about it.

"Which is kind of freeing, I hope. For you, I mean. Instead of resenting me for going against your wishes, you can just talk about how you feel. Or if you'd prefer to see another therapist, that's fine, too. Either way, you're in the driver's seat. But keep in mind: I'm under the same ethical strictures as Regina. If I learn his name, I will report him. No question about it. So, what do you think?" I relaxed back in my chair, waiting for her answer.

She started crying. Therapy began.

Since Regina had been killed at the shelter, detouring into the Reyes affair was a long shot and I feared getting too distracted. However, I also couldn't ignore it. Plus Regina had made a habit of roping her colleagues in the community to volunteer hours at the shelter. Theoretically the killer might be someone only tenuously connected to the shelter. Unfortunately, that meant I had to go to the only person I could think of who might know the background on the Reyes case. If he was still in town, that is.

Later, as Hannah and I were preparing the big room for the grief group, I dithered back and forth about asking her if she knew Marshall's whereabouts. I'd come to terms with the fact that Bettina might never feel comfortable revealing her lover's identity, but that didn't mean I wasn't going to try other means to see if it tied in to Regina's death.

I finally blurted out my question. After asking, I couldn't figure out what to do with my hands, so I pretended to fuss with the stack of paper cups next to the water pitcher. There is only so much arranging you can do with a stack of Styrofoam cups—one really tall stack or two short ones. I went with two.

Hannah watched my machinations, then gently asked, "Do you want me to find out?"

Abandoning my cup maneuvers, I flopped down on one of the folding chairs. At first glance, it seemed a remarkably straightforward question. *Did I want Hannah to find out if Marshall was in town?*

But it meant more than just a yes-or-no answer. It meant purposely arranging a meeting with a man who obviously didn't want to be with me. Not an ego boost, that. Even if we met for professional reasons, there would be all sorts of hot and cold undercurrents swirling around the conversation. Very high school-esque. Very distracting.

Perhaps this wasn't the best time for distractions.

CHAPTER THIRTY FOUR

I tossed and turned all night obsessively pulling petals off an imaginary daisy. *Should I call him? Should I not?* Siggy stuck with me until about midnight when he grew so disgusted with my shifting that he deserted me for the couch pillow. Around 3:00 a.m. another avenue occurred to me.

Lisa, of course.

I got to work early, bringing our office manager her favorite breakfast: a half-dozen crullers and a bucket-sized cup of coffee. Ever suspicious, but not one to turn down fresh-baked bribes, Lisa busied herself with cream and sugar.

"Hey, Lisa, I've got a question for you."

"No shit." At least I think that's what she said. By the looks of it, her words had to navigate past a mouthful of cruller to get to me.

"The file you found the other day? The one pending review? Can we figure out who Regina referred the client's husband to?"

"Who referred the client?"

"No. Her husband. Regina gave the client a list of referrals for the client's husband, but she didn't document them in the client's file."

Lisa's eyes sparkled. This was just the kind of data hunt she loved. Or else it was the caffeine/sugar rush. She spun her chair to the cart where yesterday's cases were waiting to be filed. With unerring efficiency, she slid Bettina Reyes's out of a teetering stack of manila folder clones.

Flipping it open, she paged through the documents, mumbling to herself. I didn't know what she was looking for, but I knew better than to ask. After more flipping and mumbling, she slapped the file closed.

"OK, she was referred by Dr. Feldman. He's on the board at the shelter."

"I know. I met him. He's retired."

"Only semi-retired. He still takes on an occasional client. He might have, for Regina. Sometimes she'd send someone over to Kyle Channing over at Wellness Center. He's got a waiting list a mile long, so it's tough to get anyone into him."

"Why not refer to anyone here?" I asked.

"She usually would unless the client was specifically looking for a male therapist. In that case, who do we have? Marshall didn't see clients, so that would leave Bob." She snorted, efficiently expressing her opinion on that one.

"They were pretty close," I said. "Maybe she would."

"They weren't close. He was her minion, not her colleague. Except . . ."

"Except what?"

"If there was a chance of doing co-therapy, maybe. I think there have been maybe three cases over the years where Regina and Bob acted as co-therapists for a marital couple. I think that way she'd still be in charge. Bob liked it because all he did was sit there."

"Anybody else?" I asked.

"Not that I can think of. And I would probably know. If one of our therapists refers someone, we filled out a form with the contact info to make it easier on the client."

"But we don't keep a copy of that form?"

She frowned. It appeared I'd found a miniscule glitch in her system. Lisa did not allow imperfection. She reached for a sticky note and jotted a reminder. "We do now."

"Ok, so Dr. Feldman, Kyle Channing, and . . . Bob."

"Yup. So now that I've answered your question, you can answer mine. What gives?" Lisa worked on a strict quid quo pro basis. If I was getting info, I'd better be ready to give it. Instead, I pointed to the cruller crumbs littered across her desk. "That was your fee."

Her Icelandic blue eyes narrowed. "Not good enough," she said.

I dangled the bag with the five remaining crullers in it. She eyed it, but I could see her weighing her choices. She'd already had one cruller fix, but her curiosity had been let loose, too. It was a battle of the appetites.

I jiggled the bag gently, letting the pastries rasp seductively against the white paper bag. I'd always loved fishing.

For once, I didn't want the donuts anyway. My stomach had been queasy ever since the image of Bob doing the nasty with Bettina entered my mind. I kept telling myself there were two other options, but I knew Kyle. He was a good guy, mid-thirties with a charming wife and three cute kids. We often attended the same trainings and had one of those quasi-deep relationships that survived despite infrequent meetings where we had to cram a lot of catching up together over the break periods and lunch hour provided at the trainings. He was one of the few colleagues who knew about my alcoholism. Well, to be honest, he knew about it before I

did since, over the years, he'd watched me guzzle wine
with far more desperation than a dry turkey sandwich
and a boring conference would seem to warrant.

I didn't think it was him.

It could be Feldman, the shelter board member. In
fact, despite his leather sandals and scraggly, gray braid,
I was really rooting for him. Aging hippie sex was ever so
much more appealing than any kind of sweaty coupling
with . . . Bob. I gagged.

I dug through my purse looking for the card
Feldman had given me at the board meeting. I found it
buried under my wallet and makeup case. It was covered
with a fine dusting of face powder where my compact
had broken. I tossed the powder in the trash, where it
landed with a clatter in the empty basket.

I quickly dialed Feldman's phone number before I
could chicken out. It only rang twice before I hung up.
My bravery had lasted seventeen seconds. I hadn't really
thought it through, anyway. Feldman wouldn't be able to
tell me if Frank Reyes was his patient. I didn't have any
kind of authorization for release of information. It
wouldn't be possible for Feldman to confirm a
relationship with Frank one way or another. And if he
was shagging Bettina, it wasn't likely he'd admit it.

I could always stake out Bettina's house and follow
her to whichever guy she was seeing. That was not only
unethical on several levels, but far beyond my
capabilities.

So I snuck into the file room and looked for a file on
Frank Reyes. If we had one, it eliminated everyone but
Bob. I told myself that as long as I didn't look *into* the
file, I wasn't breaking confidentiality. Besides, someone
had to put Bettina's file away. So I did. Right in between
the two other Reyeses: Amelia and Francis.

Ugh. It *was* Bob.

CHAPTER THIRTY FIVE

Luckily, Bob had chosen to take one of his many long weekends and I didn't have to deal with running into him in the hallway. My imagination was abusing me enough. I felt like a kid who'd been in denial about her parents' sex lives until I walked in on them. Except sex between two consenting adults was an entirely different matter than between client, adult or otherwise, and therapist. Especially when that The-Rapist was Bob.

At any rate, I had time to consider what I should do. I really wasn't sure how or, given the way I'd discovered Bob's involvement, even *if* I could report him to the licensing board. I was only semi-comfortable with my "looking *at* a file is not the same as looking *in* a file" rationale. There was also the slight possibility that Frank had seen Bob, realized what a knuckle-head he was, and decided to go to someone else. I decided to shelve the Bob-the-pig dilemma in favor of the name-that-killer one.

Unless those were the same thing.

The whole thing hinged on whether Bob had access to the shelter or not. If he'd ever been shanghaied by Regina into providing services, then I supposed he could have figured out how to get hold of a duplicate key or something. Seemed awfully long-sighted, though. It was also doubtful that Regina would have asked Bob. As Lisa already pointed out, she didn't have a whole lot of respect for his clinical skills.

On the other hand, if Bob ever referred a woman to the shelter, he might conceivably continue on as her counselor. It would make sense for him to use the shelter's therapy office. It was possible.

Unfortunately, I had no way of proving any of it.

I decided to give Blodgett a call. After nearly a week since his attack, he might be getting restless at his enforced inactivity. Blodgett, despite his lackadaisical appearance, was not a sit-in-the-recliner kind of guy. Feeling guilty that I hadn't checked in on him or Diana for several days, I dialed their house first, hoping he'd been discharged by now. No answer.

The number I had for his hospital room rang nine times. Just as I was about to hang up, Diana answered. Before she'd said anything more than "hello," my heart sank. Even with just one word, it was all in her voice. One small word with a universe of fear filling it.

"Diana? Are you okay?" Stupid, *stupid* question. I wanted to bite my tongue off.

"He's in surgery, Letty. We were just getting ready to leave. It happened so suddenly."

"What? What happened?"

"They think he had a heart attack. We were just getting ready to leave. They were bringing the wheelchair up, you know? They make you ride in a wheelchair? Then all of a sudden, Del said, 'Di. Di.' Just that, you know? Just my name. He sounded so strange. Like he was scared, maybe. And he tried to sit down, but he missed the bed and fell into that stupid table. The one on wheels, you know? Oh my gosh, you never heard such a noise. But everyone heard that, and I was yelling, you know. So all of a sudden the room was just full of people.

Which is a good thing, you know? Because I didn't know what to do. I just didn't know what to do, Letty. He's in surgery now. They took him in so fast. Just whisked him right away."

"I'm coming, Diana. I'll be there in ten minutes."

Since I was coming from the clinic, it was a straight shot up Clairemont. Finding my way back to Blodgett's room took longer than the drive over. It was empty when I got there, so I jogged over to the nurses' station to ask where I could find Diana. A tired-looking nurse had me wait while she paged for a "walker" to escort me to the waiting area outside of surgery. With all the remodeling and the resulting rat maze connecting old sections to new, they'd apparently found it expedient to use volunteers as escorts.

Elderly volunteers, as a matter of fact.

As he rounded the corner, I felt a wave of impatience at the sight of my escort—eighty years old if he was a day—and started worrying that I'd need to borrow a wheelchair just to get the two of us to our destination.

Byron, my designated sherpa, was reed-thin, with near translucent skin and a dandelion fluff of grey hair wafting atop his head. I had visions of blowing on it and making a wish, but he moved off with such a brisk pace that I quickly realized I'd need to save my breath for the trek. Condescending forbearance immediately gave way to embarrassment as Byron bulleted forward. His long, lopey strides propelled him at such a rate that I found it necessary to shift erratically between speedwalking and jogging in order to keep him in sight. Neither pace was one that I could sustain for any length of time without passing out. I found myself grateful that we were heading to an area where I could be quickly attended to following the coronary I was certain was imminent.

We arrived at the surgical waiting area a brisk thirteen minutes later. Byron had acquired a slight pinkish hue on his cheeks. I, on the other hand, had sweat rings the size of dinner plates under my arms and a face that burned from the inside out with surprisingly copious amounts of sweat streaming off it. I bent over at the waist, willing oxygen past dry, brittle lips and praying that the people would think the rasping, wheezing sound was the air conditioner. Since it was early October, that was doubtful.

There might be something to this you-need-to-quit-smoking idea, after all.

As soon as the dots in front of my eyes receded, I found Diana and dropped next to her.

She barely registered my presence. I reached for her hand and sat quietly. I had tons of questions, but I had the feeling we would be here a while. There was time.

After several minutes, she sighed, then slowly turned to look at me. "He was going to call you," she said.

For some reason, my heart thudded heavily. Maybe it was the blank expression coating her face. "Was he?" I said softly.

She nodded. "He didn't remember a lot of what happened. During the attack, you know? The guys have been asking him and asking him. The doctor says sometimes after a trauma the brain just cancels stuff out. The accident, what happened right after, all of that stuff. Just gone, you know?"

I nodded.

"But, of course, all of his cop friends are trying to find out what happened. Who did this? Why? They've been coming in and out, talking to Del, trying to get him to remember. And Bill Stanwick's been going through his papers. I let him go through Del's desk at home and everything."

She was still staring at me, trying to read something on my face. My hands started sweating and I let go of her hand, wiping my palms on my jeans.

"Diana, what's going on? What are you asking me?"

She looked uncomfortable, her kind eyes filling with pain. Not one who enjoyed confrontation, she'd nevertheless mothered too many for too long to dance around the subject.

"Bill said the only thing they could find that didn't make sense was a bunch of notes about that lady you worked with. The one who fell down the stairs at Devlin House? Del's been pulling files on a bunch of women from there. Women who died, Bill says. He came in this morning while I was at the grocery store to talk to Del. In fact, he was just leaving when I came to get Del."

"What does, um, Del think?" I asked, stumbling over Blodgett's given name.

"He wouldn't talk about it. Not with me, anyway. But five minutes after Bill leaves, Del gets his undies in a bunch saying he's got to get home. We were already *going* home. The doctor was going to stop in and see him before lunch and then we were going to get Del released and go home. All of a sudden, Del's got to leave right away. Can't even see the doctor. Can't wait to get checked out."

She turned her face away then, but I'd been watching her expressions change as she'd talked. From blank to hurt and bewildered to accusatory. I reached for her hand again, but she pulled it away.

"Diana," I said. "Are you saying that Blodgett was attacked because of something he was doing for me?"

She whipped her eyes back to mine. "Are you saying he wasn't?"

"I don't know, Diana. I really don't. He was just looking up records for me. I never thought it was connected with . . ." My voice trailed off as I realized I was lying. I *had* wondered. Diana heard the uncertainty, too.

"You've known about this ever since Del was hurt and you never said anything?"

"Diana—"

"I'd like you to leave right now."

"But I really didn't—"

"I mean it, Letty. You need to leave."

I stood, torn between respecting her wishes and wanting, more than anything, to fix this. "I'm sorry, Diana. I really am."

CHAPTER THIRTY SIX

I didn't think I could handle returning to work, so I called Lisa and told her I wouldn't be back in. I'd tossed the words "family emergency" as I'd headed out the door earlier, so she knew there was something going on. She'd reschedule my clients, making the appropriate apologies and such.

I felt like I'd been slammed in the gut with a sledge hammer. It didn't matter that Blodgett was a seasoned cop or that, as a detective, he was sure to have more enemies than kernels on a corn cob. Diana's eyes—the disappointment in them—haunted me.

Once I made it to the car I ran a self-check: I didn't feel like drinking. I was pretty sure I didn't, anyway. I definitely wanted a cigarette. Nothing new there. But that itchy, restlessness that blossomed from the seed of guilt that had been planted didn't bode well. It was still mid-morning, but I headed for sanctuary.

There was also a stale cigarette funk that persisted despite the HP & Me club going non-smoking earlier in the year. My itch kicked up a notch. In the past, if I couldn't drink, I could always smoke, and cigarettes were proving more difficult than booze.

The club was deserted, a highly unusual event. I waited around for a few minutes in case somebody wandered in for a cup of coffee, but I was feeling too restless to stay long. I either needed a meeting, a cigarette, or a distraction.

Moments later, I jumped in my car heading out of town toward farmland and long stretches of woodland. Heading north.

To Marshall's cabin.

As a distraction, there was none better. All I had to do was allow the memory to surface of that dark, still evening where we'd lain entwined on his couch, firelight dancing like fingers over bare skin, heat chasing away the chill. I shivered just thinking about it. A small question of whether I could find his cabin teased the edges of my concentration, but despite the intervening months, I found it.

His driveway, a half-mile long dirt road, would be difficult to plow in the winter. Turning in, I slowed. Thoughts of being snowed in with my former boss made me smile. And wiggle a little, too.

But for now, autumn leaves crunched under the tires and the sharp cracks of snapping twigs brought my focus back to the present. I slowed the car even more as the reality of what I was doing shoved my lust-inspired impulse sharply to the side.

This was so stupid.

I'd reached the curve, bringing the cabin into view. If I tried to back out now, I'd *literally* have to back out, driving in reverse. Frankly, the odds were that I'd end up in the ditch, which wasn't likely to ease my embarrassment. That's what I told myself.

Besides, the sight of the cabin as it came in to view made my heart thump wildly. I'd once called it "enchanted," and it still lived up to that. I was surprised it hadn't sold, but then, the entire housing market had crashed. Riverfront property was at the wrong end of the price range for someone looking for a quick sale. Several weeks ago, I'd looked up the listing online, just out of curiosity. Marshall had priced the cabin high, at a pre-recession rate, a tactic sure to stall a quick sale. I'd hoped it meant he was ambivalent about truly leaving.

His Saab was parked in its usual place. I noted the Wisconsin license plates still affixed to it and smiled. More ambivalence? I parked next to it and did a quick, girl-check of makeup, hair, and attire. More office casual than sex kitten, but it would have to do. I spritzed a little perfume from the travel bottle I kept in my console—a girl never knew when she'd need to smell good—and pushed the door open.

Pine and wood smoke and crispness, if crispness had a smell, filled my nostrils, making me wish I hadn't spritzed. Nothing could compete with the scent of Wisconsin woods.

Walking up to the cabin, my heart thudded heavily against my rib cage. Images of Marshall streaked like shooting stars across my mind. I knocked, hoping he was wearing the red flannel jacket. And jeans. Faded, frayed, *tight* jeans.

He wasn't.

She was, however.

CHAPTER THIRTY SEVEN

Tall, statuesque, blond, and beautiful—this bitch was made for hating. I got started on that right away.

She wore fashionably faded jeans and a close-fitted, honey-hued sweater, the kind that looks like she'd skinned a kitten. I could tell the faded jeans were a calculated design detail, produced in a factory and not because she felt at home in them. Didn't matter though. She had enough confidence to feel at home anywhere.

"May I help you?" Southern accent, warm and sugary.

I couldn't answer. My voice was blocked by a clotting mixture of jealousy and humiliation.

Her smile twitched a notch wider. I sensed she wasn't trying to be mean, but was amused at my bumbling. She looked past me to where my car was parked. For some reason, I followed her gaze. She was probably looking for a delivery van. I just looked stupid.

"Is Marshall here?" I finally managed.

"He sure is. Who shall I say is calling?" Looking relieved that I'd managed to join the conversation, she opened the door a bit wider. The bits I could see of the cabin behind her looked exactly the way it had in the dreams I'd been having nightly. Except Marshall wasn't lying naked on the leather couch. Can't have everything, I guess.

"I used to work with him. I'll just, um, give him a call

later. I didn't mean to interrupt."

Her turn to fall silent. Although barely discernible, her river-blue eyes narrowed just the slightest, teeniest bit. She was looking at me differently now, eyes taking in details, categorizing rapidly. Subtly rescinding her previous welcome, she eased the door back to her side.

"You must be Letty," she said.

"Yup." *Yup?* Did I seriously just say *yup* to this southern peach princess? I cleared my throat. "Listen, could you just let Marshall know that I need to talk to him about an ethics investigation on a file? There are some questions coming up about it."

I turned away.

"Maybe you should leave your number," she said.

I looked back and we locked eyes. I smiled. "That won't be necessary," I said. "He's got it."

The door clicked firmly shut before I'd even cleared the first stair.

Marshall wouldn't have caught up to me if I hadn't had to pull over and throw up in the ditch—a behavior, since getting sober, that I hadn't expected to experience again. When I saw the Saab's grill growing larger and larger in my rear view mirror, I briefly considered a Dairy State reenactment of a "Duke's of Hazzard" back roads chase scene, but with my luck a buck would choose that moment to ornament my hood. Instead, I pulled over and popped a mint.

Our car doors slammed in unison. I walked to the back of my car and leaned up against the trunk, attempting to disguise my shaking knees with nonchalant indifference. Mentally, my brain was hopping as wildly as a sugared-up squirrel, but I latched onto my "ethics file" excuse with grim determination.

As he walked up, I took a flash glance inventory: faded jeans—the real kind—and a soft blue denim shirt. His "casual" didn't come from a factory. He took a stance directly in front of me, not saying anything. Just stood there, too close, trying to catch my eyes with his. Not likely. I already knew the dangers lurking in his dark brown eyes.

"Lisa found one of Regina's old files—Bettina Reyes?—and we've got some questions about it. It looks like some therapist has been up to some hanky-panky with his client's wife. I've met with the wife and she refuses to tell—"

"Letty, I'm sorry."

"Is this a confession? I'm a mandated reporter, you know. I'm obligated by law to report sexual and physical abuse."

"Letty—"

"Frankly, I always wondered why you took off so fast but I guess it makes sense if you were running away from your mistakes." I wanted to bite my tongue off. I'd meant to be a smartass, but bringing up mistakes reiterated his belief that our relationship was one of them. I hurried on. "At least, I can stop having nightmares about Bob prancing naked through the clinic."

"Wait. What? Bob?"

"Never mind. If you're the one who's been shagging Regina's client, then Bob's off the hook."

"Letty, stop. I don't have any idea what you're talking about, but if it has to do with seeing Bob naked, I don't want to. We need to talk."

Weary, I dropped the pretense, wrapping my arms around my center. I told myself it was chilly. "No, we don't. There's nothing to say."

He sighed deeply enough to rattle the leaves lining

the ditch next to us. He kept tilting his head, trying to catch my eyes. Finally, he reached out, grabbed my wrist and tugged me over to his car.

"Get in."

"Whoa." I pulled my arm away. "I'm not going back there."

"Of course not. Just . . . get in. You're shivering."

CHAPTER THIRTY EIGHT

I knew as soon as I settled into the seat that I'd made a tactical error. The car was too comfortable, too intimate. It felt like we were in a time capsule, shut off from the world. Plus it smelled like leather and Marshall—two scents I'd fantasized combining in various, naughty ways. Sitting there, I thought of a couple more.

He started the car, turned the heater on, and swiveled to face me. This close, it was harder to avoid eye contact, another disadvantage. I settled for staring at his shoulder. It was a nice shoulder, but unlike nice butts, I've been known to resist shoulders.

"Letty," he said. "There were so many times I wanted to tell you. It just . . . it never seemed like the right time."

My stomach did a slow roll, spreading heat throughout my body. *Times?* So many *times?* Plural? We hadn't been together plural times since his return so that could only mean he was talking about before he'd left.

"What are you talking about?" Now that I wanted eye contact, his dipped away. "Marshall? How long have you been seeing her?"

"Look," he said, "it's complicated."

I almost threw up again. "That is such a cliché. I cannot believe you would pull that rancid old line out. What's complicated? Either you were seeing her and chasing me or not. See how simple that is? Now which is it?"

"I wasn't seeing her. We're married."

Literally. Could. Not. Speak. Even when I was drunk I'd never messed with a married man. Not that I could remember anyway.

"Letty." He reached for my hand. I slapped it away. "Letty, look, we're married, but not really. I mean, we were getting divorced. I came here to Wisconsin when the director position opened, and Bobbi was going to follow as soon as she closed out her job. But she never did, and after all those months I realized she wasn't going to. She came up with all kinds of excuses, but the bottom line is she wanted to transfer to California and I hate California. Anyway, there was no way the marriage was going anywhere. In fact, once I started seeing you, I got all the papers in order and I was just waiting for her to sign. I really wanted to tell you, but there was so much going on. I mean, come on. You were being stalked. People were dying. I wanted to be there for you, but I didn't want to add to the chaos."

My eyes widened so big I was afraid they were going to pop out and roll to the floor. "So, wait a minute. Are you saying you kept your marital status a secret for me? Really? For *me*? That's a load of bullshit and you know it. If you wanted to be there for me, fine. That's awesome. But you weren't just there for me. You were, you know"— I waved my hands over my body—"*there* for me."

He grinned sheepishly, but I wasn't trying to be funny and it pissed me off even more.

"So, okay. What's she doing here now? I thought you ran away to your brother's in Wyoming. Was that a lie, too?"

Well, that wiped the grin off his face. Got a little red, too. "I didn't lie. I did stay with Allan for a while. Okay, technically I was still married, but Bobbi and I were through. It was dead long before you came along. We just hadn't stamped it DOA yet."

"You didn't answer my question. Why is she camping out in your cabin? Are you reconciling? 'Cause she sure looked settled in and cozy when I got there."

"We had some legal stuff that she had to sign for the realtor. Since we aren't legally divorced . . . Well, anyway, she's going to quit claim her ownership of the cabin, and I'm doing the same for the house in Colorado. Even trade, pretty much. And then she's free to go to California, and I'm just . . . free."

"That's not the vibe I got when we were talking at the door. She acted like she still had a claim, and not just on the cabin."

Emotions struggled across his face. My heart hurt. I turned away, propping my elbow on the window, staring out at the countryside. My breath created little puffs on the chilly glass. There was still something between them. Maybe something as ephemeral as the steam my lungs created against the window glass, but something.

"Why did you let me think *I* was the problem? That I was the one responsible for the problems between us?" I asked.

"When I left, it was because of what happened here, not because of her. You want to call it running away, fine. Maybe it was. But let's face it, Letty, you let yourself get involved in a bad situation and—"

"I *what?* I let myself get involved? Are you kidding me? I was being stalked. I was attacked. I didn't ask for—"

"You didn't back away from it either," he interrupted.

The words hung in the air between us for several

moments.

"I was supposed to back away from it?" I finally managed. "How do you do that, Marshall? Some crazed asshole is coming after me and I'm supposed to just sit there and offer him milk and cookies?"

"No. But you don't have to rush toward it, either. You could have let the police do their job. Instead, you kept things from them. You ran around like Nancy Drew on steroids, and that pulled the people around you into danger, too. Including me."

It was the "pulling the people around you into danger" that pushed me over the edge, of course.

"Hey, Marshall? You know what? I don't think Regina's death *was* an accident. I think she was stabbed with a knitting needle and tossed down the stairs like a sack of garbage. Murdered, in other words. And I'm using my role as her executor to check out the staff at the shelter and, guess what? I think they're acting mighty suspicious. Oh, and just so you know, I *did* talk to Blodgett about it, but somebody knifed him—"

"Detective Blodgett was attacked?" His face paled.

"—from behind and he's been in the hospital ever since. And I didn't"—my voice hitched—"I didn't tell Diana, but I should have." I took a deep shuddery breath.

"Letty, please, I'm not saying—"

"Bottom line? I don't believe murder is somebody else's business. I think it's everyone's business and I plan to continue looking for answers, at least until I can find enough evidence for the police to step in.

"Oh, and by the way? I think Regina knew about Bob schtupping the wife of one of his clients. So, he's a suspect, too. That last part happened on your watch, and I came out to ask if you remembered anything more about it. That's the *only* reason I came out here."

He sat staring at me like I was a lunatic. Resisting the urge to stick out my tongue, I settled for slamming the car door hard enough to set the vehicle rocking.

CHAPTER THIRTY NINE

I spent the weekend swinging on a carb-salt-sugar pendulum comprised of Haagen Dazs Chocolate Chocolate Chip ice cream and bags of Lays potato chips. Cliché, maybe, but my options for mood-altering chemicals were limited, so I took what I could get. Concern over Blodgett's health warred with the seemingly less important distress at Marshall's duplicity. In reality, the two events combined for equal opportunity despair. That made me feel even more guilty. My head knew that Marshall—a man who had dropped out of my life months before—was far less important than my friend getting attacked and suffering a heart attack. I called the hospital Friday night to see how Blodgett had fared his surgery. Once again, the nurse wouldn't answer any questions other than to say he was stable. I had to settle for that, unless I wanted to call Diana.

Which I didn't.

By Saturday night, I was sick of myself, so I dragged my butt to the Saturday Open Speaker meeting. Open Speaker meetings, unlike closed, consist of one speaker telling an audience his or her story—how it was, what happened, and how it is now. Before, during, and after, so to speak. Perfect, because I wouldn't have to actively participate. I just needed to be with people.

Thankfully, Sue didn't show up, even though she liked Open Speaker meetings. I hadn't called her to set up our meeting like I'd promised, so I was a little leery of running into her. As soon as the speaker finished, I slipped out to my car. I had enough to worry about.

At least the meeting had jarred me out of my pity pot, as we call it in AA Definitely *not* one of my favorite sayings since it had the nasty habit of being true. I hated that.

But it also got me thinking.

I still hadn't figured out who RTA was. If I could get access to the shelter's files via the efficacy study, I might be able to search for other RTA notations, but I hadn't heard from Beth. Hadn't heard from *anyone* from the shelter for that matter. My impatient side wanted to call Beth, but I knew it would be better to wait and let it play out. Bugging her wouldn't help.

So much for thinking.

The next few days were remarkable only in their utter lack of progress. One morning, early, the phone shrilled. Clotilde must have taken great pleasure in knowing she woke me up. 6:00 a.m. Who does that?

She didn't even bother with a phony "Oh! Did I wake you?" I tried to pretend that I was alert and ready to face the day, but my voice couldn't maintain the ruse. All I could manage was that one-octave-higher-but-still-sleep-graveled tone that never fooled anyone. It certainly had no chance with Clotilde.

She also eschewed niceties like 'hello' or introducing herself. All I got was "The board has agreed to your proposal. I'll meet with you this evening at seven."

"This evening? Um . . . let's see . . . Today's Tuesday, right?"

"If that doesn't work, I'm available on the 30th."

"The 30th? Of this month? That's, what? Three

weeks from now?"

Long pause.

"Tonight would be fine," I said.

Click.

That left thirteen hours to wonder what exactly I was going to say since I had no clue how to set up an efficacy study. It had sounded good when it was in my head, but like all theories, when it came down to actual implementation, it felt like I was trying to nail Jell-O to the wall.

In the end, I put together a short, five-item questionnaire and called it good. It's not like they could fire me. Kill me, maybe, but not fire me.

CHAPTER FORTY

It was one of those harried, frantic days at the clinic. Edna, my 2:00 client—a dear, sweet woman caught in a remorseless cycle of resentment, depression, and guilt after her meth-addicted daughter dropped five grandkids off for an "overnight" that had now lasted eighteen months—had whispered, "I think I'm going to kill myself" four minutes before her session ended. For the rest of the afternoon, I parked her in the staff break room, where she placidly crocheted an afghan and sipped warm Diet Sprite. In the few minutes between client sessions, I worked at arranging admission to the fourth floor at Sacred Heart for her and respite care for the kiddos. I didn't like leaving her alone for long stretches while I saw my other clients, but Lisa checked in on her regularly. I stopped worrying after I found her cheerfully cleaning out the staff refrigerator. Apparently, disclosure and the reassurance that her charges were being cared for had relieved her immensely. In fact, she appeared to be reframing her stay on the psych floor as a "vacation" as evidenced by her asking whether the hospital had a hot tub.

With five kids under twelve at home, who could blame her?

Of course, Bob needed an update, right as I was

going out the door. He'd been conspicuously absent during Edna's crisis, his office door shut firmly against intrusions.

I plopped down in the chair, trying desperately to avoid mental images of Bob doin' the nasty with Bettina. My nerves had stood all they could take. If there was a God, he would spare me this.

Bob asked to review my documentation and the suicide plan. Bored, I sat back and let my mind wander. Eventually, I was going to have to deal with the Bob-n-Bettina issue and when I did, there would be hell to pay.

Most of it directed at me. Even though I'd be doing the right thing, turning your boss over to the licensing board for unethical behavior would not be a career enhancer.

I wondered if the shelter was hiring?

I almost felt sorry for Bob, too. All he'd ever wanted was to be middle-management, tucked away in an office with a surplus of prestige and a deficit of responsibility. So different from Marshall.

My eyes fell on Bob's custom-made nameplate. He'd brought it in the second week—an office-warming present from his wife. Green-veined marble with a brass plate: Robert Thomas Aaronson.

I sat up. *RTA?*

I must have looked like I'd seen a ghost, but for once, Bob's dull-wittedness came in handy. I swallowed the multitude of questions that surged up.

Now was not the time. I needed to think carefully about what I wanted to say and ask, because there would be no do-overs.

And it could, I supposed, be a coincidence.

I was more than twenty minutes late for my meeting

with Clotilde. Surprisingly, she was still at the shelter. Although my apology was sincere, I didn't waste a whole lot of time on it. I was still reeling from my discovery and I'd never convince her that my tardiness wasn't a power play. I did wonder, though, if I could work in a question about Bob's involvement here.

Taking the seat next to her desk, I simply handed her the questionnaire and waited to hear her objections. I was sure there would be several. Her anger was palpable, filling the air around us and wielded in that chill, dark manner used by people who covet control. As she ran a jaundiced eye over the form, I watched her expression. Unlike Lachlyn, who was free with her contempt, Clotilde worked at hiding her emotions—she was the professional face of the shelter after all—but she had a "tell." I'd seen it when I'd confronted her about withholding Karissa's file from me.

There. Her upper lip flickered in a half-stifled sneer. Despite the brief welling of juvenile glee at catching her out, I kept my own expression blandly pleasant.

Briskly placing the sheet of paper on the desk in front of her, she folded her hands across the top and met my eye. "How do you propose to go about this . . . this *study*?"

"I thought it would be best to keep it simple. To begin with, I'll give the questionnaire to the current residents, and then we'll need to have them fill it out again when they leave. In the future, though, we'll administer it at admission, two weeks after, and at discharge, provided we know when the woman is leaving, of course."

"Not all residents stay two weeks."

"I realize that, but I don't think it's fair to evaluate treatment results if a woman only stays a few nights." I smiled to show her I was trying to be helpful. She didn't smile back. "We'd have to have some way of addressing that sub-group though. Maybe we should still give them the discharge questionnaire?"

Clotilde shrugged.

"Also, in order to get a baseline," I continued, "I'll be conducting a file review of the last few years to see if we can get an approximate idea of post-treatment results. I won't include that data in the final summary for the board, but it could be helpful when it comes time to apply for further grants. And it will give us an idea of what's working and what isn't."

So much for a poker face. At the mention of a file review, her lips thinned to a slash, the knuckles on her folded hands, formerly poised so genteelly over my little questionnaire, blanched white. I realized I was watching a literal struggle for control, and I found myself mentally calculating an escape route.

The space between us grew hot and prickly, tangibly tense. Neither of us spoke for several seconds—a lifetime—but despite the silence, the air seemed crowded with noise: a ticking clock, my heart thudding, Clotilde's rasping, measured breaths.

"Fine," she said.

Fine?

She didn't bother explaining herself, just stood, indicating the meeting was over. Instinctively, I rose. "The board expects a progress report in one month. Astrid will inform you of the date." Without taking her eyes off me, she walked to the door, holding it open, maneuvering my exit.

Maybe I'd ask someone else about Bob.

She left the shelter moments later. Although I hadn't needed the bathroom in the literal sense, I locked myself into the porcelain sanctuary as soon as I cleared her office threshold.

CHAPTER FORTY ONE

When I finally ventured out of the commode, I found Astrid in the kitchen, making coffee. She gave a start as I emerged, then looked at the door through which Clotilde had just slammed out and said, "Oh!"

"Oh" can mean a lot of things. In this case, it meant, "Now I understand why Clotilde was so pissed."

"I guess you heard why I was meeting with Clotilde," I said.

She looked uncomfortable. "Oh my, yes. We heard all about it this morning. Clotilde spent all morning talking to the board."

Left unsaid was that Clotilde had put in an awful lot of time trying to get the board to rescind their permission.

"Do you think it's such a terrible thing to do an efficacy study?" I asked. "Doesn't she want to know if the program is effective?"

Astrid tossed me a disgusted, are-you-kidding-me? look. "We already know that the program is effective. What could be more effective then removing a woman from her abuser and giving her shelter? There's nothing a little questionnaire can tell us that we don't already know. Besides, Clotilde has to look at the big picture. There are more things that have to be considered than just this study."

The problem with—or the benefit of—an extended lie is the liar tends to start believing it. I was working up a pretty good head of self-righteous steam, forgetting that I was, well, lying like a dirty penny in a parking lot, and close to alienating the one person who had been helpful so far. I took a deep breath.

"I know the shelter works. I've seen it for myself." We both knew I was referring to the aftermath of my own attack. She relaxed a bit, so I went on. "Look, you know grants aren't being awarded easily. This study can help with that. More grant money means more for the women. How can that be a bad thing?"

"More money is never a bad thing." She smiled wryly at the admission.

A thought occurred to me. "What other considerations?" I asked.

The smile slid off her face. "Oh. Um."

"You said there were 'more things to be considered.' What did you mean by that?"

"I probably shouldn't have said that. I mean, after all, it's all been settled. When you implied that we didn't care, I got a little . . . Look, just forget it."

"What's been settled?" I said.

She scowled. "The complaint made against you to the licensing board. Last spring? Clotilde felt it was her duty to inform the board about the allegations made against you. After all, if they are going to let you—"

"*Allegations?* Are you *kidding* me? You know very well who made that complaint and why. They were completely unfounded. I can't believe . . ." I sputtered to a halt as a new realization hit me.

"Astrid, that information came out of the group sessions I attended here. Clotilde had no right to violate my confidentiality like that. Not even to the board."

Astrid's face paled. By revealing Clotilde's anti-Letty campaign tactics, she'd let her boss in for more trouble than she'd realized. If I chose to pursue the matter, Clotilde would be looking at her own ethics investigation. Let's see how *she* liked it.

"What time does she get in tomorrow?" I asked.

"I don't know. I guess the usual time. Letty, please—"

I held a hand up. "I'm not trying to get you in trouble, Astrid. I won't even mention where I heard it, but she's crossed the line. She had no right to bring up information learned in a therapy group, and worse, to use it when she knew it was unjustified! There's no excuse for that.

"Is Lachlyn here?" I suddenly changed the subject.

Apparently, the abrupt switch unsettled her even more. Her face blotched in irregular red and white patches eerily similar to Candi Cow, the 4-H Guernsey heifer I raised in eighth grade.

Probably best not to mention that particular resemblance.

"Lachlyn is visiting her daughter. Joyce is here, though," Astrid said.

"Her daughter? I thought her daughter was dead?"

"Dead? Why would you think that?" Astrid asked.

I had one of those "Who's on first?" moments. "*You* said she was. When you were telling why Lachlyn is so craz—" I coughed and started over. "When you were telling me why Lachlyn was so dedicated to women's issues. You said her daughter's life had been ruined by some guy."

"Well, yes, she had to drop out of college. She still lives up in Turtle Lake with that jerk. They work at the casino. Lachlyn went up for little Lacey's birthday. Her granddaughter. She's five."

Lachlyn: holy sister, mother, *grandmother*? My brain reeled.

"Anyway, she's running the craft class in the group room," Astrid said. Her eyes flicked across my face.

"Lachlyn?"

"*Joyce*. You said you wanted to talk to her. Goodness, Letty, you're barely making sense today."

Completely befuddled, I said good-bye and made my way up to the group room. It would give me a chance to get to know Joyce a little more anyway. I could hear the women murmuring inside, the sound a cheerful counterpoint to my emotions. Tapping on the door, I leaned my head around the corner.

"What's going on in here?" I asked, using a faux-perky, kindergarten teacher voice.

The room hushed in one of those what-is-*she*-doing-here? moments. Utilizing my alcoholic's handy ability to deny uncomfortable truths, I forged on.

CHAPTER FORTY TWO

They were knitting. I'd met most of the women, although it looked like one of them—Candice, or maybe Barb—wasn't there. A new girl sat next to Joyce, a skein of navy blue yarn tangled around her fingers.

The rest of the women's projects seemed to have progressed in varying stages and equally varied expertise. Judging by the size and pastel colors, scarves and baby blankets seemed to be the preferred choices. Joyce was the exception, an intricate cabled sweater pooling on her lap. Blood red yarn spilled from the needles like she'd hit an artery.

I shuddered as the image of Regina's strange manner of death intruded my thoughts.

"Did you want something?" Joyce asked.

"I just . . ."

She waited, staring dully at me.

"Um, Astrid mentioned there was a craft class going on so I thought I would peek in and say hi to everyone." I took a seat next to Jan, who was wearing the same pjs she'd had on during the self-defense class.

"Crafts are an integral part of the community here. It gives the women something to do with their hands and builds a sense of accomplishment and pride in their work. We talk, too, while we work. Sometimes it's more therapeutic than the regular groups." Joyce spoke in a bright, chirpy voice. It was the longest speech I'd heard from her.

The new girl was across from me, fumbling with the shiny knitting needles. It took me a minute to realize her awkwardness with the tools was because she was shaking hard enough to rattle the metal chair she perched on. She was a skinny little thing, fresh bruises adding the only color to her face.

"My name is Letty," I told her. "I've been helping out here the last couple of weeks. I'm kind of new, too."

Her eyes darted away from me, circling the group and landing on Joyce as though waiting for a cue. Joyce, looking only slightly less strained than she, nodded grudging permission.

"I'm Maureen."

"Nice to meet you, Maureen. I'm going to have a new form for you to fill out. In fact," I included the group in my glance, "We're putting together a questionnaire to help us keep track of our performance. Hopefully, that will get some more grant money rolling in here. That would be a good thing, wouldn't it? I'm going to be passing it around for everyone here."

Dead silence.

Joyce cleared her throat. "Everyone?"

"Not staff. I'm looking to get current and past residents' opinions on how helpful they found the services here. It's called an efficacy study. Then we can use those results as evidence of need when we apply for grant money."

"Well, I *am* a former resident," Joyce said. She looked at Maureen. "That's why I stayed. Even though the memories of what I lived through are awful, I won't let myself forget. I'm on disability, but I don't like the idea of not contributing to society. I'd go crazy if I had to sit around and do nothing. Working here keeps me safe. I know what to look for now, and I know what to do if I'm in danger. I'd be dead if it weren't for this place." At the last statement she looked directly at me. Her eyes, a curiously flat shade of muddy brown, stared deeply, almost challengingly into my own.

"Right," I finally said. "It's always important to, um, stay alert. Regina taught me that. Some of you knew her, right? She used to work here?" Well, duh. Of course, they knew that. I pressed on. "By the way, did she knit?

Joyce gasped. She, at least, was aware of how Regina had died. The others just looked confused. And scared. No one answered me. Maybe it was time to go.

"Okay, well, it's been nice sitting and chatting with you all. I guess I'd better be scooting for home. I'll, um, let you know when I have those questionnaires ready." I babbled my way across the floor, heaving a whooshing sigh of relief as the door shut behind me.

The hallway was dark.

I've never been a big fan of dark hallways, which have been a frequent feature in many of my more vivid nightmares. Anybody versed in dream analysis will start prattling on about "life paths" or "transitional phase," but I wasn't worried about symbolism at the moment. Regina had died a very real death at the other end of this hall. To get to my car, I either had to grope my way past that very spot—in the dark, may I repeat—or go outside—and walk around the outside of the building.

Outside, it was.

October is the right month for Halloween. Even though we were weeks away, the night felt eerie, laced with menace. Or maybe it was the company I'd just left. Since the shelter was situated on a corner lot, the sidewalk ran perpendicular along two sides. The smart thing would have been to use it, but that would mean taking the long way. I wasn't in a long-way mood.

Instead, I cut across the lawn, skirting the edge of the house, keeping a wary toe out for the writhing root system of the overhanging fir trees. As I passed behind the sign for the shelter, I realized I was treading on the same spot where Lachlyn, Clotilde, and Astrid had stood on opening day for the shelter so many years ago.

Creepy.

The whole night felt creepy. I froze as the feeling of being watched swept over me. The fear didn't grow. It was just *there*—a thin, hot liquid eating away at rational thought.

Holding my breath, I strained to listen, analyzing each sound of the night for clues. I could almost feel my pupils dilating: eyes lemur-wide, scanning the different shades of darkness, searching for the danger. A slight breeze rattled the leaves.

Time felt wonky, too, both racing and leaden. Or maybe that was my heart. I stood still a few moments, then took a tentative, shaky step forward. If anything had rushed me at that moment, I'd have wet myself. Not an especially effective deterrent against crazed attackers, but you use what you got.

When I appeared to be both safe and dry, I took another step. And then another. And then I ran my ass off.

Which unfortunately activated the run-your-ass-off floodlights, illuminating the entire property.

Light exploded, slamming into my eyeballs like a sledge hammer. I skidded to a stop, one foot sliding wildly on the fallen leaves. For one fleeting, tantalizing moment I managed the Warrior pose that had so eluded me in my one brief attempt at yoga. Then I landed on my butt, one leg stretched forward and the other twisted underneath, as a particular knobby tree root introduced itself to my tailbone. Pain zinged up my spine.

I slowly rolled to my knees, forcing myself to stand. I hurt so bad, if anyone wanted to kill me they were welcome to it.

When I finally made it to the car, I cranked the heater up to seventy-eight and told myself that I was shivering from the chilly air, not from post-hysterical stupidity.

I decided to stop off at Gordy's Market for a fresh carton of Epsom salts and some groceries. Woman could not live by chips alone. Besides, I'd eaten them all. As I hobbled up to the deli counter, I noticed a guy setting up a ladder under one of those purple-black domes that hide security cameras.

Duh. I *had* been watched. Astrid's fancy, state-of-the-art security system included exterior cameras in addition to the floodlights. Darting through the side yard and lurking behind the sign now seemed especially stupid choices.

My stomach dropped as a new kind of fear welled up. *Had I set off the alarm?* It would be just my luck to have triggered a full-scale safety drill, with the residents panicking, thinking they were under attack, and the staff shifting into protection mode. Clotilde would kill me.

And what about the police? Would they have been called? I grabbed my purchases and scooted through the checkout line as quickly as I could. All the way home, I kept glancing in my mirror for cop cars.

Ten minutes later, I pulled into my apartment's parking lot, relieved I hadn't been pulled over. Even though taking a shortcut across the yard seemed a perfectly reasonable thing to do, it didn't feel like that anymore.

I slammed the car door and scurried up the sidewalk toward the front entrance of the apartment unit. Just as I passed the smelly garbage dumpster, the shadows shifted and the floodlights—this time in my head— exploded again.

CHAPTER FORTY THREE

How did the ground get here? The sidewalk had shifted from under my feet to under my back. A worried, vaguely familiar face loomed over me, blocking most of the dark sky, which was also strangely misplaced. Instead of hanging over my head, I seemed to be facing it. The woman above looked so concerned that I wanted to reassure her.

"The walk did a wrong thing," I said.

She looked even more scared, but my head hurt, so I closed my eyes.

Light squeezed past my clenched eyelids, daggering into my brain, which had its own problems going on. I forced myself to open my eyes, a poor choice, but necessary. Everything was white or horribly reflective stainless steel, and blurry from the tears streaming down my face. My head ached so badly that my stomach heaved in. I turned my head to vomit, which triggered more blinding pain, starting a pain-puke, pain-puke cycle that threatened to never end. It did, though, just in time for the inquisition.

"What's your name?" a guy asked. His green smock was repulsive so I puked again.

"Do you know your name?" he asked again.

Of course I knew my name. Duh. I knew it. I was pretty sure I knew it.

"What day is it?"

Now, that was just stupid. I had enough going on without some ding-a-ling using me for his day planner. "Get a thing," I said. "One of those cucumbers." OK, "cucumbers" was a mistake; I knew it, and it pissed me off even more.

"OK, one more," he said. "How about where you are? Do you know where you are?"

"The hospital, you moron." Ha! Got him there.

"Well, Ms. Whittaker, I'm sorry to say you flunked our little test. How about we take some pictures of your brain and see what's going on in there?"

Anger flooded me, spiking my headache up a few notches. I *never* flunk tests.

My world morphed to a softly humming, white tube, encircling me. It moved me along and for a moment I was convinced I was in a car wash. Only that would make me the car, and I wasn't quite *that* confused. A teeny red light above my head flashed and a spinning thing whirled next to it. The car wash slid me out. A nurse smiled down at me.

"What happened?" I asked.

I was lying on a bed. A hospital bed. A wave of relief washed over me as things started to make sense. "Calendar," I said, which scared me all over again, because it made no sense to say that. Thankfully, the nurse, swooshing the curtain back, didn't appear to have heard me. The curtains made an unforgivably loud ratchety sound as they slid along the U-shaped pole ringing my bed. I was still in the ER, it appeared.

"Dr. Billingsley will be right back," she said. "He's got some things to go over with you. Do you know when your ride will get here?"

"My ride?"

"You gave us the phone number. Don't remember that, do you?" She smiled sympathetically. "Don't worry. That'll get better. You're going to have quite a headache for a while though. Kind of like a long-term hangover."

"That is *so* unfair," I mumbled.

"Hmm?" She'd crossed over to a cabinet and was removing a blanket from it. Tossing it over me, she twitched it in place and gave my knee a pat. "Hit that button if you need anything. Oh, and try to stay awake. Rest is the most important thing, but you'll need to be awakened every few hours for tonight and maybe tomorrow."

"How am I going to rest if I keep getting woken up?" *And* who *is going to wake me?* I would have asked her who was coming for me, but she'd already trotted away.

I might have slept. Or maybe my brain did one of those skip things again. The doctor was sitting next to me on his little round rolling stool. I'd never seen a nurse use one of those and wondered if they were reserved: Physicians Only.

"You've got a whopper of a concussion, Ms. Whittaker. What we like to call a Grade Two concussion, although I'm on the fence about bumping you up to a Grade Three. And trust me: this is not an area where you will want to overachieve. We'll see how this week goes. If your symptoms persist or worsen, we'll want you to get right back in here. The good news is the CT scan shows no bleeding or serious injury to your noggin. At least not yet."

"What's the difference between Grade Two and Three?" I asked.

"It used to be whether you were unconscious. Grade Two meant no loss of consciousness; getting KO'd meant automatic upgrade to Three. Nowadays, we recognize there are more individualized responses to head trauma. We're more concerned about the degree of injury and the length of post-injury symptoms.

"You can think about the brain as being the consistency of gelatin," he continued. "When you receive a knock on the head, it sloshes around, bangs up against your skull."

Ugh.

"When we're talking about Grade Three, there's the danger of bleeding in or around the brain and possibly tearing of the nerve fibers."

Eek!

He produced a handout with all kinds of instructions and things to watch for. The text was blurry and I started seeing double so I just pretended to read it. He ended up repeating what the nurse had said about rest being the only real treatment, and suggested I take some time off work. He also suggested not getting hit on the head again anytime soon.

No shit.

At least I wouldn't have to stay in the hospital. All I wanted was to be home, curled up in bed with Siggy purring in my ear. Unfortunately they wouldn't release me until someone showed up to drive me home. I'd given them somebody's number apparently, although I had no recollection of it. I didn't want to admit the lapse in case they rescinded my release.

I knew who I was hoping for, but would I have given them Marshall's number? I'd called him for help before, one night when I was, let's say . . . incapacitated. Not that I wanted to see him, I told myself. Except I'd just admitted that I did.

I closed my eyes. My head hurt too much to lie to myself.

What if it was Sue? I could just as easily have given them Sue's number, and frankly, I didn't think I could survive her abrasive attitude in the shape I was in. I loved her like a sister, but I had not picked her to be my sponsor for her gentle and endearing nature. Staying sober, for me, meant needing someone who would call me on my own shit, and Sue fit the bill.

Sue was like a rabid porcupine.

I didn't have long to wait. Within ten minutes, the double doors in the main room opened and my ride walked in.

Made me wish for Sue.

CHAPTER FORTY FOUR

"Ma, I don't *know* why somebody hit me. They didn't leave a note."

"Don't be a smart aleck. Of course, they didn't leave a note. I'm not stupid even if I didn't go to a fancy college. But if someone is sneaking up behind you and bamming you on the head, you must have some idea. If it was Kris, I'd just think it was . . ."

"Was what? What's going on with Kris?" The mere mention of my sister's name was enough to set me off. She was the baby in the family and, for a long time, was the only person in it that I felt close to. Then I got sober and she hated me for it.

"Never mind Kris. I don't want to get into it. Isn't having another psycho killer come after you enough to worry about? How do you do this? Are you like a freak magnet? You're just lucky that neighbor lady found you. Be sure to send her a thank-you note. How come you didn't go to school for computers like I told you? I mean, what do you expect when you work with crazy people? They're gonna—"

"*Ma.* I do not work with crazy people. I work with people . . ." I trailed off.

"With people what?"

"What?"

"You work with people, you said. Then you stopped."

"Ma, I can't do this now. I have a headache." I

pressed my hands to my head. If she didn't stop talking
my head was going to explode. And then I'd have to
listen to her bitch about getting gelatinous brain goo all
over her car seat. She still hadn't forgiven me for a red
Kool-Aid incident when I was twelve.

I slid against the window, resting my face against the
cool glass. She kept yakking, but by then I'd resorted to
the quasi-fugue state I'd learned to employ as a teen. A
parental nagging OFF button.

Even blackouts can be useful.

Back home, it took nearly two hours to convince my
mother that the doctor had overreacted when he
suggested I have someone stay with me all night. She
was distracted by her self-appointed inspection—and
subsequent reorganization—of the contents of my
kitchen cabinets, refrigerator, freezer, and closets. All
accompanied by a running commentary on the
undesirability of having a cat as a pet. I finally pointed
out the cat-behaired couch would be her bed. I
telepathied an apology to Siggy, but he'd already fled to
the dark space under my bed.

Siggy was a survivor.

The next day, Wednesday, I called Lisa and asked
her to cancel my clients for the next week, explaining
only that I'd been involved in a crash. I didn't specify
that the crash had involved a blunt instrument and the
back of my head and not an automobile, but she wasn't
picky about details. She even offered to run over at lunch
and bring me some soup. I almost cried.

In fact, I divided most of the morning between
feeling sorry for myself, panic at the thought that
someone had actually tried to kill me, and a rising fury
that someone had *actually* tried to kill me. Again.

It didn't help that in order to "rest," I had to practically lay on my face because the back of my skull hurt so bad. This confused and frustrated Siggy, who was used to sleeping in the nook created by the curve of my legs, not on the twin—and ever growing—hillocks of my ass.

We were both cranky by midafternoon.

It wasn't until I was brushing my teeth that I saw the thin, red welt on the side of my neck. I patted myself, groping for the chain my eyes had already told me was missing. Along with Regina's cow charm. Ripped off my neck.

I decided to use the down time for strategizing. Unfortunately, my brain was working at "See Spot run?" level. My "plan" was reduced to showing up at the shelter's team meeting tomorrow and watching peoples' faces to see if anyone looked killer-esque.

Around 4:00, Pete Durrant called. He'd somehow found out that I'd been injured. It was possible that Sue, his girlfriend-my sponsor, had told him, but then how had *she* known? I hadn't called her yet. Through her years spent teaching and her underground networking in A.A., she had a lot of resources, but this was an amazing feat even for her mighty gossip skills. Speculating made my head hurt worse, so I finally just asked Durrant for an explanation.

"Sue? What are you talking about?" he asked. "Sue wasn't there. You told me not to call her."

"I did? When?"

Long pause. "Last night. In the hospital. Don't remember, huh?"

I tried so hard to remember that I felt my brain split in two and start to leak out my orifices. A closer inspection revealed I was crying. Shit.

"What were you doing there?" I asked.

"Well, believe it or not, we consider someone attacking you a crime. Understandable, maybe, but still a crime. When that happens, they generally let the police know so we can serve and protect and all that law-and-order stuff. I guess I don't need to ask if you've remembered any more details of the attack."

Strangely, his sarcasm had a lifting effect on my spirits. Only people who really love you will use your worst moments to score on you. Besides, he knew I was crying; it probably unnerved him.

"I can see why you and Sue get along so well," I said through my sniffles. "Is being a smartass a new interrogation technique?"

"No, just a facet of my own scintillating personality. Besides, Sue's mad at me again."

"Understandable, maybe, but still a mistake."

"True, very true. So let's start over now that we're all on the same page. Hello, Ms. Whittaker, this is Officer Durrant. I'm following up on the unfortunate incident yesterday evening. How are you feeling?"

"Like dog poop. Thanks for asking."

"You're very welcome. Have you been able to recall any additional information relating to said unfortunate incident?"

"I remember being scared. Or . . . no, wait, that was earlier."

"Scared of what?" His tone instantly reverted to cop-voice.

"I don't . . . I think someone was watching me." Snatches of images clicked through my mind like a stutter-stop slide show: running in the dark; flashbulbs exploding; the newspaper photo of Clotilde, Astrid and Lachlyn standing next to the Devlin House sign; snarls of bright red yarn twining like snakes around my feet. I knew, taken as a whole, the images didn't make sense, but they felt true. True, but not factual—what the hell did that mean?

Durrant had no clue either.

CHAPTER FORTY FIVE

I hadn't been to an AA meeting since Saturday, but I wasn't well enough to go, despite Wednesday nights being my favorite meetings. The thought of enduring the shrill cacophony of women's voices made my head pound in anticipation. I told myself I wanted to be rested before the shelter's staffing the following day.

I should have realized I wouldn't escape that easily.

My phone rang just after 8:30 p.m. I'd fallen asleep on the couch and woke up with a drool slick on the cushion. Siggy hovered on the arm rest, eyeing me in a state of catly disdain. This from an animal who licks himself.

"'lo?" I cleared my throat.

"Seriously? It's not even 9:00 and you're sleeping?"

"Sue?"

"Why aren't you here? And why didn't you call me to set up your Third Step meeting? What's going on? You know what? Never mind. Put the coffee on."

Click.

I stared blankly at the phone receiver as my brain processed the ugly fact: Sue was coming. . . and she was *pissed.*

With everything going on, I'd been lax in keeping her updated—a big no-no with sponsors. For all she knew, I'd been on a wild drinking spree. Sponsors hate being the last to know those things. Part of me felt slighted that she might not trust me, but then again, I'd only been sober a short time and lately, with Regina's death and all, I'd slacked off on more than just staying in contact.

A tiny voice—one so new to me I barely recognized it—niggled at my conscience. Why not be honest? I hadn't been working the Program since before Regina died. I'd have to ponder that later.

Right now, I'd need all the mushy, bruised cells in my brain to figure out what I was going to tell Sue, especially when she noticed my banged up cranium. After supporting me through the aftermath of last summer, she wouldn't take kindly to hearing how entangled I'd become with Regina's death.

She already knew about my initial reluctance to acting as Regina's professional executor, and she knew that I'd needed Beth's support to stay involved with the shelter. Come to think of it, she knew about Blodgett's assault, too; she'd also helped me track down Pete Durrant so I could find out what had happened. But unless Pete told her about the attack on me last night, she didn't know that I'd been hurt, too.

Lying was not an option. Sue knew me too well and had long ago developed shit-detection to an art form. I needed to find a way to tell her the truth in such a way as to not let her discover what the truth was.

My head hurt.

Besides, she was already knocking at my door. I shuffled across the fake hardwood flooring to let her in.

"Well, good evening, sunshine! It's so nice to see you again." She came in like Wisconsin winters—deceptively serene, potentially fatal—her cheeriness as illusory as the warmth of a December sun.

I flinched as she pretended to buss my cheek with a social kiss. Flinched because Sue was neither social nor a kisser. I was afraid she was going to bite me.

She walked over to the empty coffee maker, glaring balefully at it as though by force of nature she could will it to perk. Siggy appeared and started twining around her feet. Like most felines, he could tell when somebody didn't like cats and exerted a version of passive-aggressive revenge. She nudged him away with her foot.

"Oh. I forgot to make coffee," I said.

Sue turned the chilly gaze to me, making me flinch again. I cleared my throat. "Um. How about we sit in the living room?"

Siggy followed us in and perched on the arm of the couch next to our guest. Ignoring him, Sue waited until we'd settled before starting in. "Letty, what the hell is going on? I haven't seen or heard from you in days, and now you're avoiding me."

"I haven't been avoiding you!" Therapists don't avoid. We just find things to do that take priority. "Taking on Regina's case load was a lot more complicated than I thought. I know I've been missing some meetings, but—"

"This started long before Regina died. It was hard enough getting you to do your Second Step, but every time I try to set up a time to talk about the Third, you beg off. When I tell you to call me to set something up, I never hear from you. The one time you *did* come over to my house to work on it, you got leprosy and had to leave."

"That was hives. I think it was the tuna fish salad I ate for lunch that day."

"Oh, bullshit. It wasn't the tuna fish. Stress causes hives, too. Now, I have been very patient," Sue said, pulling a saintly, beatific expression out of her retired-teacher's bag of tricks.

Unfortunately, it was true. She had been very patient—a characteristic I wouldn't normally associate with my sponsor. A thought broke through my sluggish brain. "You love me."

"*What?*"

"You must really love me or you wouldn't be so patient." I threw my arms wide. "Give me a hug."

"I'll give you a smack on the head is what I'll give you, especially if you keep trying to distract me."

Siggy jumped into her lap. Sue picked him up and deposited him on the floor.

"Look," she continued, after taking a deep breath. "You're right. I do love you. If you aren't ready to move on to Step Three, that's fine, but you can't work the Program if you don't. In fact, it's obvious that you're not even fully committed to the Second. Maybe we need to go back to that one. If you don't work the Program, then you *will* drink. And if you drink, then we say good-bye because I can't sit around and watch that."

I was used to Sue being cranky. Frankly, her bitchiness was entertaining especially since everyone knew it masked a marshmallow heart. Quiet sincerity from her was distressing. I didn't know what to say. I didn't want to be flip but everything that came to my mind was either an excuse or a joke. So, I kept my mouth shut for once.

After several minutes, she sighed. Fear bubbled up inside me, finally forcing words out.

"Are you firing me?" Sue hadn't dropped me after I'd relapsed a few months ago, but she could have.

"No, I'm not," she said. "And I'm not trying to nag at you, but I need you to know how serious I think this is. You can coast for a while, Letty. People do, all the time. But if a drunk doesn't get right with herself and her

Higher Power, she's gonna drink. You need to figure out what's stopping you from moving forward on this Step. Is it a God thing? Lots of people can't stand the thought of God, or what they think is God. We can talk about that. But you can't keep running away and, eventually, you might come to a time when you realize how badly you need that relationship. You can't always do life on your own. You're going to need someone and that someone might just be God. It makes sense to get to know him before you get to that point."

"How do I know if there even *is* a God?"

"Ask him," Sue said.

"Ask him? How?"

"Pray. If he doesn't answer, he doesn't exist."

"What if he answers?" I mumbled.

Sue smiled.

"But how do I turn my will over to something I don't even understand? I mean, I believe in God, but . . ." I trailed off, realizing I wasn't making sense.

"Okay, stop there for a minute," Sue said. "This is good."

Tears slid down my face. I told myself it was from my headache, which had grown exponentially during our conversation. Siggy abandoned his quest to irritate Sue, jumping into my lap and began inspecting my wet cheeks. His whiskers tickled.

"This is *good*? What's good about not knowing if you believe in God?"

"You believe in God. You just said you did. You just don't know if can you trust him or not."

"And what's so good about that?"

"You stopped running, Letty." She reached over and patted my leg. "That's enough for now."

I inhaled a deep, shaky breath. I felt weird—emptied,

but peaceful. I felt better. Relieved, maybe? I'd felt the same thing the first time I'd sat in an AA meeting and admitted I was an alcoholic. I stroked Siggy, listening to him purr, a warm lump in my lap.

"Feel better?" Sue asked.

I nodded.

"Good. Now tell me what the hell happened to your head."

CHAPTER FORTY SIX

After Sue had dragged the full story of my recent endeavors out of me, I had my hands full convincing her not to kill me herself. I finally pointed out it was ungodly to kill your sponsee, but she took some persuading.

The conversation was helpful, though, because it really showcased my rampant stupidity. At least one person, probably several, were dead and two attacked, and I was still running around like Nancy Drew-on-steroids, as it had so eloquently been phrased.

I was out of my league. Maybe even out of my mind.

Running to Blodgett wasn't an option. In fact, a twinge of guilt—more like a cramp, really—reminded me of just how badly I'd been neglecting my friend. Instead of facing Diana, I'd been calling the nurses' station to check on him, even when I knew they wouldn't tell me anything substantive. I needed to make amends, but I decided to hold off until I could get the rest of this settled. Maybe, by then, I'd have answers. Maybe I'd be able to tell them that his attack had nothing to do with Regina's death or the shelter. Or me.

I made myself three promises: I'd hand over my suspicions to Pete Durrant, I'd pull out of the shelter before anyone else got hurt. And *then* I'd apologize to the Blodgett's. I'd make it right.

I tumbled into bed and slept like the dead.

After sleeping so much the day before, I woke early. Way too early. I felt okay about my resolutions, but there were still too many dangling questions to feel truly comfortable. It felt like I'd been dreaming all night, but when I tried to focus on them, they floated away like spider webs on a breeze.

Durrant's call was another thing that had left me uneasy. Scared, really. The snatched charm proved, to me at least, that the attack on me was directly connected with Regina's death. Any other day this might have felt like simplistic reasoning. Achieving it with a bruised, Jell-O brain made me feel like I'd been inducted into Mensa.

Since I was doing so well, I worked on recreating the events that had left a blank spot in my memory. I found I had pretty good recall up until just after my meeting with Clotilde. Looking at my calendar had helped jog that loose.

Edna, my suicidal client, was the easiest to remember. Details about her situation kept pouring in— her navy-blue dress; the afghan she'd been working on; God bless her, the refrigerator she'd cleaned.

It was time for some music/hydro/aroma/chocolate therapy. I made a cup of rich, hot chocolate, ran a bath sprinkled with flowery bath salts, and after putting some light classical music on, settled in for a soak. I promised myself I wouldn't push. I wouldn't beat myself up. Bits and pieces of the blank areas, like confetti, started drifting back.

The red yarn. I'd told Durrant something about red yarn. A crystal clear image appeared—Joyce and the blood red yarn spilling from her fingers. I shivered.

Try as I might, I couldn't remember anything after

telling Joyce's knitting group about the study. There were still holes, but I could only hope that more of it would come back.

The image of Joyce stayed with me. I toweled off, hurrying to Regina's files again. The copy of the newsletter was underneath the stack. I flipped to the board members. Joyce Trent.

Google to the rescue, where I found another hidden history. There were a lot of hits. The first, an article from seventeen years ago, described the acquittal of Joyce Trent for the manslaughter death of her husband, Phillip.

Her case, one of the first battered women defense efforts in this area, pulled a lot of media attention. The extent of her long-term victimization shocked the community, spawning questions about women's rights and the unusual defense that was being used. Clotilde was quoted several times, and one whole article focused on Devlin House and the work done there.

After the announcement of the jury's decision to acquit, there was silence, broken only by one mention of the case at the year anniversary mark that coincided with a similar case. That woman was found guilty, I noted. Whether Joyce had wanted to be the poster child for women's rights, which I doubted, she'd practically taken a vow of silence afterward. Nowadays, she'd have been booked on twenty talk shows and have had a movie in development before the jury even deliberated.

With a start, I realized I was going to be late for the shelter's team meeting.

The side drive was full of the shelter staffs' cars, although I hadn't been around long enough to know who drove which car. I parked out on the street and entered through the back kitchen door, hoping to nab some much-needed coffee on the way through. No such luck.

Giving up on locating a source of caffeine, I moved farther into the shelter. As I got closer to the group therapy room—the only room besides the kitchen large enough to hold all of the shelter's staff—I expected to hear people talking; maybe, since it was early, to hear people shifting chairs and tables around trying to fit everyone in.

But all was quiet. Too quiet?

I opened the group room door cautiously, half afraid Lachlyn was going to spring at me like a demented jack-in-the-box—all freaky, bizarro clown face and maniacal laughter.

She was there. They all were, including several women I'd only had minimal contact with, and all so quiet that at first I feared I'd interrupted a prayer service. But the feeling emanating from the gathering was not peace. A fission of emotion seeped through the air—palpable anger, a touch of fear? *Whose?*

A half-dozen metal chairs had been added to the group circle. The staff sat frozen, utterly silent, all eyes glued on Clotilde who had pulled her chair back and away, creating a break in the circle, a sickle moon shape of women arcing around her. If she was serious about running for office, she could certainly count on a cadre of women helping her rise to power. An image flashed through my mind—female acolytes serving at the feet of their warrior priestess.

"Hi, Letty!" A hoarse faux-whisper from the corner behind me made me squeak and jump in surprise. As I flipped around, I heard the rustle of clothes as the entire congregation swiveled with me to stare at the source of the whisper.

Paul?

He sat tucked against the wall, segregated from the women and perched like a Victorian virgin—bolt upright, knees together, hands clasped in his lap—on the edge of his seat. Wide, anxious puppy eyes told me where the "touch of fear" emanated from.

"What are you doing here?" I asked.

Before he could answer, the hair on the back of my neck zinged up; Paul's gaze jumped from my face to just over my shoulder. I spun around so quickly that I gave myself a free buzz.

Clotilde stood directly behind me. Lachlyn had taken up a post at her side, apparently resuming her bodyguard persona. This didn't seem like the time to point out they were both invading my bubble.

"I see you two know each other." Clotilde said.

"Um, kind of. I mean, we have some mutual friends—"

Suspicion curled around the barely suppressed anger already marring her face. Her eyes took on that blank, inward gaze that occurs when two disparate ideas combine in our minds to make a new whole. The light bulb moment. Only it didn't make her look bright and sparkly.

"I need to talk to you two. Go wait in my office."

"Now?" I asked. I'd been gearing up all night to announce my leave-taking and this seemed anticlimactic.

"*Now.*" She spun on her heel and walked back to her chair.

"Sure. No problem." I struggled to play it off, but my face was suffused with heat and my voice shook. I'd never been sent to the principal's office, but from the dread-heavy feeling roiling loosely around my bowels, I now knew what it felt like. I struggled with the urge to protest my innocence, especially strong since I actually *was* innocent.

Lachlyn stepped back and gestured toward the door, effectively escorting us out of the room. She trailed after, apparently not trusting us to do what we were told. She was right; if she weren't between me and the door, I would have bolted.

I couldn't leave Paul, though. I doubted he could keep up and he'd be like a little, lost gazelle for the lionesses to feast on. With Lachlyn at his back, he crowded up on me, stepping on my heels three times before we reached Clotilde's office. Lachlyn, still silent, watched us take our seats, then pointedly left the door standing wide open as she left.

Surprised she wasn't going to take a sentry stance outside the door, I barely waited for her receding footsteps to reach the group room before turning to Paul.

"What the hell are you doing here?"

Despite the circumstances, a happy grin flashed out. "I'm going to intern here. Cool, huh?"

"What . . ." I stopped talking and mashed my palms against my eyeballs. I knew Paul wasn't stupid, but he was one of those common-sense deficient people who make you want to issue helmets and guardian angels at birth. "Paul, this was *not* a good idea. They're going to think that I—"

The group door banged open. Clotilde strode into her office, circling her desk like a panther on steroids, and slammed an armful of folders and paperwork down. The pile teetered precariously, then slid sideways knocking a recycled play dough cup full of pens over the side with a clatter.

Paul stopped grinning.

CHAPTER FORTY SEVEN

Clotilde glared at us over the desktop. Turning to Paul, she said, "Spell your name."

He paled, mouth agape as though coming face-to-face with his worst show-up-naked-to-class-and-take-a-pop-quiz nightmare. "My name?" he said. It took longer than two syllables normally would because a stutter stretched it to twelve.

Clotilde sat motionless, glaring with flat, unblinking steadiness.

Eventually he managed to connect a series of letters that sounded like P-p-p-p-pee, a-a-ay, yu-yu-yu-l. He waited as though hoping that, as in A.A., first names would suffice.

It didn't. Clotilde maintained her dead-eye stare and Paul embarked on his last name. It was a long name, too, or seemed like it. Sweat beaded across his forehead, then trickled in salty, erratic paths down his face. Because of A.A.'s first-name-only policy, I couldn't even help him, making my stomach cramp with a bilious mix of fear and frustrated enabling tendencies. Eventually, utilizing Miss Marple-like decoding skills (which involved dropping a letter if he repeated it multiple times,) I came up with "Paul LaFontaigne."

I was so relieved, I almost clapped when he finished. Paul slumped back in his chair and we beamed at each other.

Clotilde remained unimpressed. She was a hard-hearted little cookie. If anything, she looked even more malevolent.

"Paul LaFontaigne," she said in a flat, monotone.

Paul nodded.

She repeated it, quicker this time, and that's when I understood.

"You thought he was a girl," I said. "Paula Fontaigne. That's why you accepted him as an intern."

"I didn't accept him. Astrid did. Over the phone, I might add, and as a favor to Kaylee Schroeder at the college. They're sending the paperwork over today. Nobody else wanted him."

Paul gulped. He bowed his head, staring at the cheap carpeting. I watched a red stain creep up the back of his thin neck.

Now I was pissed.

"A favor to the college? Really? Because I doubt you had a lot of interns lining up to get in here. In fact, the board said you didn't have any. What's the matter, Clotilde? Are people hearing what it's like to work here? It can't be fun. The pay sucks, the building is decrepit and falling down around your ears, you've got practically no funds, and frankly, the staff are a bunch of mean, bitter zealots who have lost sight of what it means to help others."

"Lost sight?" she hissed. A teensy arc of spittle made me grateful for the desk between us. "Just what is it you think we do here? We're here, every day, day in, day out. *Every* day!

These women come to us because they know that we'll—"

"Yeah, yeah, I get it. Warrior women on a mission. I've heard all that. And you *do* help. I never said you didn't. I said you've lost sight of what it *means* to help others. You and your minions have gotten so caught up in making this a war that you've turned the rest of the world into an enemy."

We'd locked eyes and were both leaning forward as though ready to launch ourselves across the desk at each other. She gripped the arms of her chair so hard I expected her fingernails—short and stubby as they were—to snap off.

"You'll never understand what we're doing here and you never will. But if you think you're going to stack the deck with all your friends, you are sadly mistaken. I will not tolerate it. You will *never* be—"

"It's just for a semester," a tiny voice next to me said.

Startled, we broke the stare-off and turned toward it.

Paul. I'd forgotten about him. I realized I'd gone too far, disclosed too much. Lost control. Maybe Clotilde thought so, too, because just then we seemed to share a disturbing moment of synchrony as each of us sat back, took two cleansing breaths, and willed our muscles to relax. Therapists are so predictable.

"If you think we're so misguided, why are you here?" Clotilde finally asked. Control had descended like a shroud, enveloping her features with a veil of inscrutability.

A multitude of answers flooded my brain. Exhausted, I reverted to an AA basic: K.I.S.S.— keep it simple, stupid. "Because Regina needed me to be."

"Then why are you still here?"

"Because I'm not done." Technically, I *was* done with the original task, but Regina still needed me. "And despite what you may think, Paul has nothing to do with this."

Silence descended. Clotilde's jaw muscles pulsed and

she shifted her eyes away, thinking. After a few
moments, she said, "I will not have the women upset by
his presence." She refused to look at Paul. "Since you've
forced yourself upon us, you can be his internship
supervisor. If you screw it up, he flunks. He can help you
with the efficacy study paperwork, and he can observe
the group counseling sessions provided he says nothing,
sits in the back, and only if either you or Lachlyn are in
attendance. If I get any complaint, even one, he's out. Do
you understand?"

"Yes," I said.

And she was out the door.

CHAPTER FORTY EIGHT

A s soon as I was sure she was gone, I scurried around her desk and started yanking open the drawers.

Paul was horror-struck. "Letty, should you be doing that?"

"It's okay, Paul. I'm just looking for a file I'm supposed to have."

I glanced up. His face was a strange conglomeration of bewilderment and despondency. "Letty, I can't just sit there in groups. I won't pass my internship if I can't say anything. I'm not supposed to just observe. Plus, I'll look stupid."

"I know, Paul. Listen, don't worry about it. I'll think of something. I promise." The drawer that Clotilde had pulled Karissa's file from was locked. I jiggled it in frustration.

Paul sniffed. As soon as he saw me looking at him, he ducked his head, but not before I saw the tears welling up in his eyes. Unexpectedly, he dropped to his knees and started crawling around on the floor.

"Paul, what the hell are you doing?"

"She dropped her pens."

"Are you kidding me? You're picking up her pens?"

He set the cup on the desk and stuffed a handful of pens and pencils inside. "Good thing, too. She dropped her keys." He plunked them on top of the pile of folders that Clotilde had brought in.

Halleluiah.

My hands were shaking so bad it took three tries before I found the right key.

"Letty, I don't think you should be doing this."

"Keep watch," I said.

"What?"

Good lord, hadn't he ever played cops-n-robbers? I shooed my hand at him, pointing to the open door. "Go watch out for people." I started pawing through the drawer, unearthing legal pads and stationery and the various office flotsam that people end up stuffing in a drawer instead of filing it.

Or things they want hidden.

I pulled a file out—Karissa Dillard's—not the one I had, but a duplicate. Or rather—the original. The door to the group room opened and a mishmash of women's voices floated down the hall to us.

Paul squeaked. His version of "hssst!" I supposed. He had the door cracked an inch or so and was peeking out from it. Because a lone eyeball staring out at the hall from Clotilde's office wouldn't be the least bit suspicious, would it?

In three strides I was at his side, the file clutched in my sweaty little hands.

"You can't take that," he said. His face was ashen and he was shaking so bad I thought he would fall down.

"I know I can't," I said. "I don't have anywhere to put it. That's why you're taking it."

I grabbed his belt, spun him around, and stuffed the folder down the back of his pants. His suit jacket—worn to impress his internship supervisor, I was sure—covered the bulge well enough that I was sure we could get out the door.

"I c-c-c-c—"

"Yes, you can, Paul. Otherwise they're going to find you with a confidential file stuck down your shorts, you'll flunk your internship, never graduate, and end up on skid row talking to dumpster rats. Just follow me and stop sweating so much."

And I whisked his poor, tremulous self right out the back door and straight out to our cars.

We fled to a nearby Mickey D's and grabbed a booth back in the children's playland section—a cross between an aquarium and a hamster trail composed of red and blue tunnels and slides. Privacy was practically guaranteed given the fact that no one could hear anything over the shrill shrieks of an assortment of excited toddlers turned loose. Sanity was not so assured.

Paul hadn't quite recovered from our "adventure," as I was choosing to call it. He'd been hiking back and forth to the bathroom every five minutes, growing paler with each trip. We each reacted to stress in our own ways—I had both hands wrapped around a bucketful of peppermint mocha coffee with extra whip cream, and Paul had a small diet Sprite. We were both shaking so hard that our drinks had ripple effects going on, suggesting that either Wisconsin was experiencing a slight earthquake or Paul and I were experiencing stereo-palsy.

Paul had used the first of his emergency bathroom trips to remove the file, bringing it back to me with a reproachful look plastered on his face. My head throbbed. Avoiding his eyes, I dug through my purse looking for Tylenol.

"We shouldn't have done that," he said.

"You mean, *I* shouldn't have done that, Paul. I didn't

give you much choice in the matter." I finally met his eyes. "I'm sorry. I really am."

He didn't argue and he didn't look any happier with my admission. I was so used to Paul's abject adoration that I almost felt a pang at its loss. It looked like I was going to have to tell him everything.

He knew about Regina's "accident" and my suspicions that files had been tampered with, but I went back and told him everything I suspected.

Paul darted to the bathroom twice more during my little recitation. Apparently the news that Regina had been murdered and I'd been attacked the night before last wasn't soothing his intestinal discomfort. But at least he'd stopped looking at me as though he'd caught me shoving bamboo shoots up Mother Teresa's fingernails.

"So what do you think is in here?" he asked, tapping Karissa's file.

"Good question." I pulled it over and began paging through it. I'd have to compare it page by page to the file I already had at home, but I'd been over the information in that one so many times I was sure I'd catch any obvious discrepancies.

And, of course, there were. Two, in fact. The first was the discovery of the original contact information form—the one I'd previously discovered had been copied. When Clotilde or whomever duplicated the file, she must have accidentally switched the two. The second discrepancy was more interesting.

A discharge summary.

CHAPTER FORTY NINE

I'd assumed the absence of the discharge form from the file I'd reviewed at the shelter was due, in part, to Karissa's taking off the morning Regina's body was discovered. It would be an easy thing to overlook since the therapist, Regina, obviously wasn't available to complete it. It was one of the things I had planned to address in my review.

But one *had* been filled out—by Lachlyn, no less, who certainly should have noticed that it was missing when she'd been supervising my review. There was no question in my mind now that she'd known about the duplicate file.

I skimmed the page, then went back and re-read it more carefully. Although Karissa had agreed to meet with Lachlyn before leaving, she refused to let her talk to the kids. Lachlyn had noted "permission withheld" and underlined it twice. Irritated, perhaps?

The information was sparse, but the sight of a forwarding address made my heart pound briefly. Briefly, because directly underneath a different hand had scribbled 'nonexistent' in blue ink. So much for that.

Apparently someone *had* tried to follow up . . . and failed. Had Karissa given a false address on purpose? Actually, remembering her cantankerous personality, I could see her withholding the information just on general principles. She didn't strike me as someone who tolerated others messing in her business. Grandma Crazy-Pants would certainly agree with that.

That got me wondering again about where the two had run off to and why? Who had been out to the trailer that Saturday and subsequently scared off both Karissa and her feisty grandma? A tall, professional woman with short hair, Tallie had said.

I'd been assuming it was Lachlyn. But what about Clotilde? The two could be sisters. Astrid, too, as far as that went. Hell, maybe it was Bob in drag.

I needed to find Karissa.

I turned my attention back to Paul. He hadn't made a bathroom run in the last ten minutes and his shaking had calmed. He looked better.

Color flooded his face when he saw me studying him. "Find anything?" he asked, shifting uncomfortably in his seat.

"Maybe. A discharge summary that didn't exist in the file I saw, for one thing. Listen, Paul, this isn't going to work. You need to get transferred to a new internship. This shelter, it's not a good place. It would be wrong for you even if . . . Well, even if there wasn't some crazy person running around killing people."

"People? You mean, more than one? More than just Regina?" Whatever color he'd managed to regain evaporated. This could not be good for his blood pressure.

"Anything's possible," I said. "Regina might have been killed for, well, personal reasons, for lack of a better term. Like if she pissed somebody off all on her own, which she was certainly capable of doing. But something weird is going on with the shelter's files. Why bother duplicating this one? That's illegal, for one thing, so why do it if not to keep me or others from seeing it? And why did Regina snatch the others? What was she looking for?"

Paul tapped the file between us. "If it's just the discharge summary, why bother creating a whole 'nother file? Why not just keep that one page out?"

"You're right. I haven't looked at the other forms. I'll have to do a line by line comparison for that, but it makes sense that there's something hinky about them as well." I sighed.

"So, let me get this straight. You think Regina was killed because she knew something. Something about other people getting killed. And those files she took, those are the people you think were killed?"

"I looked them up on the Internet. They're all dead. Of course, they all returned to their abusers, but the coincidence of Regina having those particular files and all the women being dead has to mean something."

"That's something I don't get. Why would anyone go back to someone who hurts them? That's crazy."

Eyebrows raised, I gave him my professionals-don't-use-the-word-crazy look and then said, "It's a lot more complicated than that, Paul. Sometimes a woman isn't as weak as we're stereotyping her. Sometimes she's warm, loving, and just wants so badly to change her guy. It's her very strength and compassion that snares her in the abusive relationship. Sometimes it's about money—not about wanting more, but about not having enough. One of the first things a dominant personality is going to do is tie up the money, keep the victim dependent. It's all fine and dandy to say 'Well, money doesn't matter. If it were me, I'd just pack up and go,' but the truth is money has to be considered.

"Has the woman been allowed to have a job?" I continued. "A credit card? Access to the marital accounts? Did she finish school, get a degree? What will she have to give up? A house? The car that's in *his* name? What kind of life will she be dragging the kids into? Will he come after them? Are they going to have to switch schools or towns or states to get away from him? And will the courts even allow her to take them that far anyway? There are tons of considerations. Now, I'm not saying she should stay with him, but nothing is black and white in this job, Paul. Nothing."

His forehead furrowed, and I could tell he was trying to take it in. "You would think getting away would just be simple, survival instincts, but I see what you're saying. If I was the one trying to help that would make me crazy. I bet the burnout rate is pretty high in this field, huh? I guess that's one reason everyone is so cranky at the shelter, huh?"

No denying that. The "why doesn't she just leave him" question is one that rankles everybody faced with domestic abuse. Family and friends aware of the situation often get so frustrated with the victim's supposed inaction that they heap their own kind of abuse—shame—which only makes a bad situation worse. Even experienced professionals fall into the trap, especially, as Paul said, when burnout clouds the issue. It can be so frustrating, make you feel so helpless, that it becomes easy to strike out at the very person you want to help.

An idea stirred in the back of my brain.

Paul sucked the last of his pop from his cup, then burped quietly. "Excuse me."

I sighed again. "Are you going to transfer your internship?"

"I can't. This was the only thing I could get, and it's not even a paying job. You would think in this economy that agencies would want free labor, but they don't. All the ones I've been to say they don't have anyone who could supervise me."

I nodded. Times were tight and jobs had dried up everywhere. I also remembered something Clotilde had said. "You tried to get in at the shelter, though," I pointed out. "Clotilde said Astrid agreed as a favor to Kaylee Somebody. So, be honest, you pushed for this. Can't you go back to Kaylee or whoever and get reassigned?"

He shook his head miserably. "I'll flunk out. I have to have this internship or I don't graduate. That's why I can't just sit there and not say anything. How is that going to teach me anything? I can't learn that way."

"Okay, look. I need you to at least try to transfer. I can't watch you and deal with all this at the same time. It's too dangerous. They obviously think you're some kind of plant and that we're in this together."

He smiled a little at the "in this together" part. Until I reminded him that I'd been attacked as recently as two nights ago.

We compromised. I got him to agree to talk to his internship advisor about a transfer. Since neither of us were confident that would happen, I reluctantly agreed to put together a tentative schedule for supervision.

My headache had escalated to near-lethal levels. His involvement had complicated things exponentially, and we'd both be lucky to get out of this in one piece. As he got up to leave, I asked one more time, "Paul, why did you do this? What were you thinking?"

He looked at me, all eyes and blushing cheeks. "I was thinking about you."

It was all I could do not to thunk my traumatized head on the sticky table top.

CHAPTER FIFTY

When I got home, I sat down and compared the two files. In what I assumed was the original file, the progress notes documenting each session, had been handwritten. I recognized Regina's spiky, aggressive scrawl. The second set appeared to be created from a computer template, Regina's signatures on the bottom presumably forged. I held the papers side by side to compare. They all looked the same. I crossed handwriting analyst off my list of possible career choices.

The wording in both sets of notes matched, except for portions I discovered had been excised from the file I'd been given. Just a few sentences from each progress note, but enough to alter the meaning considerably.

The missing sections all had to do with Karissa's relationship with Mitch and her reports of his own efforts at change. Apparently her husband was involved in therapy as well as attending anger management classes. According to Regina, Karissa and Mitch were working toward reconciliation. If I had been expecting a negative bias from her to the idea of reconciliation I would have been wrong. Regina's statements were matter-of-fact, and the goals she and Karissa created— also absent from the fake file—were geared to facilitate a reunification.

So, Karissa wanted to return to her abuser and whoever doctored the file didn't want me to know that.

Why, and also, obviously, who?

I moved to the computer and, for lack of any better idea, started plugging their names into the search engine. Astrid had a Facebook page, but it was set to privacy settings and I didn't think she'd approve my friend request.

Clotilde's name had dozens of hits. All that fundraising and speechifying. She was definitely the big winner. In fact, one of her speeches had been put up on YouTube last June. Technology amazed me.

I clicked the play arrow and sat back to watch. It was a basic give-us-money-we-save-lives pitch to an organization I'd never heard of. Judging by the glittery jewelry and stylish audience, I wasn't rich enough. I studied Clotilde's face. Though her face had a high-cheekboned, graveness that suited her, she wasn't pretty. She hadn't the warrior flare of Lachlyn nor the warmth of Astrid, but she definitely had style.

Much of her speech had to do with statistics, national and local. She covered the history of the shelter. I caught a glimpse of Beth Collier in the crowd, sitting at a table with a distinguished-looking man. She wore a diamond bracelet that held me enthralled for several moments. I didn't know any rich drunks.

Then my attention swept back to Clotilde. She was talking about Cherly Bailey. About her life and death, the odds and obstacles she faced. About the need for services and programs to prevent just such occurrences.

Clotilde's plea was heartfelt and sincere. Her life had been poured out in efforts to prevent this kind of tragedy, and she was reaching out, asking for help, demanding a response.

I could almost see the people reaching for their checkbooks. I would have. Apparently, victims had uses even in death.

Something flickered across my brain again. Something Paul had said at the restaurant. I tried to remember what we had been talking about, but couldn't follow the spider web-thin trail back to its inception. I hated when that happened.

I didn't have Paul's number, but I took a chance and called the HP & Me club. An appropriately anonymous voice picked up, then at my request, hollered, "Hey, Paul. Some chick wants to talk to you." The "chick" part was his own idea.

I could almost feel waves of joy emanating from the phone as Paul came on the line. He had publically received a phone call from a woman—and it was me. He was a happy man.

Eventually I was able to control his effervescence and asked if he could remember exactly what he had said when we were talking about why women went back to their abusers.

This produced a long, painful silence, punctuated by several consecutive "ums."

"Was it about survival instinct?" he asked. "I said something about that. Remember?" I could tell from the plaintive quality in his voice that all his raw, people-pleasing needs were hanging on my answer.

"Not exactly, but that's what we were talking about. So, it was around that time. Something about . . . Argh! I don't know. I just can't seem to remember, but I think it's important."

"Well, you're still recovering from your concussion. Maybe it'll come to you if you stop trying so hard."

Good advice, but as usual I wasn't able to take it. I fretted the rest of the evening, trying to sneak up on the memory by returning periodically to Karissa's goals and staring at them until my eyes watered.

I was *not* crying.

Despite another restless night, I woke up Friday morning feeling physically a little better, but just as frustrated and emotionally lost as I had the night before. I lay in bed, trying to soak up comfort from the warm huddle of blankets that I'd twisted myself into. When it started to feel more like a straight jacket and less like a womb, I got up.

In the shower, I decided it was time to restore order in my life, starting with my legs. I'd either have to shave or braid and, frankly, I didn't think my legs could pull off the Bo Derek look. It was while I was balanced precariously on one leg and thrusting its lathered mate straight out to avoid the shower spray that I heard Paul's voice.

"You'd think getting away would just be a simple survival instinct. If I was the one trying to help that would make me crazy."

Thankfully it wasn't his literal voice or I would have sliced my knee cap off. As it was, a thin trickle of blood ran down the drain.

Seconds later, still damp and sporting one smooth and one bristly appendage, I ran out the front door.

The trailer in Lot 7 looked as dilapidated and deserted as it had the last time I'd been here. A not-so-gently used FOR RENT sign had been taped up in the window with "see Park Manager" penciled underneath. So that's what I did.

Whatever misgivings I'd left her with, Tallie had reverted to her sunny disposition. Her hair had also morphed into an unnatural, but strangely suitable buttercup yellow. Not blond, mind you. *Yellow*. Staring into her bright black eyes and listening to her chirpy greeting, I had the strangest impression that I'd caught her midway through a canary-to-human shape-shifting spell.

"Sorry to bother you again," I said. "I was hoping to find that Bernie and Karissa had returned. Have you heard from them?"

"No, I sure haven't. Bernie said she'd get back in touch and I really thought she would, even if she just wanted her deposit back. Although with the shape they left the trailer in, maybe she knew better." She shook her head, making that teacherly "tsk" sound. "I was all ready to get in there and at least clean out the trash and the fridge, but my sister up in Bloomer broke her hip. I had to run up there for a couple of days, poor thing. I guess I'll have to use some of the deposit to hire a cleaning service, although the park owner doesn't like when we have to do that."

I already knew what I was going to ask her, but I had a few more questions first. "You said they used the Wrangler to move. Did they make a few trips to get everything or just the one?"

"No, I know for a fact they left most of their stuff. All I saw them taking out was a couple of suitcases, the baby's diaper bag, and some garbage bags. That trailer is rented furnished, but it's just the basics. Thing is, though, when the fridge died about five months ago, Bernie bought herself one. Said she wanted an ice maker. She got a nice one, too. I can't imagine her leaving that behind. She really loved that ice maker."

Tallie's wistful tone left me wondering if she'd been tempted by the alluring ice maker herself. As one who lived with ice trays and tap water, I could relate.

"I'm going to have to decide pretty quick though," she continued. "All I got from Bernie was her last month's rent. She was usually behind a few weeks, but never too bad. Once Karissa moved in, they kept it up pretty current. She must have been helping out. I don't suppose you know anybody interested in a nice trailer?"

"Nice" was a highly subjective term, and not my first choice as an adjective for the domicile on Lot 7, but now was not the time to quibble.

"How much are you asking?"

"Three-fifty a month, includes utilities. First and last month down. No smoking, no pets, no kids." Her eyes brightened in "Could it be?" hopefulness.

No. It could not. However . . .

"I'll keep it in mind if I hear of anybody looking for a place," I said. "But listen, Tallie, how about if I helped with the cleaning?"

Her head tilted. "Really? How much?"

"How much?"

"How much do you charge?"

"Uh, I don't know really. I just . . ." *Just wanted to paw through Karissa's belongings and didn't want to get charged with trespassing?* "Just wanted to help. I feel bad that they took off so suddenly. It was almost as if something frightened them off, wasn't it?"

Tallie's face clouded. "I can't say I haven't wondered about that. It's just that them being scared away seems so overdramatic. Usually when people take off, it's a money thing."

"Maybe, but you said they were doing better with the bills."

She sighed. "Yeah, they were. If it was just money, I think Bernie would have come back for her stuff. Especially the deposit and that fridge. It just doesn't make sense."

We stood silent for a moment as we pondered the mystery of the abandoned fridge. Tallie finally shook herself.

"Well, this isn't getting that trailer cleaned. I've been dreading it, but if you want to take it on, that works for me. How about this: I'll provide the cleaning supplies and pay a hundred bucks a day. Don't go over three days though. What do you think?"

"Three hundred bucks?" I turned to look at the trailer. With all that had happened, I'd been off work quite a bit. I could use the money, plus this was open season on snooping.

How bad could it be?

CHAPTER FIFTY ONE

Bad, of course. Really bad. I wouldn't say Bernie was a hoarder, but if reality TV ever started a show called "Extreme Collectors of Creepy Shit," Bernie could audition. She was definitely in that pre-hoarder zone where standing amid the clutter induced an immediate case of claustrophobia. Not to mention, pediophobia.

That's fancy for "freaked out by dolls." And there were dolls *everywhere*. Hundreds of them sitting on shelves and tables, the couch and the TV and the floor. Every one of them looking at me with blank, shiny plastic eyes, propped upright in frilly dresses and frozen poses.

The whole place stunk, too: cigarette funk, dust, old garbage. The stagnant air of a home that's been shut up tight. The trailer itself wasn't horribly filthy—at least, the parts I could see—but the odor, trapped in the doll clothes and hair, permeated the room.

I paused a moment when I realized for the first time, that cigarettes stunk. I'd always known that, theoretically anyway, but for once the smell of them didn't tempt me. Progress.

Tallie had handed over the keys, along with a bucket full of generic cleaning supplies, a new pair of bright purple latex gloves, and four boxes of heavy duty trash bags. I shuffled the bucket and discovered a fifth box.

Tallie's strategy was clear: throw everything out and scrub down the rest. Not a bad plan.

I went from room to room turning on lights and trying to wrestle open the windows. I'd thought that the living room doll collection was overwhelming, but I hadn't calculated on them appearing everywhere. The second bedroom had been completely given over to them, although any attempt at organized display was lost. Plastic humanoids covered every surface, piles and piles of them. Hillocks rose where presumably the bed and dresser sat. I couldn't get to the window so I just shut the door on them.

The bathroom was the one room that was relatively free of them. There were a few, but I could see surfaces. Thankfully, the toilet only had four balanced precariously on the tank. Still, I'd hate to have eight eyes staring over my shoulder as I peed.

Two prescription bottles sat on the teensy ledge over the sink. Half full, made out to Karissa Dillard: Abilify and Zoloft. I set them back. I had to stand in the tub to get to the window, but it was stuck fast. I found myself looking straight across into the neighbors' kitchen.

They were close. Like what-kind-of-toothpaste-and-are-you-getting-enough-fiber-in-your-diet? close. Bernie may not have had much to do with her neighbors, but that didn't mean they didn't know everything that was going on in her life.

Might be a good time to see if anyone was home. It was only midmorning but retired or the unemployed—and let's face it, this *was* a trailer park—might be available. Besides, I could let the trailer air out and get away from the doll asylum.

Nobody answered at the first trailer, but I heard shuffling sounds after my knock on the next one over.

The door opened to a tall, grizzled old-timer wearing pale gray sweatpants and a two-sizes-too-small pink T-shirt with a picture of a leaping musky on the front. His fish-white belly drooped six inches lower than the hem, peeking out like a fleshy orb from underneath. I tried not to look.

I *really* didn't want to look.

"Whatever you're selling, I ain't buying. Unless it's Girl Scout cookies. I like them coconut ones."

"Do I look like a Girl Scout?"

"Maybe if we put you in pigtails and a little, green skirt." He leered. "I like cookies."

"Ew. I don't think so."

"Then, what do you want?"

The last thirty seconds of my life back?

"I'm looking for Bernie and her granddaughter, Karissa. Lot 7?" I pointed. Since it was only two doors down, it shouldn't have taken as long as it did for him to focus. "Have you seen them?"

"They left. You a bill collector?"

"No. Do you know where they went?"

"No. Got any cookies?"

"No."

He shut the door.

I trudged across the pitted concrete drive to the trailer directly across from the cookie fetishist. After knocking twice, a plump grandmotherly-type answered. The escaping aroma of baked deliciousness almost brought me to my knees. She was coated wrist-to-elbow in flour dust and wore a burgundy apron trimmed in white ruffles that looked remarkably clean given her flour-sleeved status.

"Yes?" she asked. Her smile deepened a set of dimples, making her look like Pillsbury's matriarch. If I poked her tummy, I bet she'd giggle.

I explained my purpose, a conversation made difficult because of the excessive drool that kept pooling in my mouth every time I caught of whiff from the kitchen. Louise—we'd done full introductions, including inquiries (hers) into possible relatives from the area I'd grown up in—didn't know anything about Bernie or Karissa, although she said Mikey spent some afternoons over at her house. I couldn't blame him. I wanted her as my adopted grandma, too. Before I left, she trotted back to the kitchen and brought me back three cookies— chocolate chip, warm, and melty.

Life was good again.

Still licking chocolate off my fingertips, I walked to the next trailer. The door popped open before I could knock, disclosing a fifty-something woman in a neck brace glaring at me. She needed a hair dye spruce-up since it was apparent that it had been several months since her last dye job. A three-inch strip of grey roots bifurcated her head. Again, it was hard not to stare.

"Yeah?" Smoker's rasp with much attitude.

Fifteen seconds into my "looking for Bernie" spiel, she slammed the door. Maybe she had an emergency appointment with the hair dresser. Wouldn't want to miss that.

The next two trailers were empty or, at least, their homeowners were nonresponsive. At work, maybe . . . or the liquor store. At the next place, I almost twisted my ankle on a discarded beer can buried in the shin-high scrub grass along the edge of the lawn. Nearly a dozen more lay close by. I sighed. At least I had been a tidy drunk.

The beer drinker's trailer sat directly across from Bernie's, theoretically giving its resident a clear view of her home. The trailer itself was dilapidated, the skirting missing in spots giving the exterior a gap-toothed appearance. Not the happy, in-search-of-tooth-fairy look of a young child either. More like the smashed out spaces of a has-been boxer.

I tapped on the door. A has-been boxer type in a filthy, stained, tank T-shirt answered. He stood in the doorway, weaving unsteadily, gripping the frame to keep himself from falling on his face. Instead of "hello," he greeted me with a long, odorous belch. The belch, by itself, was fairly impressive, demonstrating a range and variety of tone found in most operettas.

It really stunk though. My guess was a beer and taco breakfast with undertones of lost-my-toothbrush-ages-ago grunge.

"My lucky day," he said. Actually he said, "Mmm lickee duh," but I speak fluent drunk. His bleary eyes crawled over my body. All of a sudden I found myself nostalgic for the charming innocence of the cookie creep.

"I'm looking for Bernie and Karissa," I persevered, although frankly I don't know why. "They were renting Lo—"

"Come on in, baby!" He threw the door open. Unfortunately for him, it ricocheted off the wall and slammed into his shoulder. He stumbled sideways, his face folding into a snarl of rage. "Grrr."

"Did you just growl?"

"Grr . . . ahrooooo!" He threw his head back in full werewolf howl.

Time to split.

CHAPTER FIFTY TWO

The House O' Eyes had aired out a bit, but I knew the stench would reappear as soon as I shut the windows. Still, with a choice between stink and howling werewolves, I decided to take the sensible route for once.

They were staring at me again.

I shuddered. *How could anyone live like this?*

First order of business: immediate doll removal. I'd never be able to look for clues to Karissa's whereabouts with all those eyes. I yanked out a garbage bag and snapped it open. Grabbing armfuls, I set to. The more I scooped, the more they seemed to multiply. Doll mitosis. I started sweating and it wasn't from exertion.

Dust coated my skin. Ten minutes into the job and I already felt grungy and in desperate need of a bath. I'd probably end up trashing my jeans and T-shirt, too, which was a shame because the latter was from my favorite band, Bon Iver. For a second I thought about heading out to my car to get my iPod.

A loud bam-bam-bam on the window made me shriek, clutching the lumpy bag of dolls to my chest. A fleshy, misshapen blob slid along the lower pane.

I shrieked again. An eye—yet another one—peered in, unfocused but searching. It found me. The blob grinned and turned back into a face as it pulled away from the glass.

Wolfman.

I pulled my cell phone from my pocket, dropped it, picked it up and dialed 9-1-1. My thumb hovered over the Send button.

Wolfman laughed, then stumbled back two feet so I could get the full visual effect as he grabbed at his crotch and rubbed. Thankfully, as drunk as he was, his aim was off and he ended up fondling his belly. But I knew what he meant.

Adrenaline surged through my veins, leaving a tinny taste in my mouth. I pressed Send. "*I called the cops!* Oh God, oh God. *They're on their way!*"

Undeterred, he came back to the window, smooshing his nose and mouth into two flat circles on the glass. Then he licked a two-inch wide streak from one side to the other with a tongue as long and dirty as Keith Richards's.

I gagged. Those were *not* clean windows.

He moved to the door, jiggled the knob. I'd locked it. Once more at the window, he fumbled with the sash, pulling. *Had I locked them?* They didn't budge. Glaring in at me, he banged the pane with the flat of his hand. I thought the cheap glass would break, but it held. He stood, pondering the situation, then must have decided to heed some inner impulse from his soused brain. Staggering away, he wove a crooked line back to his trailer.

I stumbled to the window, charting his progress, making sure he left. I felt dizzy and clutched at the frame to steady my shaking legs. It shifted. Staring down in horror, I lifted. With just the slightest effort, it slid up. It certainly wasn't locked.

As my heart slowed, I realized that in all the excitement I'd neglected to actually talk to the police. I pictured them trying to triangulate my position from my cell phone, satellites connecting in space, all to ensure my safety. *Except why weren't they here yet?* By now, I should have been hearing sirens.

That's when I finally noticed how light my phone felt. The battery had ejected itself when I'd dropped the phone. The only help that could possibly have intervened in any way was my Higher Power, whom I had been steadfastly avoiding for the past few weeks.

Maybe Sue had a point.

Not wanting to test the Big Guy any more, I gathered up my purse and the traitorous battery and scurried out to my car. I was still shaking too hard to trust my driving, so I pulled over three blocks down to pull myself together.

I decided to give Wolfman time to sober up. If I came back in a couple of hours, he'd either be sleeping it off or too drunk to catch me. But I wasn't willing—or stupid enough—to come back alone. Like a homing pigeon, I found myself driving to the HP & Me club. Maybe someone there would be willing to give me a hand.

Sue was my first choice. I'd have to admit that after this incident I was slightly more inclined to view God in a more favorable light. I was fairly certain that if Wolfman tried any more breaking and entering or, God forbid, more licking, Sue would cut his tongue out with a meat cleaver and eat it on a biscuit. I'd bring popcorn to that show except it would also produce a lot of blood, which I'd have to clean up.

It didn't matter any way. She wasn't home or at the club or answering her cell. Neither did the next three people I tried. The club was strangely deserted, not even an old geezer trying to hunt up a game of Smear.

There was only one other person whose number I had and who I knew would be willing to drop everything and come to my aid. Well, two maybe, but I wasn't calling Marshall.

I had no illusions about Paul's ability to keep me safe, but at least he could be a witness for the prosecution after they dug my body out of the landfill.

He was happy to help.

CHAPTER FIFTY THREE

When I explained how I'd taken the cleaning job in order to look for clues to Karissa's whereabouts, I thought Paul was going to burst in excitement at his promotion to official sidekick. I made him drive. By the time he made it to the club an hour had passed, not as much time as I'd originally wanted to let pass by, but I figured if we came in a different car, maybe Wolfman wouldn't associate it with me and come a-courtin'.

Of course, Paul's enthusiasm dropped like a rock when I told him about Wolfman. I waited until we were pulling into the trailer park so he didn't have a whole lot of time to back out. As soon as we pulled into the "parking spot" for Lot 7—an area of dead grass in front of the rickety wooden porch—I jumped out of the car, up the steps and into the trailer. Paul's choice was to follow me or sit by himself in the car so the Wolfman could drag him off into the bushes and eat him in leisure.

The dolls stopped him cold. I couldn't blame him. I'd felt the onslaught of eyeballs as soon as I'd cleared the threshold, but I pretended to be calmer than I felt. I grabbed the trash bag that I'd been filling and got back to work. Paul stood on the cracked linoleum in front of the door, looking bewildered and twitchy.

"Come on, Paul. Let's get rid of these dolls and then we can look for something that will tell us where Karissa is."

The thought of looking for clues perked him up enough to join me in my doll eradication exercise. After nearly an hour, we had cleared the living room and master bedroom of the little beasts and had gathered the remaining stragglers from the kitchen and bathroom as well. It took three times as long as it should have, because we kept glancing out windows and jumping at strange sounds.

We hadn't touched the spare bedroom, and I decided to skip it for today. With the mounds of dolls covering every surface, it didn't look like Karissa and her sons could have been using it during their stay anyway. We'd uncovered several bed pillows and an old quilt by the living room couch and assorted kids' clothes on the floor in the main bedroom, so if I had to guess I'd say that Bernie had given over her room to Karissa and the children and taken up residence on the couch.

I also found an ashtray with some stray pot seeds and stems and a teensy nubbin of a roach. Not even enough to be tempted. It was next to the couch, but it could have belonged to either woman. We also unearthed a folder of worksheets on shapes and the alphabet, a Spider-Man lunchbox with moldy PB & J crusts in a crumpled baggie, and a pair of khaki green, no-name brand tennis shoes inside of a navy blue back pack. Mikey was old enough for pre-K or a Head Start program.

"Letty, what am I supposed to be looking for?" Paul asked. Part of me wanted to put him to work cleaning out the fridge, but he looked so eager to start clue-hunting that I couldn't ask.

"How about an address book or mail or old phone bills?"

The look he gave me was pure admiration. I didn't have the heart to tell him my methods were compiled from Kinsey Milhone books and old episodes of "Monk." This time, I didn't have to worry about breaking a password code on any computer, because there wasn't one. There wasn't even a desk, but Paul eventually found stacks of old bills and other household paperwork stuffed into an end table next to the couch. I told him to focus on the top of the stack, figuring the deeper layers would hold less potential for connection to the recent events. Eventually, however, we might require a more careful search.

The living room wasn't big enough for the two of us to work without bumping into each other, so I grabbed the trash bags and girded my loins for the fridge clean-up. Actually, I just pulled on the Barney-purple gloves, but it felt like girding.

Tallie was right. It *was* a nice fridge. Nicest thing in the trailer, actually. Nicer *than* the trailer. Luckily for me, the Stanhope-Dillard household was either not interested in perishable goods like milk or fruit, or had decided to take such items with them. For the kids' sakes, I hoped it was the latter.

The food stuffs leaned heavily toward condiments and canned drinks, not excluding four Bud Lites and a pitcher of grape Kool-Aid. One container held potato salad—nasty, but not as bad as milk would have been. It really hadn't been long enough for the lunch meats to go bad. Besides, they probably had enough preservatives to last until the next Ice Age.

"Hey, Letty, is this something?" Paul was holding up a piece of paper.

"What is it?"

"A restraining order. For some guy named Mitch

Dillard."

"That's Karissa's husband," I said. "Lemme see."

Paul trotted over, excited by his find. "You hold it." I held my gloved hands up like a surgeon. "I don't want to get rancid potato salad on our first clue."

A juicy clue at that.

It was a temporary restraining order, chock-full of good information. I particularly liked the section with Mitch's physical description: 6'1", blond, brown eyes, and a tattoo of the Grim Reaper on his left shoulder. Nice.

"Ooh, and it has his address on it, too," I said.

"How does that help us?" Paul asked. "He won't know where she is, will he?"

"For all we know, she could be back at home doing laundry and painting her toenails. In fact, that's the most likely possibility."

Paul's face scrunched up. "You really think she'd return to her abuser? I mean, I know you said some do, but—"

"They were working toward reconciling," I mumbled, but I wasn't really paying attention to him. *Something he'd said.* I held up a purple paw, my mind spinning; Paul hushed.

It clicked. "RTA," I rasped.

"What?" Paul looked worried. I couldn't blame him. I probably looked like I was having a brain aneurism. Felt like it, too.

"RTA—those initials at the bottom of all the files. They weren't initials! I mean, not for a name. They're an acronym: Returned To Abuser! That's what all of those women had in common. They went back home. To their *abuser!*"

"Their abusers killed them?"

"Someone else did. Someone who couldn't stand the thought that they went back. That's what Regina figured out. That's why she died."

CHAPTER FIFTY FOUR

We kept working for another hour, but didn't find anything else of note. I resisted the impulse to drive straight over to Mitch's house. It was dark and it made more sense to wait until the next day. I needed to fabricate a pretext, too.

Paul took me back to my car at the club, and I decided to catch a meeting before heading home. Big mistake. Nobody is nosier than a recovering alcoholic, and our arrival together was duly noted. Wolf whistles and hoots greeted us, and I felt my face flame.

I tried ignoring the whole lot, but it didn't help my composure to see Paul preening as though we really had been on a date. I fled to the bathroom until it was time for the meeting to start.

I barely restrained myself to wait for a decent hour before heading over to the address on the restraining order. Imagining a thug with a Grim Reaper tattoo being awakened at the crack of dawn on a Sunday morning helped. I stopped for coffee even though I knew I'd probably have a long wait and would need to pee.

It was just past 6:30 a.m. when I turned onto Mitch's street. Still too early to go knocking on doors, but unless he was an early-to-church riser I'd at least catch him at home. Judging by the scattering of bikes and play things littering the neighboring front yards, this looked like a family block. I drove slowly past Karissa's house. No lights on yet, but it was still early.

Their yard was neatly trimmed. A sugar maple standing at the corner of the lot was just beginning to orange up and hadn't dumped its leaves yet. A dented mailbox stood at the end of the drive, listing slightly. At first, I thought perhaps somebody had backed into it and created an imaginary scenario in my mind of a fleeing woman. However, a quick scan of the street told me it wasn't an isolated case. Several other mail boxes had been bashed in, too. If it were winter, I'd have blamed snow plows, but not at this time of year. It was far more likely that the damage had occurred in a Wisconsin version of a drive-by: a carful of bored teens, baseball bats, and a case of PBR or Leinies, if they were lucky.

Fun times.

The house was a nice ranch, nearly identical to the other homes lining the quiet street, except for the body dangling from the ceiling just inside the open garage.

I yelped and almost swerved off the road. It gave my stomach a turn until I realized it was just a gutted buck. Bow season, I remembered. Hoisted up so it could drain and keep it safe from dogs with a taste for the wild. If Mitch was a hunter, then it was possible that I'd missed him already. He could be out in his deer stand munching on candy bars and Doritos, waiting for a buck to show. Still, if he'd already gotten his buck, maybe he was done for the season. Or maybe that was Karissa's kill. Up here in the north, plenty of women hunt.

I was so busy playing girl-detective that I didn't take note of the dented, blue pickup parked in the driveway until my second swing past the house.

A rectangular magnet with "T & M Construction: Concrete and Foundation Repair" decorated the passenger door. A clue, by gosh. There were two names as well—Tim and Mitch—with different phone numbers listed under each name.

I parked at the curb two houses down and turned off the ignition. It was so quiet I could hear my engine ticking. I cracked the window so the car wouldn't fog up.

Then, I waited.

And discovered the most intense boredom ever experienced on planet Earth. How did stalkers manage this? To keep myself alert I counted the vehicles in the driveways and along the street. Then I tried to calculate a car-to-truck ratio but wasn't sure what category to put SUVs in and the math got too complicated for me, anyway. I graded the landscaping for each home, taking grass length, dandelion dominance, and general tidiness into consideration. Extra points were given for restraint in plastic lawn ornaments. Mitch and Karissa got a B+. I didn't take off for the mailbox since it seemed a recent development and nobody else had made repairs as yet. The Dillards' had some toy issues, though.

The neighbors didn't fare as well, although one house three doors down looked like a promo for *House and Garden*. Lushly manicured lawn, well-behaved shrubbery, and they even had a wheeled conveyance for their trash cans. Snazzy.

Eventually I tried imagining the people who lived in the houses, what they did for a living, what their lives were like.

I fell asleep.

The sound of a tap, tap, tapping on my side window almost launched me through the sun roof. A pale face loomed in the glass next to mine. I shrieked. Paul shrieked.

My heart was still thudding as Paul slid into the passenger seat.

"What are you doing here?" I asked.

"I figured you would be here. I brought donuts." He held up a white pastry bag.

OK, the donuts helped. I poked through the bag until I found a chocolate with sprinkles. Sprinkles are tools of forgiveness.

"So, what are we doing?" Paul asked with his mouth full of a bearclaw .

"*We* aren't doing anything. *I* am trying to see if Karissa and her kids came back home."

"How are you going to do that if no one comes out?"

I sighed. I hated it when other people made sense. We sat in silence for a bit. Then Paul said, "How about this? We could act like salesmen. I could go home and get my vacuum and we could go up to the house and tell them we'll give them a demo. We'll need some dirt, too. What do you think?"

What I thought was that it sounded like a Lucy and Ethel adventure and there was no Desi waiting in the wings to play a bongo or save our asses. I had to think of something, because Paul had his hand on the door latch, ready to run home and grab his Hoover or whatever. "Hold up, Paul. I've got an idea." I didn't really, but as leader of this dynamic duo I felt I should at least be trying. Lucy always had a take-charge attitude and I was damned if I'd be Ethel. Lucy had style. "Wait here."

CHAPTER FIFTY FIVE

I took three tries, knocking, before Mitch came to the door. I'd decided the kids weren't here since my banging hadn't started any ruckus. Their daddy was a lot less scary looking than I had imagined from the restraining order. For one thing, the Grim Reaper was more cartoonish than demonic and had the motto "Live as if there's no tomorrow" ringing it. I suppose descriptions given on a restraining order might bias a person.

His height was intimidating, but he had the tousled bed-head and sleepy smile of a young boy. Bare-chested and wearing gray, sweatpants with a red Wisconsin Badger logo that hung dangerously low on his hips, he looked like a big, stretched out version of his son. *A vastly sexier version of his son*, my id hastened to add. I told my id to shut up. I had enough trouble.

"Can I help you?"

For being woken up on a dreary Sunday morning, he was polite. He even managed a discreet body scan with a slight (gratifying) smile as he reconnected with my eyes. Apparently, it made a difference when a cute guy did it. I reminded myself of his married, abuser status.

"I sure hope so," I finally managed, sounding way too chipper. I cleared my throat to a less annoying level. "I'm sorry for waking you. Ha ha ha." Yes, I actually said, "Ha ha ha." *Geez, Letty, get a grip!* "I'm looking for a builder." *Why did my eyes dart to his muscular arms and broad, smooth chest?* "I have some remodeling work I need done. I was on my way to . . . um . . . church—" *Church? Yes, church, go with it.* "—when I saw your truck. It seemed like a sign." A sign of insanity perhaps.

My speech garnered me the sleepy smile again, which I was in no way paying any attention to.

"What kind of . . . job . . . are you looking for?" I was pretty sure his eyes dipped to my cleavage. Apparently, we had just convened the first Mutual Chest Admiration Society. I kept my own gaze pinned to his face and tried not to read anything into his question. It didn't help that he ran his hand through his hair, increasing the tousle-factor exponentially.

I'd been dating too many geeks. My bad-boy triggers were completely out of whack.

"Kitchen," I said, picking the least romantic project I could think of. Unfortunately, there wasn't a lot of concrete work needed in a kitchen. Except? "Counter," I added, feeling proud and back in control. The time I'd spent zoned out watching the DIY cable channel finally came in handy. Concrete countertops were quite popular. My libido nearly ruined it by conjuring up images of countertops and jars full of honey and . . . "Are you bondage? I mean, *bonded.* Your company, I mean. There are two of you?" I pointed at his truck, just in case he'd forgotten that he had a partner.

His mind had apparently hooked onto my faux pas, his grin flashing across his face like lightning. "Uh, what? Two of us?" His eyebrows raised, possibly wondering what my interest was in by having *two* guys for the job. "My cousin, Tyler. He's like a brother to me. We've been partners for years."

Good lord, he was still grinning. He leaned against

the door frame in that timeless, James Dean pose.

I refocused on my purpose for being here. "Oh, I thought maybe you had a little helper." I smiled, nodding at the Big Wheel in the yard.

A crease formed in his brow and he straightened up. "Uh, yeah, but they're too young to come to a job." His turn for throat clearing. My question unsettled him, but I hoped he dismissed it as a brush-off, a reference to his married state rather than someone trying to locate his wife and kids. I could tell he was trying to balance not losing a potential client with being cautious.

"Listen," he continued, all flirtation cast aside. "Why don't you give me a call when you're ready for the job. I'm gonna have to get to work now."

"On a Sunday?" I asked.

Frowning, he stepped back into the house. "I do what I have to."

"So do I," I said to the closed door.

Walking back to my car, I felt Mitch watching me and I didn't think he was checking out my butt. He had been well and truly spooked when I brought up the kids. I resisted the urge to look back, knowing that would just confirm his suspicions. Instead, I glanced at the truck trying to memorize the two phone numbers.

Paul was a jittery mess by the time I slid into the driver's seat. He had his cell phone out, holding it poised as if to dial 9-1-1 at the first sign of trouble. Which would leave approximately fourteen minutes for a homicidal maniac to dismember my body and stuff it down the septic hole in the basement. More than enough time, but I appreciated the thought.

"Down! Get down!" I shoved his head down past the dash, trying to fold his gawky frame like an accordion. "I don't want him to see you."

"Glack!" he said, or something similar that translates to "Dear god, my neck doesn't bend that way. Please stop before I'm paralyzed for life."

Digging through my purse, I pulled out an old receipt and a pen and thrust them at Paul. Despite my attempt at instantaneously acquiring a photographic memory, I couldn't remember more than three digits so I was forced to sit there and squint at the truck. They really needed to get bigger magnets. "Write this down," I said, reciting the phone numbers off the truck to my crumpled compadre.

"What are you doing?" Paul whispered, apparently forgetting that not wanting to be seen is not the same as not wanting to be heard. "Let's get out of here."

I pulled the car away from the curb, trying to drive casually—a difficult thing to portray—and not as though I were a killer-stalker hunting for his wife and children. After two blocks I told Paul he could sit up and made a series of right turns that brought me back to the corner of the Dillards's street, but on the opposite side from where I'd first parked. A large, overgrown shrub hid much of my car from casual view, but it also obscured my vision. Telling Paul to stay put, I got out and scurried up to the foliage, peeking through the branches so I could watch the house.

Paul powered the window down and whispered, "What are you doing?"

"Shh!" I flapped a hand at him. I figured we only had a few minutes before somebody called the cops. If Mitch didn't act right away, I'd have to leave.

But he did. A few moments later, he came out of the house, stopped briefly to pick up the kids' toys that were strewn about the lawn, and then climbed in the truck and drove off heading in the opposite direction—thank god—from my bush hiding place. I hobbled back to my car, knees aching from squatting for so long. Admittedly, only five minutes, but I hadn't had a chance to exercise lately. Months, actually.

Grabbing the keys and my purse, I said, "Come on. We're taking your car."

"We are?" Paul bailed out of my car so fast he almost fell over. We ran over to his Buick sedan.

"Let me drive," I said, holding my hand out for the keys. Okay, I might have snapped my fingers in that "gimme now" kind of way.

"No, you can't." He jumped in the driver's seat and I had no choice but to get in the other side.

"Then, you better drive fast. You have to catch up to him."

"We don't even know where he went. He's long gone." Paul objected, but he headed off in the direction Mitch had gone.

"Just head toward the highway. It's only three blocks up. If he turned off anywhere, we're out of luck, but if he took 53 we can still catch up."

"North or south?"

Oh, crud. I hadn't thought of that. South to Eau Claire or north. I thought of the deer dangling in Mitch's garage.

"North."

CHAPTER FIFTY SIX

W e didn't have to worry about Mitch catching on to his "tail" because we didn't catch up with him until seven miles later. Paul and I were both hyperventilating by the time we saw the back of the pickup hove into view. Me, out of fear that I'd guessed wrong; he, from the speed at which I insisted he drive in order to catch up to Mitch. I ended up having to promise to pay any speeding ticket fines, and he wouldn't let me talk in case I would distract him.

We were going 72 MPH.

Although he kept a white-knuckled grip at ten-and-two on the steering wheel, Paul relaxed enough to allow occasional speech once we had the truck in view and he was able to slow down to a sedate 71 MPH. I made him stay a quarter mile back to lessen the chance of being noticed. Most of the traffic at this time of day was heading south; weekenders heading home after a trip "Up North," so we didn't want to get too close.

As we neared the Bloomer exit about sixteen miles out of Chippewa, Paul said, "How far are we going to go?"

"For as long as we can, I guess. Why?"

"What if we need gas?"

I leaned over to look. Less than a quarter tank. *Way* less. "Really, Paul? Really? I thought you'd be one of those guys who always has a full tank. Weren't you a Boy

Scout? What if he's heading to Canada?"

"Well, you didn't tell me what we were doing. I thought we were going to just sit there. I brought donuts, didn't I? Besides, I have to be careful about how much gas I go through. D'you have any idea how much it costs to fill this car?"

I forced myself to stay calm, because if I started banging my head against the dash, Paul would get distracted. I'd been kidding about Canada, but not by much. Lots of people had cabins hidden away in isolated areas of Northern Wisconsin. For all I knew, Mitch had stashed his wife and kids in the family cabin clear up in Hayward or Spooner or points north.

"Besides, I don't want to put too many miles on. My . . . um," he broke off the sentence, his face reddening.

The blush caught my attention. I thought about his reluctance to let me drive and his concern about mileage and gas use, and took a good look around the interior of the car. Spotless. A tiny white statue of a saint, an ever-present reminder of the dangers of travel, was fixed to the dashboard. A box of tissues swathed in an intricate white-and-yellow crocheted cover rested on the seat between us. But it was the earthy, cola scent of Youth Dew that confirmed my suspicion.

"Paul, is this your mom's car?"

He went scarlet. "She just doesn't like it if she thinks I've been cruising around wasting gas."

Cruising around? I decided—for once—not to crack a joke. I'd been a little snippy with Paul lately and making fun of his mother's perception of him as a man-about-town or the fact that he was driving a mommy-mobile would be excessive, even for me.

"Maybe you could just tell her you were helping a friend," I said.

He liked the friend part, I could tell. His already impeccable posture straightened another notch and he smiled. He even punched the speed up to a rousing 76. Luckily we didn't have to maintain such a dangerous pace for long.

Mitch took the exit at Hwy. 64, heading east toward the little town of Cornell.

Half a mile later, the "low gas" light came on and the little alarm went ding, ding, ding.

I went home and took a nap. I'd run out of ideas, I'd slept badly the night before and gotten up too early, and my head hurt. Drinking was no longer an option, but self-pity sleeping ranked high on my reality evasion techniques.

When I woke, it was raining. It was also the next day. It took my foggy brain a while to accept that the clock read 5:47, because it was very dark outside. Twilight came early in the fall, but not *this* early. The glowing red AM light on the alarm clock finally clued me in to the fact that after getting home from my adventures with Paul, I'd slept through the rest of Sunday. Monday morning was too much reality to face without warning, so I snuggled back under the covers.

The steady downpour drummed on the windows, making my apartment a cozy haven. Siggy lay curled up next to me, sleep-buzzing. Unfortunately the sound of the rain made me realize that not only had I slept nearly eighteen hours, I'd not gone to the bathroom in that length of time either.

After using the facilities, I wrapped myself in a fuzzy throw blanket and shuffled out to the kitchen. The apartment was cold; I refused to turn the heat on before November, but in Wisconsin that meant wearing layers indoors as well as out. I peeked into the fridge, but there was nothing I felt like eating. I grabbed a box of cereal from the cabinet and ate a handful, dry.

Penance for my stupidity.

Of course, the phone rang just as I'd palmed a handful of dry cereal into my mouth. My greeting sounded particularly crunchy.

"Letty? It's Astrid."

Holy crap. "Astrid? What's up?"

"We had a visitor this morning. Have you been harassing Mitch and Karissa Williams?"

"Harassing? No. Of course not." Stalking might be a better term, but why quibble?

"He was really angry, Letty. I was afraid some of the women might see him and be triggered. Apparently he thinks you've been misrepresenting yourself and trying to weasel information from him about Karissa's whereabouts. Those were his words."

"Really? How weird." My heart was racing and my mouth had a pile of sand disguised as breakfast food wadded into the side of my cheek. I decided to go with part of the truth. Sometimes that worked as good as a lie. "I did go to talk to Karissa a while ago. Just to check on her since Regina had been seeing her. I told you guys that." *No, I didn't.*

"No, you didn't. Anyway, Clotilde would have a fit if she knew you were upsetting a former client. Maybe you meant well, but you've got to remember how afraid and distrustful these women have to be. They're on constant alert."

They weren't the only ones. "Look, Astrid, I was just trying to fulfill Regina's wishes. You know? And I was worried that she and the boys had been re-traumatized." *Damn!* I wished I hadn't brought that up. "By, um, hearing about the accident."

"I understand. If you promise you'll be more careful next time, I won't mention it to Clotilde. She seems to be really stressed lately. I think she's been worried about Karissa, too. Will you be coming in this morning?"

"Why do you think Clotilde is worrying about Karissa? Did she say something?"

"Oh, never mind. I'm sure it's my imagination. Are you bringing that man back? I think that's another thing that's bothering Clotilde, and I'm sorry to say I agree with her on that one. We just haven't had good experiences with male therapists working here."

"I didn't set it up, Astrid. It's just his internship. Besides, Paul is as harmless as you can get."

"Maybe to you, but this is a refuge, Letty. It just feels strange. He did look pretty mild, though, from what I saw. Just follow Clotilde's instructions and keep a close eye on him."

CHAPTER FIFTY SEVEN

anging up, I sat back to ponder the conversation. Mitch must have gone straight to Karissa after we'd talked. She'd have told him about my visit to the trailer and he'd have connected the dots pretty quickly. On top of my worry that he might pursue the complaint—and how would I explain my "kitchen work" ploy?—was the sour realization that if we'd just stuck with him, he'd have led us straight to Karissa. Now I didn't know how I'd ever find her.

Before dropping me off at my car, Paul had made me promise that I wouldn't do anything without him. He had way more faith in my ability to come up with a new plan than I did.

Unfortunately, I could foresee no clever ideas on the horizon. I stretched out on the couch and entered into a serious funk over how I'd blown it. Despite Paul's lack of gas-preparedness, I knew the real failure had been mine. I'd spooked Mitch and now he was on alert. For me, in particular. If that meant he'd be more protective of his family, in general, that was good. Unless he was so busy watching for me that he'd let Lachlyn slip by. Or Clotilde. Or Astrid, or Joyce, or whoever the hell it was. Even if I went back to him and tried to explain who I was and what I was doing, he'd never believe me. And if I tried staking out his house again, he'd either call the cops or kill me dead. The man had access to concrete and basements after all.

Siggy hopped up on the coffee table.

"Siggy, get down." I flapped a hand at him. He ignored me with catly indifference and began biting a slip of paper. He loved chewing paper. Maybe he needed more fiber in his diet.

I took the paper away, receiving an irritated tail flick in response. It was the scrap that I'd had Paul write the phone numbers on. No help there. It wasn't like phoning Mitch or his cousin would be of any use.

But I could Google the cousin's number.

I snapped myself up and flung myself across the room toward the desk. Plugging in Cousin Tyler's phone number brought me to one of those "find your high school boyfriend" sites, and for a mere $39.95 (with 20% off, mind you) I could find not only his full name and address, but his marital and divorce history; relatives, including those living at the same address; bankruptcies; property ownership; sex offender status and criminal background. I shuddered at how easy it was to invade nearly every area of a person's life in this new age. The loss of privacy was staggering.

Then I got my credit card out.

I'd promised Paul I wouldn't go off on my own. It wasn't that I hadn't broken promises before. I had. Lots of them. But I'd never broken a promise—not since getting sober at least. It would suck. I'd have to admit my dishonesty in a meeting. Sue would kick my butt. Worse, I'd have to look Paul in the eyes if I broke my word. And I *had* been a wee bit bossy with him yesterday. So I owed him honesty, at the very least.

Of course, he was home and happy to join me. Lucy and Ethel ride again.

I picked him up just after noon. When I GPS'd the address that Big Brother had helpfully provided, I found that Cousin Tyler lived just north of Bloomer on County Highway F. Rural. Very rural. Even if we had followed Mitch we probably would have had to abort the mission because there'd have been no way to blend into the surroundings traveling down those back roads.

It was a beautiful drive, especially when we turned off on F. Autumn had sparked off a thousand different shades of orange and red. It wasn't hard to find the mailbox with the address painted on the side. Bright green-and-yellow John Deere with a teensy little tractor fixed to the top. Quite the eye-catcher.

I slowed on the gravel driveway, not wanting to ping rocks off my car. Someone was keeping up with the maintenance on it, though. It looked recently graded, and I wasn't scared of dropping into a crater hole. The driveway was at least a quarter mile, but it was hard to estimate the length because it curved around the side of a hill, causing the house to be nestled in a nice windbreak. A big, old wooden barn stood a short distance away from the house, outbuildings and pole sheds scattered around it like satellites. An elaborate wooden swing set off to the side indicated the presence of children.

I'd expected an old-fashioned, two-story farmhouse but found a tidy little ranch, almost a clone of Mitch and Karissa's, instead. My heart skipped a beat when I sighted the Wrangler parked out front. I pulled in and parked next to it.

"Think anyone's home?" Paul asked.

It was quiet. Nobody came to the door or window to see who had pulled in. It *felt* like somebody was home, though, and I could only hope that the somebody wasn't currently loading the "Welcome, strangers!" shotgun.

Paul and I got out and he followed me to the front door. "Don't look so scared," I said, voice trembling.

"I'm not," he whispered.

I knocked. We waited. Knocked again. Still nothing. Gesturing to Paul to stay put, I walked back out to stand on the sidewalk in front of the windows.

"Karissa?" I called. "We're not here to hurt you. I know what happened. I just want to make sure you're safe." I kept my hands out a little from my side, palms open, standing in full view. "Karissa?" I tried again. "I know what happened to Regina. I know that you know what happened and that's why you're scared and running. Mitch is helping you, too, isn't he? I'm sorry if I scared him yesterday. I was just . . . just trying to help."

The door flew open so fast I thought it was going to knock Paul off the stoop. Without the wedges, Karissa looked like a pixie. A thin, haunted pixie with circles under her eyes so dark they looked like bruises. I double-checked to make sure they weren't.

"That was you?" she said.

"Yeah. It was. I'm not here to hurt you, I promise. I think I know what's going on."

"Oh, now you *think* you know what's going on, huh? A minute ago, you knew."

I swallowed. Possibly because I'd just noticed the fillet knife she held at her side. I had history with knives, and it wasn't good. "I know Regina was killed. It wasn't an accident. She was pushed, wasn't she? Did you see it?"

Her face paled. "No. I didn't."

At first, I thought she was denying the whole thing, but then I realized she was just being literal.

"I've got Mo-mo," I said. "I should have brought

him." A seemingly stupid non sequitur, but she understood and nodded. Neither of us wanted to say it out loud. She hadn't seen Regina killed. Mikey had.

"How is he doing?" I asked. Paul stood next to me, a bewildered look on his face, but he had enough sense to stay quiet. Maybe he'd seen the knife, too.

She stood silent, eyes boring into my own. Reflecting the horror and futile anger of a helpless mother. Helpless, because she couldn't change the past. Couldn't go back and erase it from her child's mind.

She opened the door wide, motioning us in.

CHAPTER FIFTY EIGHT

She stopped off in the living room to pluck her fourteen-month-old out of an old-fashioned wooden playpen. The new-and-improved Elmo lay on its side in a corner. Mikey had, indeed, moved on.

Karissa led us to the kitchen. After dropping the knife in the sink, she settled the baby in a high chair and scattered a handful of cereal on the tray for Myka to pick at. The rest of us sat at the table, hands wrapped around cups of hot coffee trying to find solace in the warmth.

"He's having nightmares about it. At least, I think so."

"What do you mean 'think so'?" I asked.

"He won't tell me about them. He wakes up crying, though. And he's wet the bed twice. He stopped doing that years ago."

"Have you asked him if he saw anything?"

She looked uncomfortable. "I'm afraid to. I didn't want to make it worse, you know? I figure he'll forget about it a lot quicker if we just leave it alone. That's why I brought him here. He knows he's safe here."

The house was quiet. Grammy didn't seem to be around and Mikey had yet to make an appearance either. "Where is he now?"

"He's got a fort up in the barn loft that he plays in. He likes to pet the horses, too. I took him out of school for a few days."

I licked my lips. "Is it just the nightmares that he won't talk about? Has he said anything at all? That night, maybe? Or the next day?"

She just shook her head, looking away, out the window to the barn. If she didn't ask Mikey what he'd seen that night, then maybe it wouldn't be true. Maybe there wasn't a murder. Maybe they weren't hiding from the killer.

"Do *you* know who it was?" I asked.

Again, Karissa shook her head. "I was afraid to ask. I still am." She started to cry. Denial can only carry you so far, and then you have to face the truth. Unless you're an alcoholic—then it'll last as long as the booze does.

Myka studied her solemnly, then his face crumpled and he started to whimper. He had stray cereal O's stuck all over his face and body. One dotted his cheek, like a grainy teardrop.

Paul walked over to the drainer and poured a drink of water. He brought it to Karissa, then stood next to her, resting his hand on her shoulder. He didn't pat. He didn't fidget. I was proud of him.

Karissa took a deep, shuddery breath, drank the water off in one gulp, and pulled herself together. She smiled at Myka and gave him some more cereal. Thankfully, the baby calmed as soon as his mother did. Paul sat back down.

"You're a shrink, right?" she asked. "Can you talk to him?"

"I can, but the important thing is to make sure he's safe. You need to go to the police, Karissa. He has to tell them what he saw, *who* he saw."

I felt her retreat emotionally. I understood; I'd been indoctrinated in an avoid-the-police-at-all-costs mentality myself.

"I don't like the police. What if they take him away?" Her voice cracked on the last sentence.

"Why would they?" I asked.

She met my eyes. "Because I didn't keep him safe," she whispered.

"That's not your fault," Paul said. "You can't help it if someone at the shelter is bad. And you *are* keeping him safe. You got him away."

"But there was that thing with Mitch. You know . . . going to the shelter in the first place and all that. That was all my fault."

Paul and I both frowned at the classic victim mantra.

"No, really," she said. "I mean, he pushed me, yeah, but he was pushing me *away*. We were arguing about the bills again and the baby started crying. I was so mad I went after Mitch. I didn't see him pick the baby up or I wouldn't have . . . Anyway, he just stuck his arm out to fend me off, kinda." She paused as though there was something more she wanted to say. Her face registered guilt.

I waited, but when it seemed like she wasn't able to go on, I asked, "Were those your meds at the trailer?"

"What were you doing in there?"

Whoops. I reverted to honesty again. It was getting to be a habit. "Looking for you. And cleaning. Tallie needs to rent it out. You guys left a lot of your stuff behind."

"Grammy did. All those dolls." She shuddered. "Can't say I'm sorry to see those go."

I made one of those therapist "mm hmm" sounds designed to acknowledge a comment without judging. Handy things, those. Without it, I might have whooped in agreement.

"I wanted to send Mitch over to get our stuff, but we

were afraid someone would see him and realize he still had contact with us. How did *you* figure out where we were, anyway?" Her face grew tight again. Apparently, reminders of my snooping were not confidence builders.

Again, with the honesty. "Through Tyler's phone number on the side of Mitch's truck and, um, we followed him on Sunday. Only to the Cornell exit. Not all the way here." As if only partially stalking wasn't creepy at all. I left out the part about nearly running out of gas. Maybe if she believed we had second thoughts, she'd ignore the utter disregard for her and her family's privacy. For good reason, though. Time to remind her of that.

"Who scared you off, Karissa? Tallie said a social worker came to your grandmother's house. You took off right after."

"Tallie's got a big mouth." After a short pause, she said, "It was Clotilde. She said she was just following up. Checking on us since we left under such 'tragic circumstances.'" Her fingers wiggled quote marks over the last two words.

"Did she ask you to come back to the shelter?" Paul asked.

"She tried, but Grammy ran her off." We smiled in mutual Grammy-appreciation. "I knew something was wrong. I even knew it the night it happened, but I didn't know exactly what. Mikey had been off playing. He can kee"p himself busy, not like some of those kids with their noses stuck to the TV. When I found him, he was hiding in our bedroom and had peed hisself. He wouldn't talk to me. Not at all. I thought he was upset that he'd had an accident, so I just got him changed and made him go to bed.

"The next morning . . . That's when I figured out

that he'd seen it. But I didn't think it was . . . I mean, I just thought he'd gotten scared at seeing her fall. I pulled him in the bathroom and asked him did he see her fall, but he still wouldn't say anything. And then I got afraid."

"Afraid?"

"Afraid because he wouldn't say what happened. I thought, maybe . . ." Karissa's face convulsed, tears and snot streaming. She put a shaking hand over her mouth, unable or unwilling to speak her greatest fear out loud. Just like her son.

"You thought maybe Mikey did it?"

She covered her face and sobbed. And *sobbed*. Paul went for more water and I started a search for tissue. Not finding any, I located the bathroom and appropriated a roll of toilet paper.

Several moments later, as Karissa came up for air, I noticed her son crossing the lawn in front of the barn. Karissa saw him coming, too.

"Oh, crap. You guys have to go."

"Karissa, you have to let us help you. If we found you, so can they."

"I don't want him to see you. You need to leave." She began herding us out of the kitchen, shooing us ahead of her like errant chickens fleeing the coop.

It wasn't really fair to press the point, but this was about a child's life. She was under so much pressure, operating on instinct alone, and she was getting stubborn in her fear. I stopped in the middle of the hall, refusing to budge. "The police can keep him safe, Karissa. You *can't* take the chance."

"I'm *not* going to the cops. What if you're wrong about this? What if Mikey was just freaked out because he saw her fall? Or saw her body? That would scare a kid, too. Or what if they blame him? They can twist things, and Mikey gets confused easy."

I'd been raised by a woman who would have sung the Halleluiah Chorus to that speech. And raised by a man who'd died while under police "care." But I also knew some cops—two, in particular—that I felt I could trust.

I told this to Karissa and practically begged her to let me talk to one of them. Mikey was coming in the door, his shoes rasping across the porch outside the kitchen door as he took them off.

"Fine! Whatever. Just go." She shoved me out the door, closing it with a snap.

CHAPTER FIFTY NINE

aul chattered nonstop for the first three miles. I only half listened, my mind going back over everything we'd just learned. Mikey was in danger. I was sure of it. He'd seen or heard something. Something that had scared him so badly that he couldn't even tell his mother about it. And it was Clotilde who'd visited them after I did, inciting their retreat to the farm. As much as I disliked her, it didn't fit with my suspicions, but maybe I'd been wrong. Maybe it *was* money that was the driving force of the murders.

"It's a good thing she agreed to let you talk to the police." Paul's voice broke into my reverie. "Are you going to talk to Pete?" Paul knew Durrant from AA too. Pete was one of the few men who willingly hung out with Paul. His awkward neediness scared most off.

I answered the first part of his comment. "Paul, she agreed because she's not going to be there when we get back. She's taking off again. She's a runner and she's scared."

"What?" He swung around in the seat, looking back through the rear window. "If she leaves, we might never find her again. We have to go back. We've got to keep talking to her. Doesn't she—"

"No. We have to get to Durrant and get him out there before she can take off. I'm guessing Mitch will go with them this time. And you're right, there's no telling where they'll go so we have to hurry."

I was doing 78 mph, bracing on the curves and hugging the center line to keep clear away from the soft gravel edge that would suck me down into the ditch if I wavered too far over. Paul clung gamely to the grab bar over the door and didn't complain. I was reluctant to take Hwy.53 back to town. At the speed I was going, I was sure to attract the attention of a fine officer of the law. I wasn't worried about the ticket, but I didn't want to lose the time.

Problem was, I didn't know the area very well. As tempting as taking a back road short cut might be, too often they'd take you miles out of nowhere. They enticed unwary drivers. They *seemed* to lead in the right direction, looking invitingly straightforward. A clear shot from here to there. But often, after several miles of confident I-found-a-short-cut joy, the road would take a sharp left (or right, depending on which would be most inconvenient). More times than I cared to count, I'd find myself winding my way around farms and creek beds only to have the road suddenly peter out into a cow path, or turn to gravel, or dead end into a corn field.

I took the highway.

We made good time, hitting Chippewa Falls in just under twenty-five minutes. I tossed my purse into Paul's lap. "Find my phone, okay? I don't have Durrant's number but—"

He held the purse away like it'd been dipped in cow shit, horror slicking over his face. "I can't look in there. That's . . . Geez!"

"Paul, it's not kryptonite." *And you're not Superman.* Didn't say it. "Just find it so I can call Sue and get Pete's number."

He peered into its depths warily. Dipping a tentative hand in, he brought out my wallet. Another dip: my makeup case. If he looked inside that he might find my spare tampon. It would kill him.

Grabbing my purse back, I started rummaging around the bottom. Like most purses these days, it had come with a nice organizer pocket for a cell phone but, for some unknown reason, my phone usually slipped out. Digging deeper, I brought out a pack of gum, a grungy lip balm, and a rectangular, turquoise bit of plastic that I didn't recognize. It looked like a memory drive, but I didn't have a turquoise one.

"Shouldn't you be looking at the road?" Paul asked.

I pulled over abruptly, slamming the car into park.

"Letty? What is that?" He started to reach for the devise, but I pulled it away as dread rose like bile in my throat. "Letty?" Paul tried again.

"It's a Buddy tracker," I said.

Going back, I buried the speedometer. Paul made little squeaky sounds. I think he was praying. Someone needed to. For once I was hoping I would pick up a police escort. I planned to enter the farm's driveway with a string of cop cars behind me like a parade.

No such luck.

We'd been gone less than an hour, but a different car was parked next to the Wrangler when I skidded up to the house. It looked familiar, like maybe one I'd seen at the shelter, but I wasn't a car person, and wasn't certain. Just seeing it made my heart thud against my ribs.

Nobody answered my knock. I didn't try a second time. The door was locked and I went in, Paul following at my heels.

We found Karissa on the floor, the steak knife next

to her. Red splotches of blood spattered across the counter and walls--an impressionistic interpretation of horror—and her head lay in a pool of it. Her breathing was thin and raspy. The baby wailed from somewhere deeper in the house. Grabbing a kitchen towel from the counter, I threw it at Paul. "Help her!" I took off at a run for the back rooms.

Myka was in his crib, red-faced and screaming full throttle. He was safe. I left him there. A quick run through the house told me we were the only ones there. When I made it back to the kitchen, I found Paul kneeling next to Karissa, heedless of the blood, holding the towel to her head. His cell phone was open on the floor next to him and a woman's tiny voice issued from it, giving first aid instructions.

His face had gone ashen and he was shaking so hard that his glasses shook on his nose as he looked up at me. But he held the compress tightly.

"The baby's okay. I've gotta find Mikey." My heart was beating so hard I could barely hear myself talk. Paul nodded and turned back to his charge.

I ran for the barn.

CHAPTER SIXTY

Somebody had slid one of the big, wooden doors slightly open on its track. I could slip in quietly. The problem with that was I didn't know what—or who— lay beyond. I'd be following directly on the heels of the killer.

I preferred coming at things from another direction.

I skirted the barn looking for a side entrance. I didn't want to face her head on. I had one advantage—I was pretty sure I knew where Mikey was—and I didn't want to lose it. The weeds were fierce along the side, but a tractor trail made me think I'd find what I was looking for.

And I did. A regular, people-sized door had been placed midway down the east side. I gripped the metal, D-shaped latch, praying it wouldn't squeak. The metal was warm from the sun, another factor that worried me. I'd be blinded as soon as I entered the dark interior. Whoever was in there would have me at an advantage so I took the time to close my eyes, cupping my hand over them, willing my eyes to dilate. It gave me time to listen, but if anybody was moving around inside, I couldn't hear them.

Enough. I sucked a deep breath and slipped inside. Dark, yeah, everything in gray tones, but not as bad as it would have been if I'd walked straight in. Irregular shafts of light stabbed through splits in the weathered walls, through knotholes, and ragged gaps low along the wall where wood met stone; rat doors, my daddy used to call those. I shivered.

Senses I rarely relied on came alive. Smells rushed in: horse, the heady, distinctive smell that all horse lovers inhale like ambrosia; cow, too, but an old smell, not as insistently pungent as if they were still raised here; hay; straw; dust; diesel. Barn smells that triggered memories of my childhood home on the farm, before Daddy died and we had to move.

And hearing. I felt like my very skin was straining to hear. I could have been fooled into thinking the silence was pure had I not known that a deviant version of hide-n-seek was playing out inside. It felt like the barn was breathing. After a moment of concentrating, I was sure I heard something. Something moving deep inside, but so quietly that I couldn't be sure it wasn't my imagination.

I felt exposed standing so close to the door and slid over to the wall, a wooden partition, the first in a series of box stalls. A concrete strip ran in front of the stalls, the first thread of what I knew would be a concrete and wood maze. Farmers didn't plan for "flow" in these old barns. They'd throw a wall up here, tear one down there, whatever they had to do to suit the purpose of their current need using the least amount of money and time, with whatever tools they had available. MacGyver had probably been a farmer before that secret agent gig.

And I was stuck in the middle of it. In the dark. With a killer and a traumatized six-year-old.

Splendid.

I had to find the stairs to the hay loft. Right or left? I decided stairs would most likely be at the front of the barn and headed left. I wanted to keep to the shadows along the stall fronts, but I found if I got too close my clothes snagged on the rough planks. It created too much noise, not to mention the likelihood of running a needle-sharp splinter into my skin.

Moving away from the side door meant moving away from the light. A feeling of Jungian foreboding swept over me as I moved deeper into the darkness. Instinct wrestled with irrationality as my senses continued on the high alert designed to keep me safe while, at the same time, I fought a battle with hysteria.

Involuntary shrieking has a tendency to give your position away.

As a child, I was always the first one found in the marathon games of hide-and-seek—the normal kind—that my cousins and I played every summer. I'd find a fantastic, guaranteed can't-find-me hiding spot and then be consumed by the urge to giggle or to make peeping sounds, giving my position away. I always felt sorry for the kid who was It. Co-dependency starts early.

I felt no such urge with this It.

A third of the way down the hall, a narrow offshoot aisle created a dilemma for me: keep forward or turn toward the barn's center? Usually I liked options, but this time all the choices felt like traps. Having a killer at the end of one of them does that.

I kept moving forward, body systems going haywire under the burden of fear they carried. The barn was cool, yet I was slick with sweat. Despite a dry mouth, I had to pee like a race horse, but the timing seemed ill-advised. Plus, I found that, in trying to be silent, I kept forgetting to breathe.

Fun fact: what would normally be black dots dancing in front of your eyes signaling impending asphyxiation turn green and sparkly in the dark. I thought they were fireflies until the dizziness kicked in.

Another problem occurred soon after when the stall fronts gave way to a long row of open cattle stanchions. Apparently, horses needed more privacy than cows, which didn't seem quite fair. On the other hand, nobody milks horses, so they didn't need to set up a system to keep them side to side in a long row. What it did mean was that I would be completely exposed if I kept going forward.

Instead, I crept up to the dividing partition that the stanchions butted up against in order to peek through the slats. That was the plan anyway. I'd forgotten one very important detail about stanchions. Namely, a gutter—the concrete channel that runs behind the cow butts to deal with the stuff cows output. The gutter makes it handy for the farmer to hose the manure away. Very nice for the farmers. However, gutters are also very, *very* easy to stumble into.

I went sprawling. I managed, barely, to not scream, even after barking my shins on the gutter rim and skinning both knees. Unfortunately, a "whomph" sound escaped when I belly-flopped on the concrete pad. Crawling forward, I huddled on the floor in front of the manger, sucking back whimpers, tensed for an attack.

Nothing moved. I forced myself to breathe quietly, listening hard between each breath. If she had heard me, she was probably holding still, too. We were listening to each other listen. I shuddered.

After several heartbeats I raised myself up to look through the boards. I found myself gazing out at a large, open area in front of the double doors. A sort of lobby. The doors were still ajar and a large wedge of light allowed me to see a set of stairs leading up to what would be the hayloft. To get to them, I'd have to cross that lighted area. Right out there in the open.

CHAPTER SIXTY ONE

I wanted to cry. The whole damn barn was shrouded in darkness except for the *one* section I needed to cross. I sat back, leaning against the manger, praying for . . . anything.

Something metallic clanged. I was fairly certain it had come from the opposite side of the barn, farther back, deeper in. My heart was thumping so hard I wasn't sure I'd be able to hear a second noise, but I didn't expect one. I imagined It, frozen as I had been after my fall. If I hurried, I'd probably get across.

But she'd be listening now. Straining to hear any reaction to her blunder. If she heard me go up the stairs, I'd be leading her right to Mikey.

Just then, I heard the blessed sound of a car pulling up and the silence after the motor shuts off. My heart leapt. The cops were here. A door slammed, more gravel crunched, and one of the doors rumbled back along its metal track.

Astrid stood just inside, blinking. She should have done the eye-covering trick. If she wasn't the killer, was she here to stop her or to ally with her?

"Joyce?" she called. Astrid's voice was laced with fear and . . . deep sadness. "Joyce, I know you're here! Come out."

I heard something again. From the other side. Astrid heard it, too. She darted across the entrance, hurrying through a doorway leading toward the sound.

I took off at a dead run, hit the stairs and, for once, God help me, kept my balance. I prayed Astrid's noise would disguise my own and took the stairs two at a time.

The hayloft was huge. A great, open space with timbers curving gracefully overhead like an upside-down Noah's ark. Long ago, as a fully working farm, this space would have been filled to the rafters with hay or straw bales, stacked crisscross, as tight as bricks to keep the moisture out. Now, not even a quarter of the space had been used for the current stack. They'd used small, rectangular bales here, not the great round bales that start dotting the fields in the fall.

If Mikey had a fort, it would be a space dug out on the flat top of the stack, bales arranged to make a cozy hidey hole. Perfect for a little boy running away from the world.

Or a girl. Been there.

The stack was a flat wall rising twenty feet or more. A corner had been chipped away as the bales were removed, one by one, to feed the horses. It was too early in the season for them to have been used much. Pasture grass was free and plentiful.

That meant that, although I had a few feet of dislodged hay bales to make it easier to clamber up, most of the stack rose straight up in a vast, green wall. But there were always handholds and places to cram your foot if you were adventurous or dexterous enough.

I was neither, but I got up, anyway.

At the top, I flung myself flat out for no other reason than my thigh muscles had separated themselves from the parts of my leg that they were supposed to stay tethered to. My arms were scratched into hamburger, wrist to elbow, from the spiky stalks and my shoulders burned like someone had poured acid down my back. If Joyce came for me now, I'd hand her the knife.

Except I *really* didn't like knives, and the thought of one roused me enough to peek over the side of the stack to see if Joyce or Astrid or some murderous combination thereof had followed me up the stairs. Nobody in sight, but I could hear them. Not the words, but their voices, shrill and angry, somewhere down below.

I had to find Mikey. I started making my way across the "floor" of the hay stack, watchful of gaps between the bales where a misstep could break my ankle. It took a few minutes, but I found a break in the pattern, a spot where the bales had been realigned, widening a hole so a kid could slither through to the dark space beyond. The fort. I dropped to my knees, sticking my face close to the hole, hoping Mikey wasn't armed with a BB gun or blow dart . . . or machete.

"Mikey?" I whispered. It is inherently difficult to inspire trust in a whisper. Whispers are, by nature, designed to signal danger, mistrust, secrets. Had to work with what I had, though. "Mikey, I know you're there. It's okay. I'm here to help. Your mom's gonna be okay, buddy, but we have to get you out of here. The police are coming." *And so was Joyce if I didn't get him out of his burrow.*

Nothing. I prayed I wasn't wrong.

"Mikey, I'm going to have to move the bale. Don't be scared. I just have to get you out of here before . . ." Right. *Don't be scared.* There's a crazed woman, whom you've witnessed killing your therapist and brutally attacking your mother, hunting you down, but don't be scared. Good lord, I was an idiot.

"Okay, go ahead and be scared. I know I am. But we have to get out of here. We have to get outside where the police can help us."

I heard a stirring. A pale splotch rose up through the black opening. Mikey's tear-streaked face came into the dim light. "You came to my house."

"That's right. I talked to your mom and your Grammy."

At the mention of his mother, Mikey face crumpled. "That lady killed her, didn't she?"

"No. No, Mikey. I found your mom. She's alive." *Oh God, don't let me be lying.* "She was still breathing and a friend of mine is helping her. He called an ambulance. We're going to be hearing the sirens any minute." I held my hand out. It would have been more reassuring if it wasn't shaking, but I'd already told him I was scared, so maybe it added an aura of truthfulness. He let me pull him out, and we crab-crawled to the edge.

Part of me wanted to stay here, dig another Letty-sized burrow next to Mikey's and take up residence. It was doubtful that Joyce would ever think to come up here. But if she did . . . we'd be trapped like rats in a bucket.

The sounds from below were not encouraging. The arched, gambrel roof heightened the acoustics. They'd stopped yelling, but I could still hear something. Scuffling and thumps. Grunts. The dull thud of flesh against flesh. I recognized that sound. So did Mikey.

"She's fighting someone. Is that your friend?" Mikey's voice quavered.

"I think it's Astrid. She came in after me. She's trying to stop Joyce, I think."

It sounded like they were duking it out right at the bottom of the stairs, explaining why the sound traveled so well. And then, a guttural scream lifted to the rafters, darted around the timbers, and filled our ears. Mikey ducked his head, covering his ears with his hands. The smell of urine overtook the faded green scent of hay as his bladder let loose. I hoped it was his.

Something bad had happened down there. Something really bad.

A raspy panting floated up the stairs. Astrid or Joyce? If Joyce came up, I'd have no choice but to take her on so Mikey could get away. As long as he didn't rabbit for the fort, he'd have a chance. I found myself gripping Mikey's arm so tightly, I probably left dents, but he didn't pull away. Probably didn't even feel it. We were frozen, eyes glued to the top of the stairs. Watching.

She didn't come. Instead, it got quieter. Not silent exactly, more like a brooding hush. The slightest sounds—a footfall, cloth whispering, the panting dopplering in retreat—gave me hope that she was moving away.

"Is she leaving?" I whispered to Mikey. He shook his head, confusion more than denial, I thought. "I think she's leaving."

I still didn't know who I meant by "she." If it was Astrid, she might not know Mikey and I were here. If it was Joyce . . .

Better to assume the worst. We waited. The longer I heard nothing, the higher my heart shrilled. I decided it was better to stay put until we heard sirens. We had no clue where Joyce was or if she was coming back. I listened so hard for her return that my concussed head flared up.

Unfortunately, it wasn't sound that ambushed our senses. It was smell.

Smoke.

CHAPTER SIXTY TWO

I saw the smoke before I smelled it. At first glance, I couldn't make sense of the grey, ephemeral tendrils rising from the cracks between the floor and walls on the north side. Then, Mikey and I stared at each other in horror.

Why do these crazy bitches like fire so much?

Joyce hadn't made a run for it. She was busily setting fire to the barn. To smoke us out? To finish off what she'd started with Astrid? Or, if poor Astrid was dead, was she trying to destroy the evidence?

"We got to go," Mikey said. With that, he flipped over on his belly, unmindful of the prickery hay, and slithered over the side.

Oh, crap. I followed, far more mindful of my stomach being razored open. Just in case, I tossed up another quick prayer—this time for a gravity-defying miracle that would keep me from bashing my head open on the plank flooring, nearly two stories below.

Somebody must have heard my plea, because I made it down safely.

I started for the stairs, but Mikey yelled a warning. I'd been so busy concentrating on not falling down the haystack that I hadn't heard what was going on below. Joyce had, indeed, returned and, although I couldn't see what she was doing, the smoke rising on one side of the building coupled with the sloshing and bumping sounds

I heard from just beyond the stairs told me she was kindling her fire at the front of the barn. If we took the stairs, we'd run right into her.

Mikey grabbed my hand, pulling me back toward the haystack away from the stairs.

"Mikey, no, we can't go back. We have to get out of here!"

He clamped his hand tighter on mine and kept tugging. I was afraid if I pulled out of his grasp, he'd take off on me, panicked into running the wrong way like a wild animal darting toward a car's headlights.

"Come on!" he persisted. His face, when he turned to me, was set in grim determination. This wasn't panic. He had an idea. I looked up at the bales of hay. Then, it came to me.

"Mikey, is there a hay door up there?"

"Yeah, come on!" He almost pulled my arm out of the socket.

"Mikey, it's three stories down! We can't jump out of there!" *But wouldn't that be better than sitting on the floor waiting to burn?*

The smoke became more insistent and the wind outside seemed to be rising, too, a blowing, susurrant sigh that seemed to encompass the whole structure. I would have expected a breeze to dissipate the smoke. Instead, it hung suspended in dense veils, solid and unshifting. If anything, it seemed to be thickening.

Because, of course, it wasn't wind. It was fire.

In the distance, sirens wailed.

"ABOUT DAMN TIME!" I bellowed.

But were they too late? A surge of resentment clouded my thinking. The one time I was ready to trust my life to the authorities, and they'd taken so long, it had turned into a weenie roast. I decided if it got too bad I

could try to free-fall on top of a cop. At least my mom
would have one small pleasure from my death, and it
would serve them right for taking so damn long. Mikey
scurried up the stack like a trained squirrel. I got about
six feet before I remembered something.

I dropped down, landing with a thud that rattled my
teeth and sent shooting sparks through my legs. Mikey's
worried face appeared over the edge of the topmost
bales.

"Go on," I told him, waving him away. "Go find the
door. Wait as long as you can for the police or firemen
before you jump. They might be able to catch you."

He reached a hand over the side. "Come on! You're
gonna get burned up."

"I have to get Astrid. She's hurt down there. I have to
try. You go on. Get going!"

His face scrunched up and he started to cry again.
But he left.

I headed back to the stairs, arguing with myself the
whole way. *I don't even like Astrid. I didn't like Regina,
either, and look what happened.* The closer I got to the
stairs, the harder it got to see. And breathe. *She
probably isn't even down there anymore. Maybe she
crawled to safety.* I took my shirt off, holding it to my
face. I found the first stair by tapping forward with my
foot, churning the billows with my frantic jabbing
motions. *This isn't my job. I shouldn't have to be doing
this. The only thing I should be worrying about is
myself . . . And Mikey. Okay, two things. Isn't that
enough? Do I have to save* everyone?

The farther down I went, the hotter it became. The
heat and smoke became solid, a pressure, something I
had to push against to get through. The big double doors
were aflame. Tongues of fire flowed along the edges,

biting and hissing at the century-old wood. More flames danced along the walls, racing up the timbers, sucking at the oxygen, and growing as they fed.

I found Astrid by tripping over her body. I fumbled over her, blinded, eyes burning. Feeling my way to her face with hands that quickly grew sticky with blood. All I could hear was the fire, roaring now, an element of combustible rage.

She wasn't breathing. I couldn't find a pulse. I made *certain* there was no pulse. That was the most I could do.

I crawled back up the stairs, coughing and choking so hard I saw dots again. The smoke burned down my throat and air suddenly became a thing to be diligently sought after rather than taken for granted. I stumbled my way blindly across the loft floor until I ran headlong into the wall of bales.

The only direction was up, and that's where I went. Midway, a bout of coughing almost launched me off the side. Snot and tears ran freely down my face, but I dug my hands in between the bales, hanging on til I could force a foot up. Then, the other. And kept going up.

I got confused at the edge. I couldn't find any more "up" and my mind was too busy wrestling with the lack of oxygen to make sense of my position. Hands grabbed at me, twining in my hair and pulling.

The roaring had risen to an ear-splitting howl. The barn, all around us, moaned in its death throes. I couldn't think. I crawled, following Mikey's heels, knowing that if I lost him now . . .

A piercing screech of metal added to the cacophony, as Mikey shoved one side of the sliding door sideways. He'd found it. I lunged forward, thrusting my head through the space into the air. The craving for clean air more urgent than any thirst.

Smoke billowed skyward, black plumes blotting out the sun. Despite that, this half of the barn didn't seem to be completely engulfed, though in a structure stacked with hay and made of dry, aged wood, we only had a few moments at most. Mikey clattered the other side open and stood peering over the side. I struggled to my knees and fought to speak.

"Wait . . ." A coughing spasm wracked my body, twisting my insides into one convulsing, cramping muscle. I grabbed Mikey's arm and waited for it to pass. ". . . heard sirens," I managed. "They're coming." But *when* had I heard sirens. How long ago? Did they even know where we were or that we were even here?

Mikey knelt down next to me, placing his black-streaked, earnest face nose-to-nose with mine. His eyes, big and imploring, stared into my own. "There's a wagon. We jump in it. Just do what I do."

And, in front of my disbelieving eyes, he stood, squared off on the edge of the three-story high opening . . . and jumped.

He fell through the grey swirling mass and disappeared beneath it. Leaving me alone, staring out into a day turned into writhing night.

I didn't hear him land, but that might be because of all the screaming. Mine, of course, and the barn's. And then I coughed so convulsively I hit my head on the floor, banging my nose so hard I thought I heard it pop. Again with the stars.

Grabbing the edge of the wall, I leaned out as far as I could, blood running in rivulets from my nose, adding a new twist to the tear/snot/smoke effect.

"Mikey!" I screeched. "*Mikey!*"

"I'm okay! Jump!"

"Are you freakin' kidding me? I can't *jump*! I can't

even see you."

"Just jump where I did. You'll land in the wagon."

A thousand questions ran through my head—all of overwhelming importance and entirely unanswerable. *How big was the wagon? Exactly where was the wagon? Would my heavier mass create greater velocity, thus slamming my body through the wagon and halfway to China? Why hadn't I paid closer attention in physics class? Was there going to be a pitchfork issue at the bottom? Was Mikey out of the way? Was I really as high as logic told me I was? What if I missed?*

How long could I wait for the firemen before burning up?

Another coughing fit brought me to my knees, and I realized I wouldn't die from the flames. It would be smoke that would do me in and a lot sooner than the fire. I'd pass out very soon and lie here, unconscious and unfeeling, on top of the hay at the edge of the world.

And *then* the fire would charbroil my stupid, chicken-shit ass.

I sent up one more prayer to the Higher Power that now had my full attention, if he wanted it. Then, I pushed out, aiming for the spot where I'd last seen Mikey, and let myself fall through the dark and the grey and the air and the emptiness.

CHAPTER SIXTY THREE

There is nothing remotely fluffy about a wagonful of straw. When I hit, the breath whooshed out in a rush, and all I could manage was short, shallow gasps—a respite from the coughing jag, but worrisome in its not-enough-oxygen, gonna-die implications.

Finally, my lungs hitched in enough air for my panic to lessen. Slightly. I was still lying on a bed of flammable straw on a flammable wooden wagon adjacent to a flaming inferno.

Not to mention a killer sill running around, literally fanning the flames and (presumably) cackling with glee.

Mikey.

I crawled over the sidewall and flopped to the ground, setting off another round of coughing. I hacked up phlegm, half expecting it to be as black as ashes, but it wasn't. Mikey was at my side in an instant, grabbing my arm, asking if I was all right. His concern almost did me in. Tears had runneled two clear paths down his black, sooty face. For a moment, I lost track of who was taking care of whom, and then it came to me that, aside from hollow reassurances, I'd pretty much been dead weight for him.

I wiped a tear from his cheek and he flung himself at me, wrapping me in a full-body, all-boy hug. Maybe dead weight has some uses, after all.

It was too soon to relax. "Mikey, we've got to find the cops." Never, *ever* thought I'd say those words. "And the firemen. Hear the sirens?"

Don't know how I'd missed them in the first place. The strident wails and siren blasts added to the confusion. "Come on," I said. "Joyce is still . . ." I stopped before giving voice to the fear. "We can't quit now, big guy."

We staggered along the side of the barn, pushing through knee-high weeds that clutched at our feet as though the earth was in league with the killer. The smoke wasn't too bad on this side, making me worry we'd run into Joyce as she made her rounds. When three black-suited firemen came tearing around the corner, I let out a shriek that would have broken glass.

The sight of us caused a bit of excitement for them, too. They were on us like we were the winning lottery ticket in Saturday's MegaMillions drawing. The weeds ceased to be an issue as I was half-lifted, half-dragged between two of the firemen to the front of the building, where all hell was breaking loose. Or, rather, where trained professionals from three adjoining communities were battling to shove hell back into its cage. Mikey was carried to the closest ambulance, of which there were plenty.

Cop cars, fire trucks, too many to count; at least four ambulances; pickups with little swirly blue lights— personal vehicles of the on-call emergency workers— filled the farmyard like an Emergency Vehicle Expo. With relief, I saw that Paul had called out the cavalry. One of the ambulances had parked outside the kitchen door, the driver just barely waiting for the doors to close behind its occupant before wailing away. Paul stood on the porch, blank-faced watching the transfer of his charge; then his eyes met mine across the controlled frenzy between us. His face lit up—it might have been the sight of me in my bra—and he started toward me. A cop pulled him back, already starting the questions. Already digging backwards into this mess. The authorities were involved with a vengeance.

They could have it.

And before the wash of relief took hold—because God forbid I should feel *that* for very long—I spied Astrid safely ensconced between two paramedics with a police officer hovering just to the side. The EMTs were wrapping one of her hands with gauze and she clutched an oxygen mask to her face with the other. The scream she let loose when she caught sight of us put shame to the sirens and nearly caused the cop to draw his gun.

What the hell? Astrid? I slammed my feet into the ground, causing my firemen escorts to almost rip my arms out of their sockets. They re-gripped and hauled me to yet another ambulance, barely waiting for the EMTs to take over before racing back to the fire.

An EMT with the name Whitman stitched over her breast slapped a mask over my face, while a male counterpart hauled the stretcher out and helped me to lie down. Even as they sought my pulse and did the flashlight eye thing, I fought to sit back up.

"*Joyce* is dead?" I said. The mask muffled the words, and I pulled it off.

Whitman put it back on. "We can hear you. You have to keep this on."

"Astrid killed Joyce? Is Joyce still in there?" That was stupid. Of course she hadn't. That had been a very dead body I'd touched. And bloody. My hands were sticky with it. My stomach did a lazy, ominous roll.

"Is there someone else in the barn?" the guy this

time. "Hey! Chief!" He waved the chief over.

"What's goin' on?" The voice coming through the mask sounded all Darth-Vader raspy, but in a reassuring way.

"She says there's someone else in there."

The chief pulled a radio up to his face.

I grabbed his arm, yanking the mask off again. "That's not what I meant." A cough wrenched from my body, twisting me until I was almost hanging off the stretcher. Someone slapped the mask back on. I pointed at Astrid. "She and Joyce were fighting. I thought Joyce killed—" More coughing. It seemed to be getting worse.

"We found the body. Is that who you mean?"

I nodded, holding the mask tight enough to leave dents in my cheeks. I'd learned my lesson.
"I thought it was Astrid. I mean, I thought Joyce killed Astrid." I couldn't make sense of it.

"Was there anyone else in the barn?" The chief, understandably, was bulldog-focused on that question. He spoke slowly, enunciating each word, his face inches from mine.

"Just me and Mikey and Joyce. Astrid came in later."

"Three of you are out. One fatality. You're sure no one else is in there?"

I shook my head and he charged back into the fray, leaving me to wrestle with the facts.

I kept thinking that. Astrid killed Joyce, okay, no arguing that. Astrid: alive. Joyce, not so much. I still had blood on my hands from checking her body. But then why the fire? *Why?*

Off came the stupid mask again and I slid off the stretcher in one smooth move, then charged the fifteen feet between our ambulances. Astrid saw me coming and started screaming again. Behind me Whitman shouted, alerting Astrid's team, who jumped in front of Astrid protectively, each grabbing at me as I tried shoving my way past their protective wall.

As well she should.

"Why, Astrid? *Why did you set the fire?*" Instead shouting, my voice graveled into useless hoarse croaks. I sounded like a hysterical frog. Plus, I could barely hear myself over the din. I writhed against their restraining hands like a mad thing, trying to get close enough to Astrid so she could hear me, so I could see her face when I made her answer. "Why the *fire*? Astrid! Why did you set the barn on fire?"

They were pulling me away. I didn't have the strength to fight, so I went dead-weight, dropping out of their grasp, and then crawled through their legs. I popped back up, right in Astrid's face. Eye-to-eye. I must have looked like a beast, red-eyed, soot-blackened face, snarling and snapping. I hoped I did. "Astrid! *Why*? Why the fire? Why did you set the barn on fire?"

The cop got between us, and all the paramedics piled on, but as they dragged me away, Astrid screamed, "I didn't know! I didn't know you were in there! I didn't *know*!" She broke into hysterics, and I saw her paramedics move to push her down against the white sheets, blocking me.

That was as much of an answer as I was going to get, at least for now. The fight drained out of me, leaving me hollow, shaking and nauseous and cold. I stopped resisting. They hustled me back to the ambulance, tossed me on the stretcher, and refitted the mask. I let them do their thing. Their hands moved professionally, tending to my body; I distanced my mind, retreating.

Only once I sat up, searching for Mikey. Whitman grabbed my shoulder, ready to pounce, but as soon as I saw him, safely being loaded into his own ride, I lay back down. His ambulance peeled off, with Astrid's a few moments behind. I'd made my EMTs so nervous, they made a cop ride in the back with the male paramedic. And then we were off.

CHAPTER SIXTY FOUR

Had Astrid come to the barn looking for Joyce . . . or for Mikey? As the ambulance churned its way to Chippewa, I tried to think it through. Why would she set fire to the barn if she'd killed Joyce? To hide the body? Was it an impulsive stab at hiding her deed? It would be stupid, because of course it wouldn't work, but people do stupid things when they're freaked out. If anyone knew Joyce best, it would be Astrid; working together, side-by-side, each of them focused on the daily lives of their charges. Astrid could have guessed.

Were Astrid's hysterics guilt or fear? Or did I have it backwards? Was there a different motivation all together for Astrid to set the fire?

I put my brain in reverse, recasting Astrid instead of Joyce for the role of killer.

Astrid—the nurturer, the welcomer—feeding the women "milk and cookies and tucking them in at night." Astrid—the only one who hadn't seemed embittered, burnt out. The one who'd kept her focus narrowed, inside the walls of the shelter, turning a blind eye to the bigger picture in order to tend to the little details in the women's everyday lives. Had she found a solution to the hopelessness, a way to fight back when someone she cared for and rescued was determined to make an awful, soul-destroying choice? A choice that would undo everything she'd spent so much time patching together, returning to her abuser, taking the children, too, more often than not.

Was that what drove her?

Joyce had issues, sure, but did she have the wherewithal to plan and carry out the murders? In her earlier life, Joyce's fundamental personality style was passivity. Until she bludgeoned her abusive husband in his sleep, that is. Maybe I should rethink that "passive" bit.

But then why had Joyce attacked Karissa? It hadn't been Astrid, I'd heard her car pull up to the barn when I was hiding from Joyce. If Joyce was coming to warn Mikey's mother, she wouldn't have cracked her head open, would she? Seemed counter-productive.

Unless . . .

I thought of the blood-stained knife lying on the floor, just a few feet away from Karissa; of Karissa meeting us at the door, the same knife clutched at her side; of the warning we'd delivered, Paul and I, the panic we'd instilled. Had she gone after Joyce? Was Joyce defending herself?

So, there were two choices. Joyce-the-killer attacks Karissa and starts hunting Mikey down. Astrid comes to the rescue. There's a mighty battle where Joyce is killed and Astrid sets fire to the barn in remorse or guilt or fear or something.

Or . . . Joyce comes to warn Karissa, is attacked and forced to defend herself, then tries to get to Mikey before Astrid-as-killer adds a pint-sized victim to her roster. Astrid kills Joyce and sets the barn alight to either smoke us out or silence the only witness to her attack on Regina. Maybe she figured Joyce would be blamed for the fire, too.

Which?
Mikey knew.

The ambulance pulled into a garage bay and I was whisked down a short hall. On the way, we passed by two glass-fronted trauma rooms. The first held a squad of medical people working on Karissa; Mikey, in the next. They steered me into a third.

No sight of Astrid. Maybe they'd taken her to a different hospital. From what I could remember, though, St. Joe's was the nearest acute care center in the area.

They hoisted me off the ambulance stretcher and onto the hospital's wheeled bed. Almost as soon as I settled, a nurse popped a clip-thing on my index finger and switched me to a different oxygen mask as a second fussed with the machinery. A third buzzed in and out, doing other mysterious nursey-things, and when the doctor joined the mix, they moved around and over me in such smooth synchrony, it would've made a water ballet team weep with envy. With the oxygen, my coughing had lessened considerably, but I was still hacking up phlegm and my throat felt red and itchy. After asking me a series of questions, he ordered blood work and "chemistries" and some kind of test that sounded like he was reading the ingredients from a box of cereal—the kind nutrition-Nazis warn us about. And then he was out the door and gone.

"Did someone call Mikey's grandma?" I asked.

The nearest nurse glanced up. "The little boy? Do you have his grandmother's number?" he asked.

"Not exactly"—not at all, really, but I forged on—"but her name is Bernadette . . . something. Maybe Mikey knows where she is. Is he okay? Can I see him?"

Through the window, I saw Mikey being wheeled

323

away. I sat up. "Where are they taking him?" My heart started thudding. I couldn't lose sight of him. My sudden movement triggered a coughing spasm.

The nurses exchanged glances over the top of me. Apparently, they'd been informed about my antics at the farm. Antics. Attempted homicide. Whatever.

The nurse eased me back, his hand warm on my shoulder. "Relax. He's just going to radiology for a chest X-ray. We have one right here in our department. Isn't that cool? You'll be next."

They continued to work around and over me. I debated telling them my suspicions, but that glance between them didn't bode well for my credibility. If I made them too nervous, I was afraid they'd sedate me.

I kept an eye on the hall, watching for Mikey's return and still trying to determine where Astrid was. The newly remodeled ER had been designed with the nurses' station as a central hub, allowing them a view of most of the exam rooms. One in particular—on the far side of Mikey's, with just the edge of the door visible—had a decent amount of action going in and out.

"Is that where they took Astrid? The one who set the fire?" The questions just slipped out.

Another shared glance. They didn't answer. But they didn't say she *wasn't* there, either.

Good enough.

I became even more certain of Astrid's whereabouts when I saw a uniformed police officer go up to the door and look in. He strolled away almost instantly, so I couldn't be certain it was the cop from the farm, but if it wasn't, he was close enough to be his brother. If that *was* where Astrid was being treated, it didn't appear as though they considered her very dangerous. An impulsive arsonist, maybe, but not a crazed killer going after a six-year-old. Hell, she might even be a hero in their eyes, if she'd dispatched a real murderer.

Sooner than I expected, I saw them wheeling Mikey past my window, back to his room. He looked so tiny, a little lump, under the sterilized linens. His face, still smudged with soot, was turned toward me, mouth open just enough to see a gap where a tooth was missing. Sound asleep, too, from the look of it, and I didn't blame him.

Somebody stopped their progress, just beyond my room. "If he's stable, we're going to need help transferring the mother. She needs to go to Luther ASAP."

I heard them getting Mikey re-settled, and then the action shifted to Karissa's room. She must have needed more extensive assistance than St. Joe's could offer. Feeling the guilt of having led the killer straight to her, I said a silent prayer, promising to look after her boy.

CHAPTER SIXTY FIVE

After dimming the lights and covering me with a warmed blanket—heaven—the nurse left. I hadn't considered that they'd leave us alone. It would be easy, so easy, to fall asleep. A wave of exhaustion washed over me, making my arms and legs feel too heavy to move, my brain fuzzy. I yawned.

Then, I shook myself so hard I almost heard my brain rattle. Forcing myself to sit up, I swung my legs over the edge of the bed.

I watched.

It was just a flicker, a shadow flitting through the only bit of door to Mikey's room that I could see. But after what seemed like an eternity spent trying not to doze off, I just couldn't be sure. I pulled off all the attached medical paraphernalia and slid off the bed—a controlled fall, might be a better term, since my legs almost gave out—and ran to the door. I peeked out, not wanting a nurse to catch sight of me until I was sure I wasn't imagining things. They'd pulled the curtains on Mikey's windows. Astrid's room was similarly cloaked. The nurses' station was crawling with observant, efficient medical personnel, modern-day sentinels over their patients. Didn't anybody take coffee breaks anymore? If I was wrong and they caught me sneaking around Mikey's room, they'd decide *I* was the dangerous one. They were already wondering, I could tell.

An alarm set off behind me, its shrill beeping designed to alert the nurses that their patient had become untethered from her monitors. *Shit-shit-shit.*

Decision made.

I dropped to the floor and belly-crawled the fifteen feet to Mikey's door. The tiles were freezing but very clean, I noted, then I slid around Mikey's door.

Astrid stood poised over Mikey's sleeping form, a pillow clutched in her gauzy-mitts. With a croaky roar, I scrambled to my feet and launched myself at her.

It wasn't anything like those choreographed, action-movie scenes.

Astrid was far more skilled—and mentally prepared—for physical violence, but I was psycho-pissed and at the end of my rope. It helped, too, that she was used to having the element of surprise, sneaking up on her victims. She clearly wasn't used to crazed avengers screaming like banshees and hurtling themselves across the room.

We careened into multi-million-dollar machines, tripped over a stool, and took out a storage cabinet on wheels, shooting it across the room and tipping it over with a horrendous crash. Mikey screamed hysterically, adding to the bedlam. Astrid grappled for my throat, using strategic self-defense techniques, trying to knock my feet out from under me. I bit and scratched and gouged and kicked and went for the eyes. If she'd had balls, I would have kicked those, too. We were both wheezing and grunting like asthmatic pigs.

The room filled with blue-smocked beings. Astrid and I fell, locked in each other's arms, bringing a clatter of metal and plastic down on top of us. Hands grabbed, pulling me off, dragging me away. I got a couple of kicks in before they were successful. I fell against Mikey's bed and he latched onto me with a howl, his little fingers wrapping so tightly around my neck, he almost finished off what Astrid started. I started coughing, my tears mixing with his. A nurse tried to separate us, but Mikey let loose such a wail, she gave up.

"She's crazy! She's trying to kill me." Astrid got the first preemptive accusation in, a good move. "She attacked me at the barn, too. There were witnesses."

"The barn *fire*, don't you mean? You tried to kill us. You were trying to kill Mikey."

Mikey buried his face in my shoulder, shuddering and sobbing, "Mama. *Mama*." I patted his back.

"It's going to be okay, Mikey," I said. "It's okay now."

Only it wasn't. We might have stayed in a stalemated she-said/she-said wrangle, but just then the cop plowed in the room, way late to this particular party and pissed as all hell. Probably embarrassed, too, 'cause he was going to have to explain why his arsonist had been jumped by the crazy-lady-from-the-barn-fire in the innocent child's hospital room. Didn't look good for him at all.

Since he'd already witnessed my "aggression" earlier, he zeroed in on me. He even had his hand on his Tazer, the desire to zap me tangible in his eyes. But Mikey and I clung so tightly to each other our skin practically grafted together, and there was no way he could risk shooting me.

"Lady, step away from the child."

"I can't," I said. "He's scared." I clutched him tighter. I was scared, too. Mikey kicked his wails up a notch to prove my point. Covering Mikey's ears, I pointed a shaky finger at Astrid. "She was trying to kill us in that fire. She killed Joyce and Regina and a bunch of other women—

abused women—and she tried to kill us. And just now she was trying to kill Mikey. She had a pillow and . . . She would have done it, too."

Everyone turned to stare at Astrid.

She didn't look like a killer. She'd sagged in the nurses' grip, the gauze trailing from her hands like day-after party streamers, her face gaunt and haggard. She looked old and bewildered. Sad.

Then, her lips pulled back from her teeth in a feral snarl. "You stupid bitch." Mikey twitched in my arms and burrowed his face deeper into my breast. "Who are you trying to save? *Him?*" Astrid pointed at Mikey. "Why even bother? That stupid cow is just going to drag him back to that abusive asshole. And you can't tell me that she doesn't know better. But she'll still act oh, so surprised when he does it again. And again. How long do you think it will be until big, strong Daddy starts smacking the kids around, too? I suppose you think they can change, don't you? That if he says he's sorry, he really means it. You're as stupid as the rest of them, running around, poking your nose into my business."

Behind Astrid, the doctor signaled to one of the physician assistants in the hall. The PA disappeared.

"And that little brat is just as bad," she strained and flailed against the hold the nurses had on her. "He's just going to grow up into another asshole. That's how they make them, you know. One after the other after the other. A little asshole assembly line. The mothers are just as guilty, too, because they don't *stop* it. And they could. We show them how, so there's no excuse for it, really. Maybe we can't stop the men, but the women could learn, if they wanted to. I keep telling them and showing them. And they just don't listen."

The PA was back, edging around behind our group,

until he reached the doctor and handed him something. Astrid kept spewing her verbal vomit, but the doctor moved in swiftly, a quick jab, which made Astrid squeal in surprise. She thrashed around some more, but only for a few seconds, then she sank, finally quiet. Blessedly quiet.

The medical team snapped back into their practiced, efficient groove, tackling the debris scattered across the room and hauling Astrid out. The cop trailed after. I stayed with Mikey, holding him and crooning while he sobbed. We curled up on the cot. I thought they might try to medicate him, but instead they rolled us into my room, hooking me up to my oxygen and covering us with warmed blankets. They left us alone, checking frequently, until he fell back to sleep. Then, they shifted me to another exam room, hooked me back up to my oxygen and shuttled me down to X-ray—everything back to business as usual.

EPILOGUE

When someone mentions HBO, I no longer think of movies, but of hyperbaric oxygen therapy. HBO means lying in a clear tube for over an hour, while pure oxygen is pumped in. I advise you to not drink liquids beforehand. It actually wasn't that bad. Mostly I caught up on my sleep. The part I didn't like was staying three days in hospital, before they let me go home and do the treatment as an outpatient.

I had visitors, of course. Paul had shown up at the ER, after all the excitement had passed. He'd gotten held up, giving a statement to the police, but once he got there, he stayed until after they transferred me to a regular room. And was back the next day. And the next. He drove me home.

At least it wasn't my mom.

Marshall came, too. I think Hannah got a hold of him and let him know I was laid up. He showed up on the second day, toting a simple bouquet of daisies. I guess he remembered that I didn't like roses anymore. I'd been taking a nap and when I woke up, Paul was on one side of the bed and Marshall on the other. They each held a hand.

Awkward.

"Do you mind if Letty and I talk," Marshall asked Paul. "In private."

Paul, bless his heart, checked with me first and when

I nodded, he swallowed hard and excused himself. Before he got to the door, I stopped him.

"Paul? Would you mind getting me a chocolate shake?" He must have realized that chocolate trumps daisies. Made his day.

After some um's and throat clearing, Marshall told me he was going to give California (and his marriage to Bobbi) a try. I had to sit through the whole we've-decided-to-work-on-our-marriage speech, but to give the man credit, he looked both embarrassed and proud of the cliché. A two-fer on the emotional Richter scale.

I couldn't argue. Didn't even want to, really. There's nothing wrong with a man trying to get his marriage right, and if he was in California at least I wouldn't have to watch him do it. I wished him luck. He kissed me on the forehead, holding his warm lips against my skin for about ten heartbeats longer than he should have.

Diana came to see me, too. And to apologize. I beat her to it. Blodgett gave us about ten minutes alone to cry it out, and then shuffled in to claim the chair at my bedside. He was using a cane. He looked old. He was pretty sure, although we never learned for certain, that Astrid had been the one to crack him over the head. He'd been to the shelter that afternoon to "look around," using Regina's accident as a door-opener. Astrid was the only one he'd talked to, but he couldn't remember anything more than that and there really wasn't any proof.

He held Diana's hand as he told me he'd decided to retire. He was tired of waiting. Diana was, too.

It was on the third day, about a half-hour before I was due to be discharged, that Clotilde showed up. I could have done without that.

She looked like she could have, too, so I'm not sure what compelled her to come. Paul braved her presence, refusing to leave even when she glared at him. He flinched, but he stayed.

"What do you want, Lachlyn?" I was too tired and too beat up to be polite.

"I'm not sure," she said. "I almost didn't come."

I waited.

"If you're wondering whether we knew Astrid was killing our women, then no. We didn't. But I suspected something was wrong. I . . . " She stopped, clearing her throat. She glanced at my water pitcher and I waved a hand at it, giving permission. She shook her head, but Paul poured her a glass anyway.

"Actually, it was Regina I noticed," Lachlyn continued after taking a sip. "She was acting very strangely. Distant. I don't know when it occurred to me, but I suddenly realized I was watching *her* watch Astrid." She lifted her hands helplessly—a gesture that seemed alien to her. "When she fell—"

"She didn't fall. She was pushed." I wouldn't allow euphemisms for Regina's death.

Lachlyn gave a nod of acceptance. Another alien gesture. "She was pushed. So, I started watching Astrid. But I didn't know what I was supposed to be watching for. And then you showed up." She took a deep shuddery breath, looking away. "I thought maybe Regina had told you what she was afraid of. But then you seemed as much in the dark as me. It made us certain though, that there was something really bad going on."

"Us?" I repeated.

Lachlyn flushed. "Me. Just me. Clotilde . . . I never spoke to her of my suspicions." She made direct eye contact, no blinking.

Such a rotten liar.

"Regina hadn't told me anything," I said, moving her

away from the subject of Clotilde. "The circumstances of her death felt strange, but I probably wouldn't have thought any more of it, if you all hadn't been so resistant to letting me do my job."

She smirked. "Your job? That should have been my job. I'd known for years that I was supposed to take charge of Regina's case load if anything should happen; and she, mine. Can you imagine how it felt to know that Regina didn't trust me? She was my . . . Anyway, I knew there was something about the paperwork that had worried Regina and when she appointed you, then it meant she expected you to find it. Maybe she believed that I would have ignored it. Or hidden it."

"Would you have?" I asked.

She didn't answer. "Astrid . . . I know you'll never understand this, but she was a good soldier in this war. It just . . . She saw too much. It got too hard. Something broke inside her, a long time ago." Lachlyn raised a hand to her heart. "I know what that feels like, especially now. I guess Regina felt I wouldn't be able to do . . . what needed to be done."

"Maybe Regina chose me because she knew how difficult it would be for you. Maybe it didn't have to do with trusting me or not trusting you. She could have just been looking out for you. You've been in this battle for a while, too. Maybe she just didn't want you to suffer anymore than you already have. Maybe she wanted to make sure you didn't break, either."

Lachlyn looked startled. Her hand dropped to her lap, and a little iron returned to her posture.

"Maybe," she said. And then she left.

They closed the shelter. Most of the women had been relocated to other facilities during the media uproar that erupted when everything came out. They just never re-opened. I heard from Beth that Clotilde is gearing up for a run at the state capitol. More power to her, I guess. At least, figuratively.

I never heard from Lachlyn again. And that was okay.

What wasn't okay was not getting a chance to say good-bye to Mikey. Karissa and Mitch took off with their kids as soon as she was physically able to make the move. I could probably have tracked down Bernie or even gone back to the cousin's farm, but it seems too stalker-ish. I just hoped they gotten him some help, wherever they went. If they were able to trust the system again. Which I doubted.

One good thing? At her last session, Bettina told me about running into "her man" and the missus while they were dining at Houligan's Pub. I couldn't tell her that I knew, so we had to play the story out with a pseudonym. She chose "that fat asshole." Worked for me. She said she realized how stupid she'd been—her words—and that she was going back to try to make her marriage to Frank work. Seemed to be a lot of that lately. Unfortunately, she never gave me permission to report him. I had no choice but to let it go. His tires were mysteriously slashed, three days in a row. Coincidence?

That was a hell of a lot of good-byes, now that I looked back on it. But not everyone left. Paul didn't. Sue didn't. Ma wouldn't, although I tried to convince her that the weather in Florida would suit her arthritis better. She reminded me that she doesn't have arthritis.

I can dream.

Thank you for reading THE ONE WE LOVE.
I hope you enjoyed it! Please check my website
http://www.donnawhiteglaser.com/ for more Letty
Whittaker 12 Step Mysteries coming soon.

CONNECT WITH ME:
Twitter: http://twitter.com/readdonnaglaser
Facebook:
http://facebook.com/donnawhiteglaser.com
donnawglaser@gmail.com

ACKNOWLEDGEMENTS

I know I'm going to forget someone and then I'll be in trouble. There are so many people in my life who let me do what I need to do in order to make this happen.

In no particular order, I want to thank Marla A. Madison, April Solberg, Marjorie Swift Doering, Dave Tindell, Helen Block, Darren Kirby, and Gail Francis. You've all been so much a part of this process that I can freely say it wouldn't have happened without you. Thank you for making me a better writer. (At least, I think you did.)

The Sisters In Crime organization has been an invaluable resource. If you are a mystery writer, join. You won't regret it. And if you do join, make sure you sign up for the Guppies. There is no better place in the world for a writer to be than in this community of amazing women and men.

To Jes Springer, Katie Swift, and Tamilyn White for understanding that when they see that blank expression on my face, it's not stupidity. (Well, not most of the time!) I'm just working out a way to kill people and not get caught. In my head. It's research, I swear.

To my family. Always.

Want a sneak peak at Letty's next adventure?

THE SECRETS WE KEEP:
A Letty Whittaker 12 Step Mystery

ONE

After Trinnie relapsed, I'd hear about her every now and then. The usual reports came back. Somebody saw her at the bank; another talked to her at Wal-mart- that kind of thing. Everything pointed to the fact that she was still drinking and the damage was beginning to show. After each rumor, I'd end up meeting with my own sponsor, Sue, trying to figure out how to "let go and let God." After several months the rumors died down. People focused on some other train-wreck.

What made it bad for me was that, shortly before, she'd asked me to be her sponsor right before she'd "gone back out," as we say in A.A. I knew she'd been struggling and I hadn't been there when she needed me. The excuse that I'd been in the hospital recovering from a barn fire I'd barely survived only soothed my intelligence, not my emotions.

I am also a licensed psychotherapist. A *frustrated* psychotherapist who should be able to have worked it out on her own. Instead, I stuffed my guilt in a dusty corner of my heart and went on with my life.

Of course, that's when she called.

That's why, after so many months of silence, I climbed into a brand new, Gotta-Have-It-Green, Mustang driven by another A.A. buddy. I'd met several months ago when I'd volunteered some time at a domestic abuse shelter where she sat on the board of directors. Beth was the richest alcoholic I'd ever met.

As I settled in, she turned her emerald-green eyes on

me. "Well, Smiley. What are you looking so pleased about? Feeling good about this little road trip?"

"It's a gorgeous June day and there's a lot to feel good about," I replied.

"You've got the gorgeous day part right, but the rest is wishful thinking. I'd ease back on the expectations if I were you."

"More like hopeful thinking, but I get the point."

Beth needed to know Trinnie's background, so I gave her the highlights. Trinnie had first gotten sober last year. She'd come to meetings fairly regularly, but she hadn't chosen a sponsor. Until me. I was only supposed to be temporary, since I hadn't worked all Twelve Steps myself.

I swear I didn't mention anything about my own emotional reaction to Trinnie's relapse, but she picked up on the key issue with chilling speed.

"The real question for you, honey," Beth smiled crookedly, "is why you feel responsible for her in the first place? You might want to keep that in mind during our little chat today. Provided she's sober, that is."

She was right about my over-developed sense of responsibility but I was sick of trying to sort out the nuances of my bond with Trinnie. I was missing something important and it pissed me off when I couldn't figure it out or analyze it away. I looked out the window at the passing scenery as Beth wound our way toward the neighborhood behind the library. Most of the houses that we zipped past were old Katrinans in varying stages of disrepair.

"Tell me a little about what to expect out of this girl," Beth broke into my funk. "I mean, besides being hung-over."

"That's the only thing I can guarantee. She was

completely sloshed when she called last night."

"What is it with drunks and middle-of-the-night phone calls? Maybe there's a latent vampire gene triggered by over-consumption of alcohol."

"No kidding. From what she said, she's been on a week-long binge and decided to call everyone she's ever met and make amends."

"Oh, that's priceless. I'm sure she blew them away with her sincerity as she slurred her way through her apologies. Why didn't I think of that?"

"Thing is, she's got a good heart. Aside from self-inflicted misery, she'd never hurt a fly. Kind of surprising, considering her background."

Beth swung her gaze from the road and her stream-lined eyebrows arched a question.

"The usual divorced family drama with *lots* of money thrown in. Made for a really nasty custody dispute when she was a kid. They got fed up with her drinking and cut her off without a penny. We never got deeper than that, but from some things she said, I wondered about some kind of trauma history."

The houses started looking familiar and I concentrated on finding the right one. The combination of nearly a year's absence and the massive renovations of the neighborhood homes made it difficult.

"I think her house is toward the end, on the left. The downstairs tenant has some kind of rose fetish. Look for a huge rose garden out front."

A few houses down, we spotted it. Beth glided the Monte onto the gravel drive and cut the engine.

"How do you want to do this?" I asked. "Do you want to take the lead?" Given my history with Trinnie, it would be hard to be objective.

Beth's mouth pursed as she thought about it. "You

do the intro. If she was that drunk, you might even have to remind her that she called you last night. You never know. Sometimes they call in a black-out and act totally offended when you show up the next day. They forget they talked to you. If she's still good to go, we'll play it by ear. If you're losing it, I'll say so."

I agreed and, gripping my copy of A.A.'s Big Book, led the way down a path that was more sinkhole than sidewalk. Rounding the corner, we headed toward the exterior staircase that led to the upper apartment. As we went along, I caught the thick fragrance of roses. Looking over my shoulder, I saw that the back yard had also been claimed by the Rose Queen. In the late afternoon sun, the vast beds of roses gave off a sense of tired tawdriness, looking burdened by their obligation to cheer. I turned back to the door wanting to block out the cloying scent. Taking a deep breath, which didn't help, I knocked on the peeling paint of Trinnie's front door.

I waited a few seconds, then knocked harder. No answer, telling me Trinnie was either not home or hung-over and still in bed. Of course, having been on a week-long bender, the latter wouldn't be too surprising. On the plus side, a monumental hang-over might make this Twelve Step call look like a sign from God. At the very least, she'd be in too much pain to holler or throw things.

I sighed. I really didn't want to slog all the way back home and be forced to reschedule. Out of sheer wistfulness, I reached down, tried the door knob. It turned and the door creaked open a couple inches. "What do you think? Should we just go in?"

Beth hesitated a second. "You know her best, Violet. If we go in is she gonna come after us with a frying pan?"

"Not Trinnie. She's not the type. Besides, she should be expecting us. If she remembers calling me, that is."

"If she's even here. Our luck, she woke up at noon and went back out to the bars." Beth nudged me forward into the kitchen.

For someone who was at the bottom end of a eight-month binge, the place wasn't too bad. I'd seen worse. To be honest, I'd lived in worse. Bottles and glasses everywhere, but it wasn't rancid with filth the way a lot of dumps get. Maybe she didn't use the kitchen as anything other than a liquid re-fueling station. The stove top was free from grease, the curtains over the sink white with yellow flowers. An empty ice tray sat on the counter, but no visible signs of any food source other than several booze bottles existed. Sunlight shone through the clear glass of one of the bottles that stood on the window sill, casting a tiny rainbow on the far wall.

Beth popped open the refrigerator. She pointed at the bottles of wine standing alone on the top shelf. "We'll have to get rid of these for her, if she plans on going through with it. The one part of a Twelve Step I hate is the smell when we pour out the booze. Makes me sick to my stomach."

"I know. And don't you love the treasure hunt for secret stashes with the ones who live with family? At least with Trinnie being single, she can stick her stuff right out in the open." I set my book down on the table, automatically straightening a chair.

Finishing her examination of the fridge, Beth headed through the open archway into Trinnie's living room. The closed curtains created a dark cave, so I flicked the lights on. The matching blue-and-white striped couch and love seat were in pretty good shape, looking as though they'd been expensive once upon a time. In contrast, the cherry coffee and two side tables clashed with the golden teak tones of the couch set. The tables looked like they fit. Burn marks ran down the length of the outer edge of the coffee table and a side table. Trinnie had the dangerous habit of resting her cigarette on the edge of the table instead of in the overflowing ashtray. Mismatched lamps gave off a grimy light and had a low-end Goodwill store feel to them.

An empty pizza box and several sticky glasses covered the coffee table, further indicating where Trinnie spent her time. An old-fashioned, plug-in-the-wall phone sat in the middle of the couch, next to her copy of the Big Book. The book, navy blue and steady-looking, perched sedately in the midst of the alcoholic mess.

Beth propped hands on hips and peered down the hallway. "Must be sleeping pretty deep if she hasn't heard us clattering around in here." She fashioned a megaphone out of her hands and yodeled down the hall. "Yoo-hoo! Anybody home? You have company!"

We stood a few minutes in indecision. With a sigh, I headed down the hall. Trinnie slept in the back bedroom, but I paused to listen at the first. *Why would anyone want to be a burglar?* The adrenaline rush made my mouth taste tinny and I had to pee like a racehorse.

On the off chance that she had passed out on the floor, I peeked into the bathroom. Sometimes drunks need a little siesta on the tiles. When you're an active alcoholic, you think this is mighty clever.

Other than the tan, seashell-dotted shower curtain, the room was a jarring Pepto-Bismol pink. She'd carried the seashell motif even further, gluing a wavy strip of wallpaper border waist high. She'd either had an inner-ear infection or was drunk when it was applied. Several threadbare towels lay piled on the floor in a damp, musty heap.

An old-fashioned bottle of coke syrup and an

economy size bottle of Extra-Strength Tylenol balanced on the rim of the sink. I'd almost forgotten that trick. Drunks will try anything; I did. This particular method worked fairly well, if you discounted the enormous damage to your stomach lining.

At the end of the hall, I paused again, hand hovering over the knob of Trinnie's bedroom door. *Maybe we should just leave?*

"What the hell is taking you so long?" Beth's funneled voice echoed down the hall scaring the crap out of me.

My nerves unraveled, sliding over the edge into mild hysteria. I slapped a hand over my mouth. Snorts and whiffles escaped from between my fingers, making me sound like a hyperventilating pig.

Beth joined in. We were going to wake Trinnie for sure. The thought of her catching us creeping around her apartment while she lay crashed out with a hang-over didn't help.

"I'm going to start the treasure hunt in the kitchen," Beth said, between hiccups. "Is it only booze I'm looking for or does she dabble in other stuff, too?"

"Just booze, I think." I took a deep breath, and opened the door.

CPSIA information can be obtained at www.ICGtesting.com
Printed in the USA
LVOW11s0557150914

404070LV00001B/28/P

9 781480 009882